I0724912

Spied

Copyright © 2016 by J. M. Miller

All rights reserved. No part of this book may be reproduced, transmitted, downloaded, distributed, stored in or introduced into any information storage and retrieval system, in any form or by any means, whether electronic or mechanical, without express permission of the author, except by a reviewer who may quote brief passages for review purposes.

This book is a work of fiction and any resemblance to any person, living or dead, events, occurrences, or locales is purely coincidental. The characters and the story lines are created from the author's imagination or are used fictitiously.

Second edition - 2024

Cover and Interior Design by J.M. Miller

Editing by Lawrence Editing - www.lawrenceediting.com

ISBN-13: 978-1-955472-13-5

J.M.MILLER

This one's for Stinky.
Missing you.

1

Gia

Sweat lined my jittery palms, transferring some moisture onto my phone screen, while drops gathered along my forehead and more slipped down my spine. The day was hot. Sticky, icky hot. Florida's humidity was only partly to blame. The other part was the passion unfolding in the courtyard just beyond the set of townhouses I lingered between. Secretive and seductive, the act was enough to make my skin flush and my thighs tense.

Hands moved everywhere. His hands were large, roaming her bikini-string covered back, up and under her long black hair, only to switch direction again, skimming fingers down to dig below the curve under her butt, pulling her closer to him. Her chin tipped up, lips moving, uttering words I couldn't hear because of the rattling air conditioner my butt was perched upon. Any other person would skip the racket, favoring a quieter place for a covert op, but I had a gift of everyday invisibility. I'd blended in throughout my life. Noise didn't matter much—short of screaming directly at them, of course. Since there was no real concern with getting caught, the only real problem was that I couldn't hear any words they said or noises they made. I could imagine, though, and for some strange reason I was doing just that. *Breathy whimpers*, her silent mouth emitted as his lips assaulted her neck. Her eyes pressed tight and he mumbled words against her skin, like "You like that, muffin?"

Mmm. Muffins. My stomach growled. I was kind of hungry.

I pushed the thoughts of food away and refocused on them—their movements, their passion. What the clanking air conditioner took away in sound it certainly gave back in sensation. The fan inside rocked the metal frame, jolting my butt and shaking some friction relief between my legs, like an off-kilter spin cycle.

Good God. Apparently, it had been too long. Clenching my teeth, I silently scolded my neglected libido and got back to the task at hand. I didn't know what had gotten into me. The hungry thing was nothing new, but watching people make out never had so much of an arousing effect. The guy ... his hands. That had to be the difference. There was something about the way he touched her that reminded me of my ex, Landon. The familiarity was intense, obviously strumming my sexy chord if I was down to let an air conditioner get the job done.

So embarrassing.

I was used to being reminded of him when I saw these couples, just with a totally different set of feelings. Anger mainly. Because they were cheaters, either one or both. That was what I was reminded of whenever I took the next job since I had caught Landon. My everyday invisibility had turned into a curse that stabbed me in the heart. Not long after, it turned into a gift bearing cash.

Duplicity, my side business, had taken off faster than I thought it ever would, garnering me word-of-mouth chatter of suspicious girlfriends and even relatives or best friends who were afraid to be labeled the bad guy by spilling the cheater beans. The clients didn't want a PI, didn't want to get legal. They just wanted peace of mind. Ninety percent of the time, their suspicions were right. As long as

I was given accurate information to follow, most situations were cut and dry—a trip within the local areas of Destin and Pensacola, watching targets in a hotel lobby or a vacation rental parking lot, a few quick burner phone snapshots stripped of metadata then texted to the client and/or the victim, and that was it. Voilà.

People rolled their wheeled luggage down the sidewalk behind me, not caring about the phone in my hand or my targets groping each other in the middle of the courtyard. People always had somewhere to go on vacation, something to see. They didn't usually pay much attention to anything at all, especially during summer. And this was just another average end-of-summer day.

"Excuse me," a deep timbre spoke, loud and close enough behind me to cut through the clanking of the air conditioner and stop my heart.

I jumped up with a frantic spin, landing awkwardly on my own feet for a second before falling backward onto the grass. My eyes trailed down my sprawled body—sweaty tank plastered to my boobs, knees parted and pointed to the sky—then traveled up the owner of the voice. Short work boots, khaki shorts, green polo—standard maintenance gear for the East Bay Resort property. Even over the noisy air conditioner, I heard the guy's rough laugh. My eyes snapped up to his face right as his hand covered his mouth to stifle the sound.

I huffed and shook my head, disappointed that I'd been caught off guard. The noise, the situation ... it had all had me ... preoccupied. Considering that preoccupation and the dull ache still thriving between my legs, I looked down, catching the guy's eyes roaming over my jean shorts at the same time.

Just when I thought it couldn't get much worse, I saw the ring of sweat down south. *Fantastic.* Swamp ass. The air conditioner was running hotter than I'd thought.

The guy dropped his hand away from his face, revealing lips pressed firmly together to tame a smile. He extended his hand with a step closer. "I'm sorry. I didn't mean to interrupt you from ...?" His eyes flashed to the damp imprint of my butt on the unit.

I leapt to my feet, dodging his hand and hoping my face wasn't as red as it felt as I switched off the thoughts of the air conditioner and the day's targets—who had since disappeared. Tucking my phone into my back pocket, I replied, "I had to sit down for a second." *Oh, that was weak.*

The guy tilted his head and narrowed his eyes, dropping his already heavy brows lower.

He wasn't buying it. I needed a different approach. Quickly taking more of him in, I noticed some things. Manly things. Strong hands, toned arms. There was a slightly rugged look to his typical beach-boy body. And his skeptical eyes held a hint of humor with maybe something a little more. Attraction? Flirting wasn't exactly my forte; it was Kass'. My older sister had the entire process down to an art. Being a girl. Using her girlie bits. Even my quiet younger sister, Viv, had some talent in that department. I wasn't as fluent, but I probably had to try in order to get around him. Otherwise, there was a chance he'd report me. I'd gotten onto the property using the Silhouette Bridal Boutique access pass, bluffing my way past the gate guards by claiming a bridal emergency. If I ruined the company's standing with the resort, Aunt Aimee would have my head. And of course word could spread through other local resorts, those who often referred us when any of their destination brides hit distressing bridal snafus.

I had to turn it out. Put on the goods. "I, uh ... it's so hot out here." I hooked my fingers under the hem of my tank and pulled outward, the material peeling away from my skin as I arched my shoulders back. "And I was, uh, feeling a little dizzy ... so—"

"So you decided to take a seat and record two people making out?"

Well, shit.

"Judging by the deflated look on your face, I'm willing to bet you aren't a renter or an employee. Are you local? A vendor?"

"I, uh ..." I had nothing. My damn invisibility had failed me.

"I'm going to have to report this. Voyeurism in not tolerated at this resort."

My mouth dropped open. "I ... Oh my God, no. I'm not ... I-I wasn't ..." Well, maybe I kind of was, but that wasn't the—He didn't need to know that. He didn't need to even think that.

A laugh burst through his lips and his shoulders shook. "Wow, you are flustered." He opened his own mouth, mocking my reaction with a bit of a smirk that made me instantly notice how good-looking he was while simultaneously irritating the crap out of me.

Anger flared. Directed at myself. At my girlie bits. At him. He was messing with me. Well, I had news for him. "Okay, you got me. I'm just not used to being caught," I said, doing the flirty eyebrow lift I used to practice in my bathroom mirror when I was still in high school, praying that a few years had worn off the awkward. Kass would be proud. Or laugh. Yeah, she would probably laugh, which meant I likely wouldn't tell her.

I stepped slowly to him, watching his mouth snap shut and ignoring the rubbing noise my sweaty jean shorts made. He hadn't seemed to notice that, though. His eyes were honed on mine. I bit my bottom lip and pulled it between my teeth dramatically when I stopped close to his side. His body started to shift toward me, but I placed a hand on the bare part of his bicep to stop him and glanced up. "I mean, did you see them? They were ..."

His Adam's apple bobbed.

Touchdown! Goal! Whatever! I'd hooked him.

The circumstances were almost too bad. He was pretty adorable. His stormy blue eyes were easy to look at and the light scruff along his jaw was inviting me in for a feel. Not being able to pursue my prize catch was a shame. But I had to get out of this situation and avoid the East Bay Resort for as long as I could. If Aunt Aimee needed us to go for a bridal emergency, I'd have to ditch somehow. I couldn't risk seeing him again and him reporting us for my stupid side biz antics.

I skimmed my finger down his arm and slipped my other hand into my pocket for my keys. "Good luck fixing the air conditioner," I said, then I took off running.

"I was joking, you know!" His shout was mixed with fervent laughter.

There was no chance I'd turn around because there was no way I would trust him. I never trusted *them* anymore.

"Mark!"

I shook my head and turned around, the noisy air conditioning unit coming back into focus along with John's pissed off voice and face. "What's up?"

"What's up? What the hell are you doing?" He hooked his hands on his hips and glared from behind his Ray-Bans.

I glanced at the unit, at the tool bag on the ground, and shrugged. "I heard the call for this one, so I figured I'd stop over and take a look. I thought it might be a belt problem, but it sounds like we'll have to order a new blade. The things shaking pretty good." I smiled to myself, thinking about the girl who had just run away, the way her body rocked while sitting on top.

He shook his head an annoyingly little amount, as if his neck only moved an inch under the stress of its overexerted muscles. "And why were you shouting? I know this is loud, but there's absolutely no reason to shout across the parking lot. You'll scare the guests."

"Seriously? Let's talk about scaring the guests for a second, Hulk."

John's muscles bulged at the insult. "I can't help it if my physique intimidates people," he said, allowing his vanity to dilute the superiority cloud always hovering around him for a single moment. He thought being ten years older gave him authority even though we held the same position and started working for East Bay at roughly the same time.

I laughed with a nod, knowing a change in direction was the best way to deal with him. "Well, I couldn't help what that girl's physique did to me."

"What girl?"

"Oh, man. She was pretty hot."

John cracked a smile and the patchy beard he called a babe-catcher twitched. "Oh, yeah?"

"Yeah, she was ..." She was cute. And hilarious. I had no idea what the hell she was doing, but I hardly cared. Messing with her was fun. The way she bristled, getting all bent out of shape for a minute before trying to seduce me.

"She was ... what?" John's pushy voice broke through my thoughts.

I turned back toward the parking lot and wiped the sweat off my brow. "She was something." I just didn't know what.

"Wow. Riveting," he scoffed. "Whatever, man. Just go turn in your shit. Your shift's up and you know they're not paying unnecessary overtime."

"Yeah," I agreed, grabbing the tool bag as my phone rang a high-pitched horror ringtone. After plucking it from my pocket, I glimpsed the caller name out of habit even though I already knew it was Pacey. "Later," I said to John then hit the answer button and started to walk. "There's the gorgeous bridezilla!"

I immediately heard an exaggerated sigh at the other end. "You sound chipper. You finished work?"

"Yeah, heading to clock out now. What are you up to?"

"I'm up to my ears in this wedding crap. I just … Why did I even think coordinating it myself was a good idea?" She sighed again. Not a good sign.

"Listen, Pay. It's all going to be fine, all right? And it'll be over before you know it. It's less than a month away. Isn't everything already done?"

Her scathing laugh was so loud I had to yank the phone from my ear. "Ah, ease up. Shit."

"Of course you men have no idea. Do you think things just come together with no orchestration?"

Didn't they? "Of course not."

"I've had a few cancellations already," she continued, "jacking the seating up again. Then there's the freaking videographer. I don't even want to start on that. And now Leah and Maria bailed on my fitting tomorrow because they're sick."

"Fitting?"

"Pretty sure I've mentioned my dress before." Her voice was light, teasing, but the higher pitch was indicative of her annoyance.

"Oh, the dress. My fault," I said, walking around the corner to the maintenance building's entrance. "I'm sorry things aren't going easily. Do you need my help with anything? I mean, I know that I'm—"

"You can come to my fitting tomorrow," she interrupted.

I chuckled at her as I moved through the locker area, ditching the tool bag by the storage racks. "Sorry, I have to work tomorrow."

"Bullshit," she snapped, and I laughed some more. She never fell for my crap. She was immune before she learned her first cuss word.

"Honestly, none of your other wedding fembots can help with this? I would think I'd be the last pick for that. Well, maybe not the last pick."

"Of course you're not the last pick because you're actually allowed to see the dress without ruining everything. And yes, with Leah and Maria puking their guts out, my other choices were Mom—who is busy—and Guy's stepsister, Edena—who's also busy with work and preparing an early family dinner tomorrow or something. Everyone has plans. I swear, Leah is bombing her maid of honor duties. She's trying to kill this wedding. I know it."

"That's a tad dramatic. But yes, of course I would love to fill in for the sick maid of honor and go to my baby sister's dress fitting for her too soon wedding." I nodded a silent greeting to a couple of guys in the employee lounge then stepped outside to head over to my condo building. Being within walking distance of my place was one of the biggest perks to living on the resort property. I had no complaints. The District inside East Bay was its own little community and it had everything a single guy needed. Food. Bars. Events. It was a hot spot for everyone, locals and vacationers. The gardens located on the same side of the resort were also where Pacey's wedding was booked.

"After everything I just told you, your razzing is uncalled for." Her pitch climbed a notch again.

"You're right. You're right. No more razzing. Just text me the time and I'll come pick you up."

"Thanks."

"Welcome. Now go get yourself a drink and chill out. Oh wait. That's right, you aren't quite old enough."

"Mark!" she screamed into the phone.

I pulled it away from my ear again, cringing and laughing. "I can't help it."

"Okay, asshole. Since you started it. Do you have your plus-one yet?"

I grumbled and glanced over at the packed pool across from my condo building, staring at all the bare skin and string bikinis as I passed by. The plus-one dilemma was one I'd rather avoid. I never dated locals, and convincing a vacationer to go to a wedding would be a pain in the ass. Someone who worked at the resort might be down to go. Tonya, the lifeguard, or Cari, the cutie from East Bay's main reception ... But taking someone to a wedding was a bigger deal than other dates. A beer at the bar and dinner at the harbor was completely different than doing the Cupid Shuffle and introducing drunk Uncle Harv. I didn't want anyone getting the wrong idea.

"I told you to stop the razzing, but no." She dragged the O sound out through mocking tones like she was eight again. "Now you have to deal."

"Yeah, yeah." I sighed. "I'd rather come alone. But it's your day, so I'll have to get back to you."

"I figured. Sooner than later, okay?"

"Sure—"

"And you're still meeting up with Guy on Friday, right? What bar?"

"Right. How could I forget the start of the fun weekends leading to the wedding?" I couldn't contain my sarcasm. The pre-wedding events sounded less than thrilling, but she was my sister and I wanted everything about her wedding to be as special as she needed it to be. That required me sucking it up and attending some corny functions. "It'll be here, at The Dive. Don't worry, I'll look after your precious reality star and make sure no one messes up his pretty hair."

"Quit."

"Quit what? It's just ..." It was just his claim to fame and the winnings that didn't sit well with me. They met at the University of West Florida a year before he went on the live-in reality show Beach Bum and won some cash. His proposal to her was right after his time in the spotlight, and I didn't exactly trust that he wouldn't succumb to the idea of fame. Where would that leave her?

"I don't need the 'no one will ever be good enough' fatherly crap right now. I thought you liked him?"

"I'm more worried for him, really," I teased and laughed again, attempting to defuse her.

"You're such a jerk," she replied with a soft laugh. "See you tomorrow."

"Later," I said and hung up.

She'd be married soon. That messed with my head. Four years separated us, but that didn't stop us from being close. She had always looked up to me, so it felt weird for her to be taking this step so soon. She wasn't even finished with college.

I bypassed the indoor elevators and jogged up the stairs to my pricey one bedroom on the third floor. It was worth it to live in The District. I liked the convenience, the constant noise, and the rotation of renters. There was something about it all that made me feel free. Maybe it was the anonymity. Despite working on the property, I was able to keep to myself. Unless I actually wanted company. Then all I had to do was walk the block to Main Street and hit up any of the bars or restaurants. There was always something happening.

I tossed my keys on my small coffee table, grabbed a Corona from the fridge, and moved out onto my small balcony to look toward The District. The mass of voices drew me in, but I had no desire to be engulfed by it. Thoughts of Pacey's wedding had me too mellow to go lose myself in a crowd ... or a woman.

A pair of brown eyes flashed to mind. I tipped the beer to my lips and smiled just thinking about the girl sitting on the busted air conditioner while spying on someone in the courtyard. Was it an ex of hers? She wasn't mad enough for it to be a current relationship. That would have involved tears, screams, or both. So what then? Maybe she was enjoying the show after all, or was drawn in by a hot moment. I only caught the tail end of what looked like a nice make-out session. My attention was mostly on her. Her chestnut ponytail was pretty long, some strands sticking to the damp skin of her neck. Her tank top also stuck to her skin in the most delicious looking way. I could still feel the heat from her eyes when she glanced up at me, from her touch when her hand grabbed my arm. That moment had been intense enough to stop all my thoughts.

I shook my head and stared at the trees lining the horizon. She didn't back down from my shit, that was for sure. It would have been interesting if she hadn't taken off. I had a feeling I wouldn't see her again, though. And that was a real damn shame.

3
Gia

Working at Silhouette Bridal Boutique was a special kind of hell most days. Not because I was a wedding hater per se. I was more ambivalent about the whole institution, really. I'd seen so many marriages fall apart, so many relationships crumble. Lives changed forever because one person—or both—decided they didn't care enough about the other to say "Hey, you know what? I want to go bang other people, so let's just call it a day." Okay, maybe that wouldn't help all that much. Lives would still be changed forever. But I still believed the sting of it all would be far less if the person was just honest. On a level of one to shitty, deceitfulness was right up there beside the act of sticking anything into another woman's fun hole.

That was my opinion anyway. And I had expressed that very opinion to my asshole ex, Landon, with a slew of profanity and punches after he and another chick's fun hole had stumbled into his dorm room at Florida State while I was naked on his bed, waiting to surprise him one life-changing night. He had his dick out, she was on her knees, and I was fully dressed before either had noticed me. The drive home from Tallahassee was splendid. Fun times.

He was just one of the many selfish asses who wanted their cake and ho-bag muffin too. Lies didn't matter. Lives didn't matter. Love never mattered. The only thing that mattered was his mediocre pecker and the five minutes it took him to make the O face.

Yes, of course I was still pissed six months later. Those kinds of feelings didn't just go away overnight. That was the reason I started Duplicity. I felt bad for other people who were being lied to, the other girls—sometimes guys—who couldn't track their significant others without being detected. They needed justice too, and I was happy to help them because I was rewarded with the victorious high of catching the assholes. Call it cathartic. The money was nice too.

My Velostar's tires squealed when I slammed the brakes in one of the parking spots that lined our storefront windows, making some patrons emerging from Fresh Brewed clutch their to-go coffees a little tighter and scowl in my direction. The local favorite coffee spot was our building-mate in a multi-sectioned strip mall, not far from Destin Harbor and beautiful beaches along the Gulf of Mexico—where a majority of our clients' nuptials were professed ... and sometimes flushed.

After grabbing my own cup of late-morning caffeine, I yanked the glass door open and stepped into Silhouette's with a sigh. Another day, another couple of helpless romantics to assist in the start of their journey leading to eventual regret. With a deep inhale, the familiar stale smell of fabric and false promises hit my nose. As usual, though, the intensity of my bitterness was drowned out by comfort. The black and white decor and the patterned wall displays instantly made me think of my mom. The boutique was her and Aunt Aimee's dream, something she treasured daily until her death two years prior. It was a huge part of her life, so she was everywhere inside. That would never change.

The latest in top-forty pop music pumped cheerfully from our surround speakers, filling the whole space up to the open ceiling, but all else was quiet. The reception desk was empty. There was no movement around the headless mannequin dress stands or back toward the more crowded rack displays, no people lounging in the waiting area's upholstered chairs or in the two bigger dressing areas along the side of the store—the privacy curtains hung wide open.

I knew Aunt Aimee had some high school stuff to handle for the start of Viv's senior year, but Kass was scheduled to work. She was the only other person who was qualified to make alterations for the two fitting appointments scheduled for the day. It wasn't exactly like her to leave the store unattended, even to grab a quick coffee next door. The store was her life too.

Loud thuds from the back of the store traveled out over the music. Fearing the worst, I slipped across the hardwood floor, ditched my purse and coffee, then snatched the closest display shoe for a weapon. I smacked its heel across my palm, testing the level of pain it could render until I remembered its price. Bloodstains wouldn't sell. The silver jewelry T-bar displayed on the accessory ledge was a better bet. I grabbed it instead and shook the lacy garters off. It was heavy enough. The ends were blunt. I swung it through the air once then moved toward the back of the store.

The back storage and alteration room door was closed, so I leaned in and pressed my ear to the wood. Someone spoke, a thick voice. *Not Kass.* I cranked the lever and shoved through the door with the T-bar cocked back, prepared to crush whoever was trespassing like a spider. A big, fat spider, hopefully one not armed with a gun.

Kass jumped backward, dropping her leg off the table, and so did the guy beside her. Tall. Blond. Shirtless.

"Shit, Gia," she said, sweeping her long dark hair away from her face then straightening the waist of her canary-colored maxi dress. "Put that down before you hurt yourself." Her cheeks were a shade of red, definitely not caused by embarrassment. Kass never did the walk of shame. She sauntered to the next bed.

Mr. Blond and Gorgeous chuckled at the situation—or me—as he pulled a T-shirt over his head.

I let my weapon fall limply to my side and stared her down. "Really?" It was a question she was used to hearing from me. Not that I objected to her vagina's 'all dicks welcome' policy as much anymore. It was her life. But I was a little miffed that she had brought the latest one to work.

She only rolled her big icy blues at me then flashed them to her daytime date with a quick bat of her lashes and kiss of her naturally plump set of pouters. "Thanks for dropping by."

"My pleasure," he assured, then gave me a cocky grin before heading toward the back loading door.

We watched him silently. As soon as the steel door shut, I slugged her in the arm.

"Ow," she whined, but moved past me without bothering to acknowledge it otherwise.

"C'mon, Kass. You know there's no dick time at work." I skimmed my fingers across the table, moving some cut tulle and lace. I was always worried about her being safe, but I'd never lecture her. Remembering where they'd just had sex, I quickly wiped my hands down the sides of my high-waisted pencil skirt. Hopefully that hadn't gotten any sweat—or other stuff—on the loose material.

She stepped beside the mannequin that sported the start of her latest design. Her fingers tucked the edging of the unfinished bateau neckline. "It's not like it was the first time." She tried for snarky, but the soft words betrayed her. "Don't worry, it won't happen again."

We moved out to the front. She grabbed a water from the guest refrigerator and dropped onto the small love seat. I returned the T-bar to its display and stepped behind the reception desk, pulling up the inventory information, noting that Viv had already updated the latest shipment. Taking a long drink of my mocha latte, I flipped to the daily schedule.

"You have one of your own on the schedule today. In fifteen minutes. Pacey." We carried several designers and some off the rack extras, but Silhouette's special tags were custom made by Kass. She designed and created gowns, proud to give some brides the opportunity to wear something completely unique.

Her full lips smiled so big I thought her face would crack from the sudden, unfamiliar pressure. "Oh, right. Pretty Pacey. The fit and flare special. She's the one who's marrying Guy."

I lifted a brow at her but dropped my eyes back to the monitor.

"You know. I know I told you. The guy named Guy from that local reality show a while back. What was it called? Where they had all the people in that Pensacola house and did beach challenges. People voted via text." She stretched out her long legs, allowing the maxi dress to pool like melted sunshine on the floor below, and propped her feet onto the low birch wood coffee table. "Beach Bum. That was it. Some of those guys were hot. Girls too. I can't lie."

"Never watched it, but I know her dress. Crepe and lace filigree sweetheart neck. Today's her final fitting, right?" I downed the remainder of my mocha latte in a long gulp, needing the caffeine to push faster. Looking at the schedule, I could already tell the day would drag. Things had been too slow lately.

"Yeah, should be. The last adjustments were minor, so I'm praying she doesn't kill me by switching bras or something." She sighed loud and deep. "I'll pull the dress in a minute. I'm exhausted." She took another sip of water and laid her head back.

"I bet you are," I quipped with a laugh that morphed from girlie giggle to full-on ho cackle.

She joined me, and we drowned the latest top-forty title with our oldies sister song that didn't play often enough.

When my unexpected hysteria and her amusement died down, she said, "Oh, I needed that just as bad as I needed his wide seven. He did this thing when we were standing—"

I held up a hand. "I don't need to know. All your recounts mix together anyway, so spare me."

"I'm not sparing you anything. You need this. It's not like you've been having your fill," she teased and let her head fall back again, closing her eyes. "The only action you're getting is what you're spying on. How's business, by the way?"

Staring blankly at the appointment schedule, yesterday's Duplicity job flickered to mind. The heat between that couple, the heat between my thighs. The maintenance guy.

"Hey!" Kass said, breaking my thoughts, snapping her fingers. "What's that gaga look on your face? What happened yesterday?"

I shook my head and glanced around the room. "I caught the guy. Nothing new. I already pushed the pics through to the client. Viv said payment was made."

"Nah-uh. Something else happened. I can see it on your goofy face."

I huffed. Of course she had to be super sister and notice crap I didn't want her to. "Well ... I was spotted—"

"Shit." She sat up and tucked her bare feet beside her on the couch. "But you didn't get busted?"

I smiled and bit the side of my lip, thinking of the maintenance guy.

"Oh, you're seriously holding out. It was a guy. Was it *the* guy?"

"What? No!" I scrunched my eyebrows at the thought. I mean, it hadn't been too difficult to watch the cheater in action, but he definitely wasn't as hot as ... "There was this maintenance guy at East Bay. He saw me spying on the target."

"Go on," she drawled.

I chuckled. "I tried to work some girl magic and flirt to get away. At first he didn't seem to buy it, so I improvised ... then bolted before he knew what was happening."

"No follow through?" She stood up and hooked her hands on her narrow hips.

"Like I had a choice. He thought I was either a dirty perv or illegally snooping." I dropped my eyes to the screen. "I couldn't bank on him not reporting me, and I still can't chance it, so I won't be able to go with you if there are any wedding day emergencies there. At least on the bay side. The gulf side is probably safe."

She walked closer to the desk. "I'm willing to bet you could have hooked it up. You have it all, Gia. You just need to get around yourself and your hatred for all things with a penis, show a little confidence, and cut loose. Commitment is overrated anyway."

"Okay, Blanche." She had a point, but I was tired of hearing it. She'd been trying to get me past the Landon issue for months. Nothing worked. Following her advice, I'd plunged into a couple name-optional bar hook-ups to clear my head. They just didn't clear my heart.

"Better Blanche than Dorothy," she retorted with a shrug. "Anyway ... Do you have any new cheating gigs? Need me to catch any guys?"

"No new hits on the website, but I'll let you know if I need those C cup snake charmers again." Baiting a cheater wasn't really the direction I wanted Duplicity to take, but we'd had one request for a gentle nudge toward unfaithful and Kass had been a sure thing. She got the job done.

The phone rang beside me and Kass backed away from the desk with a spin. "I'll go grab Pretty Pacey's dress from the back."

"Silhouette Bridal Boutique, Gia speaking," I answered, staring out past the parking lot at the busy lunch traffic. As I was wrapping up the phone call, a sleek Charger pulled in and parked beside my car, sporting similar dark gray paint. The car doors pushed open and two people got out. "Yes, that's correct. We'll see you—" I gaped at the two people outside, blinking furiously, worried I was hallucinating but knowing there was no such luck.

Moving onto the sidewalk was a petite brunette I recognized as Pacey, and beside her was the dark-haired, stormy blue-eyed maintenance guy. *He can't be her fiancé, right?* No matter how contemporary, not many brides wanted their husbands to see the dress before the big day. He wore plain khaki shorts and a solid blue T-shirt, with adorably messy hair and a smile that made my mouth fall open. He looked even better than I remembered ... and was about two steps from entering the store.

I tossed the phone into the air with a yelp and ducked below the desk, smacking my forehead in the process. "Ouch."

"Gia! What the hell?" Kass yelled from somewhere in the middle of the store.

The door swooshed open, sucking the air out of the room, out of my lungs, as I squatted in fear under the desk. I was in a horror movie. That was the only explanation. I was the lead extra about to die of horrible embarrassment within the first ten minutes, right after the opening credits.

Who was he? I covered my heart in a useless attempt to quiet its raging drum solo.

"Hi, Pacey. Welcome back," Kass greeted the bride-to-be.

"Hey, Kass," Pacey's sweet voice replied. "This is my brother, Mark. The girls bailed today, so I twisted his arm."

Oh, here we go. I bit down on my lip. All hope of him doing the guy thing and dropping her off was out the window. One look at Kass and he'd stick around, killing all chances of me going unnoticed.

"Nice to meet you, Mark." Kass' voice was dipped in way more sexy than usual. The tone was soft and silky, and it stabbed me right in the gut. *Crap.* Maybe I didn't want to go unnoticed after all. The dilemma twisted inside. If I outed myself, could I chance that he wouldn't report me after the fact? Could I risk any repercussions it might have on the boutique?

"Nice to meet you, too. I'm not sure I'll be much help, but I'm here." Oh, his voice ... did things. It sounded so much better when it wasn't being drowned out by the clanking of a broken air conditioner. Smooth, resonant, something I wouldn't mind listening to on the regular. In my ear. In my bedroom. Against my skin.

"I'm sure just being here is helping tremendously," Kass assured. "So, Pacey, this last one shouldn't take long at all. The dress is hanging in the first room there. Feel free to show Mark and I'll be right back to help you into it if you want."

Bare feet shuffled hurriedly on the hardwood toward the desk. Kass' legs came into view, followed by her face as she bent to see me. "What are you doing?" she whispered.

"It's him!" I whisper-mimed back.

"What? Him who?"

"That guy. Mark. That's the guy from the East Bay Resort yesterday."

Her eyes bulged. "Seriously?"

"No, I'm just squatting here because I wanna be a duck ... Yes," I hissed. "I should try to get out of here."

"Okay, I'll distract them."

I nodded, and she pointed at the dressing room before standing and heading that way.

"What do you think about it, Mark?" Kass asked.

I waited for him to reply then crept out along the side of the desk. Kass had positioned herself at the back of the store, forcing them to face her. I crouched low and started for the front door, one eye on them and the other on the escape, hoping my flats wouldn't squeak on the floor. Kass let out her patent flirtatious laugh and touched Mark's arm, halting me for a moment. Her eyes locked with mine, staring then shifting wildly, willing me to move. I shook my stutter off, but as I took another step, Mark followed Kass' nervous gaze and his eyes landed right on me. Then widened.

4

Mark

"I was just heading over to grab a coffee. Does anyone want anything?" The sweet words came out of her cute mouth as if she hadn't just appeared out of thin air, as if I wasn't stalking toward her, as if she didn't recognize who I was.

"Right," Kass spoke behind me. "I'm so sorry I hadn't offered. Would you guys like something from next door? We have water here, of course, but if you'd like something else ..."

Kass knew her. That much was clear. So who was she and how did she get here? And why was she at East Bay the previous day? I would get answers before she could disappear again.

"Mark?" Pacey called from behind me, ignoring Kass' questions. And I ignored hers, continuing my walk across the wood floor to the girl who looked way more professional today but just as sexy.

She held her stance, only shifting a little when I took my final step. We were nearly as close as we had been the day before. She bit her lips together and her eyes shifted toward the door.

"I'll help grab drinks. I'll be right back to see the dress," I called over my shoulder to Pacey, then leaned closer to the girl to push the door open behind her.

She sidestepped through, not fully turning her back on me to exit.

As the door closed and the outside noise and warm breeze off the gulf surrounded us, I let my eyes wander over her. The high-waisted, tight skirt and loose, sleeveless top she wore was all business compared to the sweaty tank and shorts from the day before. It gave her a confident look that I'd only glimpsed at the resort in the seconds before she had taken off. What really made me smile was the flush in her cheeks, which made her look a little flustered, like when I'd first caught her. There seemed to be a battle raging inside her as her body bounced lightly in place and her hands twisted, igniting my attraction. I wondered if the situation was the cause, or if I was. Either way, it had to be why she attempted to duck out without being seen.

"Are you just going to stare at me all day or are you going to put me out of my misery?" she said, taking a slow step toward the coffee place.

I laughed lightly. "I was going to ask if you were following me, but since Kass covered your exit attempt, I'm guessing you work here."

She nodded and glanced around with a nervous smile, not offering more information.

"Yesterday, I would have guessed a gentlemen's club," I continued, watching her eyes snap back to mine, narrowed with fury. "Or maybe an adult store of some kind ... since you like to watch and all." I tossed all the chips in with a grin and waited. She'd either find it funny or offensive. After our rather flirtatious discussion about voyeurism the other day and the way she had ditched me, I was betting on funny.

The corner of her lips tipped up painfully slow, triggering a small amount of air to slip past my lips in relief. Her eyelids closed and she shook her head the tiniest bit, not even causing a ripple in her sleek ponytail. She opened her eyes again, soft and amiable.

Their brown color matched her hair, chestnut with lighter streaks catching in the sun. "Both would be okay jobs, I suppose, but I prefer lace and idealistic brides to leather and sweaty dollar bills."

I laughed, trying really hard to focus on her eyes and not picture her in lace or leather, which was almost impossible. "Is that right? I can see how it might be more appealing." With a nod toward the coffee place, I took the lead in that direction then opened the door and followed her inside the empty shop.

A rainbow-haired barista joked about her being back again so soon and asked if she wanted her usual. She accepted with a polite, "Hold the scone again and on the tab, please."

I would have offered to pay, but she was too quick, and I was too busy watching her. There was something easy about her movements, graceful and comfortable. Her body was fit but not overly so, with the kind of curves on her hips and thighs my hands itched to explore.

"And what will you have?" the barista asked, stealing my attention.

Despite the delicious and enticing smell of the shop, coffee was the last thing I wanted. But I pulled my wallet out anyway and fished for a few bills. "Tall, black."

The girl let out a breathy laugh and moved toward the serving side of the counter. I handed the barista the bills, quickly dropped the change she handed back into the tip jar, and followed behind the girl. I still didn't know her name.

"Something funny?" I asked, turning sideways and resting an elbow on the high ledge.

Her nose wrinkled a tad and the barista chuckled, eavesdropping from behind the milk steamer. Conspirators.

"Nothing," she replied with a sweet grin, "just a boring order. Very ... maintenance man."

"Should I have ordered something a little more gentlemen's club? Like a stripped latte or a ... lappuccino?" I closed my eyes for an extended moment, immediately regretting the cheesiness of the last one.

"Oh, that was so bad." She smiled, fully, bright white teeth gleaming at me, and I couldn't help but smile back.

"I know. I'm so disappointed in myself. My pun game is usually on point."

Noticing her drink order on the counter, she reached up to retrieve it. "Are you sure Pacey doesn't want anything?"

"She doesn't need caffeine, believe me. Her energy level is spastic enough." I chuckled about my sister, but my mind was only on the girl in front of me. Pacey wouldn't object. In fact, she was probably planning my wedding to this girl while trying on her own dress.

"One of those brides, huh?"

"Mostly just one of those people. She can get hyper and overly excitable, especially when things aren't going according to plan. She's very ... together."

"Gotcha." She brought the blank cup to her lips for a sip. I scowled at it, not seeing any words or letters. After her sip, her head tilted. "What was that look for?"

"Your cup's blank."

"You're mad at the cup for being blank?"

I shrugged. "I was hoping to see your name because I still don't know it."

"Kate knows me well enough not to write it, especially in an empty shop." She shrugged right back. "And if you want my name that bad, why not ask?"

"Honestly?" I said, welcoming the direct conversation so I could stare freely, admiring her daring eyes, mousy nose, and the soft look of her lips. "I was trying to be smooth." The barista—Kate—held my coffee out to me with a smile. When I grabbed it, she winked before letting go. For the briefest moment I thought she was flirting, but then I saw the scribbled word on my cup. *Gia.* A gorgeous name. I returned Kate's wink, thanking her. Her approval was good news, especially if she knew Gia well. Maybe Gia wasn't dating anyone.

"So let's recap," Gia said. "You're not bringing your pun 'A' game and you aren't that smooth." Her voice was cool and her eyes twinkled, showing a bit of excitement to have the upper hand.

"Ouch." I took a sip of my coffee. "Oh, and don't forget that I drink boring maintenance man coffee."

"Right. Can't forget that," she quipped, biting the very edge of her bottom lip with a nod.

I knew I was staring at her like a lunatic, but I couldn't stop. I had to keep looking, to keep talking. "I feel like you know so much about me now, and I hardly know anything about you ... Gia." I watched her eyes. When they widened, realizing I had said her name, I took a sip of my coffee, making sure she could see her name on my cup.

Her nose wrinkled and her lips pursed in mock anger. "Thanks a lot, traitor Kate."

"Welcome," Barista Kate said with a giggle from somewhere behind the counter.

"You work at a bridal shop and your name is Gia. See? Your knowledge of me far outweighs what I know about you. That has to change."

"Oh, does it? I'm not so sure. I mean, I'll give you points on smoothness—even though you cheated—but I'm still not impressed by your puns."

"You don't like my puns?" I smirked, turning my body a little so she could see my butt. "I think I have nice puns. They might be a bit stiff but that's because I try to keep the cheese away—"

She laughed, full and high, holding her cup out to keep it steady. "Oh, God. Stop ... I can't—"

"What? At least they aren't stinky puns ... Well, the lappuccino might be *straddling* that line a bit."

"Okay, okay," she said, holding up her hands in surrender. "I give." Her smile was real, not generated for an ulterior motive, like free drinks at the bar, and it struck me in a way nothing else had in a while.

"Good," I said, "cause my puns were getting tired."

"Please ... they started that way." She rolled her pretty eyes at me and stuck her tongue out a little.

She handled corny well, but it was definitely time to move on. "So, Gia, bridal shop worker, you gonna tell me why you were really hanging out by the townhouses at East Bay yesterday?" Those pretty eyes glanced toward the door. *Shit.* "Sorry, that was a bit rude. It's not really any of my business."

"No, it's okay. I was just thinking that I should probably get back to work." She took a few steps in that direction. "And your sister is probably waiting to show you her dress."

"Right," I agreed, following her outside.

"It was for work," she said, answering my question. "Sometimes we go out to the wedding venues. But I wasn't exactly where I should have been."

"So you ditched me because you really thought I'd report you?" I filled in the gaps of her explanation, but I had a feeling something was still missing. There was no way I would ask any more questions about it, though. Prying further wouldn't land a date, which was definitely my goal. I needed to see her again.

"Yeah, pretty much," she admitted. "I mean, I knew you were probably joking, but I didn't want to risk anything coming back on the shop. It's my aunt's place. Family run." She tipped her head back, looking at the sign overhead. "My mom and aunt started the business years ago. My sisters also work here. So you can see why I didn't want to chance it."

"Sure, I get that. Then Kass is your sister?"

"Yeah. Older. My younger sister, Viv, and my aunt Aimee are out right now. They'll be in later."

"And your mom?"

Her lips turned down a little and her fingers tapped lightly on the lid of her coffee. "She died a couple years ago."

"Oh, I'm sorry."

"No, it's okay. I just don't talk about it with many people, especially people I don't really know." A light smile quirked on her lips. "I guess this is just an odd enough situation as it is. The way we met ... and then you showing up here."

"It is. I didn't expect to see you again, but I'm glad I did." I looked through the storefront window, watching Pacey sway in front of several angled mirrors, wearing her dream dress. "I'll have to thank my sister for manipulating me into coming today." I smiled at Gia.

She looked through the window too. "We should go in. Kass probably had to answer all the phone calls."

I nodded in agreement, knowing there was no way to ask for more of her time without crossing some psycho line. So I leaned closer to her, smelling a hint of her sweet perfume as I grabbed hold of the door handle and pulled it open.

"Thanks," she said, and I nodded again.

I followed her in, and we were both bombarded. Kass hustled across the room to meet Gia at the front desk, her bright yellow skirt trailing in a long streak.

"Hey!" Pacey yelled at me. "What do you think?"

I hadn't the first clue about wedding dresses, but I knew it made her look even more amazing. "Wow, Pay. It's beautiful."

She beamed, gently grasping the sides and swishing it around as she rocked her body. "It is, isn't it? Kass is brilliant. She knew exactly what I wanted. The fit is perfect, tight enough to allow for the usual nervous weight loss."

"No weight gain then, huh? Guess I can't buy you any mint chocolate chip ice cream until after the big day."

"I will kill you," she threatened, giving me crazy eyes with a bright smile.

"Ha!" I laughed and took a long drink of my coffee before turning my head to sneak a glimpse at Gia. She and Kass were whispering behind the desk. She glanced at me and quickly turned away.

"You've got some 'splaining to do," Pacey whispered.

"I'm not the only one apparently." I smirked. "We'll talk later."

"Damn right we will." She continued to stare at her reflection.

For the rest of the time we were there, I had to force myself not to get up and walk to Gia. She was working, and I had to stay in control. There was no way I'd blow my chance by coming off too eager. But, man, staying in control was hard. My focus was entirely on her, studying the way she moved when she went to the back of the store for something, listening to her voice when she spoke to customers on the phone or to the few who had ventured inside.

"If there are any problems we need to worry about, call us immediately. Otherwise, it'll be ready for pickup the week prior," Kass said to Pacey, walking toward the door when she was finished.

I crossed the room to toss my empty coffee in the trash and leaned onto the higher section of the desk, catching a smile from Gia as she ended a phone conversation.

"I want to see you again," I said, being direct to make up for the half hour I had to restrain myself. "Can I call you?"

She bit her lips together, squishing the smile, and nodded. "Sure."

I handed my phone over and watched her tap some info.

"I texted myself ... a coffee emoji." Her eyes closed and her head shook the slightest bit.

I tucked the phone back into my pocket, smiling at her cute reaction. "I'll call you. Maybe we can go out, somewhere other than our jobs."

She laughed with a nod and tapped her fingers on the desk beside the keyboard. "Yes, no more crashing work."

"Right. Later then." I smiled and took a few backward steps.

"Bye," she replied, and, reluctantly, I turned toward the door.

As soon as Pacey and I slipped inside the quiet car, she laughed. "Start talking."

5

Gia

"**W**ell, well, well. Looks like someone hooked something spectacular," Kass stated as soon as Mark and Pacey stepped outside, her body gliding with a peppy walk toward the dressing room to store the dress.

I tilted my face down, pretending to look at the computer screen while I continued to watch the car outside until it pulled away. Had all of that really happened? He seemed ... nice and normal. Normal enough not to report me. At the very least, he seemed to believe my reason for being at the resort the previous day. But my cynical brain still screamed at me. I wouldn't be the only one affected if he turned out to be a dick.

"Ew. What's with the face?" Kass walked out from the back, glaring at me with an evil eye. She crossed her arms. "I know that face. That's the Gia over-thinking-it face."

"Gia's over thinking it? What else is new?" Viv's squeaky voice traveled up from the back of the store, beating her petite body around the dress displays.

"Hey. Where's Aunt Aim?" Kass replied as Viv emerged, her black jeans and tank a stark contrast to the white fabric behind her.

"She ran over to AJ's to grab lunch."

"Gia's got a guy all hot for her." Kass skipped the convo back and leaned a hip against the edge of the high desk.

Viv scooped her massive blond mane off a shoulder then slid her backpack down to the floor. She commenced her normal ritual of removing her laptop and setting up her personal geek area, preparing for a shift of bridal boredom. "Wow," she said with no hint of enthusiasm to back up the statement. "Whenever did you find the time to meet someone?"

"You're hilarious," I replied, my voice mimicking her flat tone.

"During the last job." Kass fed into Viv's joke.

"Duplicity?" Viv sounded more interested now even though she continued her setup. Plugging in. Starting up. She stopped and looked at me, her gray eyes wide. "It wasn't ...?"

"No," I replied irritably. "What is with both of you? You really think I'd fall for a target?"

Kass looked at Viv, and they both shrugged. I huffed a breath out and went back to staring at the screen with no real focus.

Viv also turned her attention back to her laptop, fingers traveling the keys at crackhead speed. "Well, you really don't stray from your routine. So who then? Someone at a nearby café, like Fresh Brewed Frank?"

Kass snorted as she moved to the couch and plopped down.

Frank was the coffee shop creeper who showed up most days just to watch us and our clients from his car. Pretty sure he was doing what Mark had accused me of. *Mark.* I thought of his smile at East Bay Resort, teasing me about the air conditioner. "There was this maintenance guy ..."

Viv side-eyed me. "Sounds porn-worthy."

"Go on," Kass' voice bellowed with her face tipped up toward the ceiling, dragging the words as if she'd just gotten in from a night of drinking Jack ... or doing a guy named Jack ... or both. She still wanted the full story, but there was no way she'd get it.

I rolled my eyes and flipped through inventory lists, still with no focus. The only thing I could picture was his eyes. Blue. Deep blue. The kind that got all the phone numbers. The kind that made promises to souls. The kind that retired brand new panties. The kind that twinkled "I love you" in Morse code as they watched hearts break open.

"Stop it!" Kass called from the couch. "I can read your man-bashing mind from over here with that over-thinking-it look on your face. Twenty-two is too young to be such a hater. Not all guys are the same, Gia."

"Duplicity would suggest otherwise," I mumbled, having seen it time and time again. Cheating. Lying. Greedy men readily ditching their relationships to plunge into a brand new fun hole.

"Well, you may want to get a different hobby then. It's corrupting your mind."

"There's no way you're dropping Duplicity," Viv butted in. "Not after the work I've done. The site is locked tight, and we're making a decent amount of money." I really had her to thank for most of the technical work. She was the computer brain of the family, and after I'd come to her with the early ideas for Duplicity, she helped push it all into reality. Without her, I'd be meeting clients in a trench coat and exchanging manila envelopes instead of using burner phones and encrypted access codes.

"The money may be good, but it's fueling our sister's ugly man-hating fire." She sat up and looked straight at me. "Seriously, though, if you don't go for Mark, I will. He was ... oomph." Her lips pulled into an open-mouthed smirk and she ran her tongue along the edge of her top teeth.

"He was oomph?" I questioned with an exaggerated eye roll. That was an understatement, but I wasn't about to admit that to her. He was so much more than oomph. Over at Fresh Brewed, he had my body buzzing hard enough to last a full week without coffee ... or pastries. And when we'd come back to the boutique, I couldn't even think with him sitting in the same room. *We sell wedding dresses? What wedding dresses?* Most of the phone calls I'd taken were dead air for a full minute before I'd realized the callers had already hung up.

"Did you see his arms? And that ass ... yum," Kass blabbed on.

The thought of her having him in the back room like Mr. Blond and Gorgeous made my stomach flip. "You got a good view of his ass because he wasn't looking at you."

"Oh snap. He didn't even look at Kass?" Viv's eyes popped wide, still looking at her screen.

"No, he didn't," Kass confirmed with a chuckle. "His eyes were occupied fully with Gia's goodies."

"Hold up, though," Viv said. "I thought you saw him on the job? He was here too?"

"He's Pretty Pacey's brother. One of the two October brides who bought my tag. She dragged him here for her final fitting. Gia must have made an impression yesterday because he was on her like—"

"You on any dick?" Viv interrupted.

A laugh burst through my lips and Kass joined in, nodding at the truth.

"What's so funny?" Aunt Aimee stepped through the front door, holding a to-go box in one hand and using the other to push her sunglasses through her dusty blond hair. With only twelve years separating her from Kass, she was the young aunt we always liked hanging with even before our mom had died. Her fragrant perfume mixed with her lunch spread an odd floral-seafood scent into the room.

"We were just discussing Gia meeting a guy."

I glared sideways at Kass. Nothing good would come from disclosing more info to Aunt Aimee, only the risk of her finding out about Duplicity. And there was absolutely no reason for her to know about the cheater business yet. It would only worry her. Then I'd have to hear a million warnings about spying on people and protecting myself.

Aunt Aimee's sandals smacked along on the wood as she crossed the room. "That's fantastic, Gia. Glad to hear about someone besides Landon, who by the way moved back from Tallahassee if you haven't heard. His dad mentioned it when I stopped over at The Grand Destin to restock Silhouette fliers."

So much for my dreams of him staying gone forever.

In addition to going to the same high school, The Grand Destin was how Landon and I had gotten together. Landon's dad was an executive. Naturally, we'd crossed paths ... and spent some time in a few rooms. Him being back in the area was worrisome, but what was worse was how Aunt Aimee had gotten the information. She was making more promotional rounds than usual, and her typical cheerful demeanor had dropped a few pegs. She hadn't spoken much about it, but the boutique's revenue had been on a downslope. Despite the approach of busy season, the number of brides had decreased and our slimming inventory reflected that. It was another reason I needed to push Duplicity to the next level. If there was a problem, I needed to help.

"So what's the deal?" Aunt Aimee continued. "Are you going on a date?"

"Yeah, Gia. Are you going on a date?" Kass prompted with a sly grin.

"Maybe. I have his number," I said, resigned.

"Good, sourpuss. Maybe if you get lucky, you'll quit scaring the clients out of marriage."

"That was one time," I mumbled. "And she was on the edge anyway."

"Let's hope a sour *puss* doesn't scare her new date away," Kass teased.

"Oh, Kass, that's just gross," Aunt Aimee chided. "And if it really is sour, maybe you could help her out … since you're such a douche." She barked out a laugh, clearly proud of her joke, and disappeared to the back office.

I shook my head. "You guys are hilarious."

Two chicks with wide smiles walked in through the front door, immediately pointing to the first dress display and baaing excitedly like happy little wedding sheep. I was no longer in the mood for this dress petting zoo.

"I got 'em," Kass said, noticing my eye twitch. She hurried off in their direction.

"We have a new job," Viv murmured, turning her laptop's screen toward me.

I glanced at the site she had created for Duplicity. Simple design. Black and white. No frills. Just the plain truth to reveal the lies. "They got the codeword?"

"You know they wouldn't be able to access the info otherwise," she confirmed and scanned the info. "Maria is the contact listed."

"Hard to forget that one. The target was her sister Leah's boyfriend, Arnold. Caught during Billy Bowlegs Pirate Festival floating on a party boat on Crab Island with some waitress. I had to hitch a ride on a pontoon boat and navigate the sea of drunks that day. Who's the target for this one?" I loved asking that question. It made me feel like a secret agent. *Cheater catcher Gia. Gia undercover. Special agent Gia ... air conditioner lover? Ugh.*

"I'm forwarding the pictures and info to your next burner phone." Her bony fingers danced across the keys. "Even though I'm sure they know the target's identity will be discovered while you investigate, the client wants anonymity for them and the target. No names to start."

"What?" I whispered, watching Kass usher the giddy chicks to the next designer's section. "No way. We have it stated as a requirement. I can't just trust this person isn't some psycho ex plotting revenge."

"I'm guessing the reason is to prevent us from doing preemptive research. You might want to reconsider, though. They're offering five thousand."

"What?" This time I yelled, drawing every eye in the shop. I held my hand up in an apologetic wave but quickly dropped my attention back to Viv's screen. The highest amount we'd charged before was $1,000. Skimming the info, I read and surmised, "They're close enough to the target and client to care, suspect something just isn't right, but haven't been able to prove infidelity."

Viv nodded. "The five K pays for three weeks, whether you find evidence or not. Specific itinerary included. Half up front when you reply with your location approvals. Pictures of the target from each approved location are required to receive the balance."

"If they're willing to pay that much, why not hire a licensed PI?"

"Maybe it'll cost more for that amount of time. Or maybe they really trust Maria."

"Maybe," I agreed. "If we do this, we'd have some extra cash. It could help the boutique by buying some of Kass' materials. I also could add to my funds for a real shot at this PI business. School. Certification. Get legit."

"You sure that's what you want?"

"Sure. I mean, I am pretty good at it." I scrunched my face thinking about getting caught by Mark. I'd have to work on my invisibility skills.

She shrugged her shoulders and turned her smoky shadowed eyes to me. "Being good at it doesn't necessarily make it your destiny."

I had a feeling she wasn't just talking about me anymore. It was the start of Viv's senior year, which meant more introspection lately. She was deciding her destiny too. "You know, some things work and others don't. The real question is if you enjoy it, right? At least, that's what it should be. And for me, right now, Duplicity is heavier than Silhouette on the enjoyment scales."

She nodded with a soft grin, understanding my subtle advice without needing more. That was our speed.

"So let's take a look at my schedule and sign off on the locations. What's the first time and place?"

"Friday night at The Dive," she replied.

"The Dive? In The District at East Bay Resort?" I asked even though I knew it was. I'd been there several times with friends through the years to shop and eat. The setup had a New Orleans vibe with multi-colored building facades and balconies.

"Yup."

Great. That was the last place I wanted to go. Despite what I'd told the estrogen queens earlier, I really had no intention of calling Mark and would hate to bump into him again. This job was officially more important. He would only be a distraction.

But he worked maintenance, and chances were good that he worked the day shift. That meant bumping into him on a Friday night where he worked was pretty unlikely.

"I'm in."

6

Mark

The Dive was packed. A cool breeze and slight temperature drop brought everyone out for a Friday night at The District. A local rock band was playing at the small stage across the pond, their music drowning the normal restaurant and bar chatter. The sun had just dipped below the horizon, calming the chaos of the day. It was the best kind of night. Relaxed, but busy enough to break the monotony. It almost made me overlook the fact that I was tasked to hang with my soon-to-be brother-in-law.

I placed my beer bottle back onto the bar, rubbing residual condensation between my fingertips as I shifted my eyes away from the crowd and back to Guy. He'd arrived ten minutes prior, and we were already struggling with conversation. Luckily, I'd gotten to the bar early and was already a few beers in. Before tonight, our interactions had involved other people—Pacey, the family—padded interactions where I'd mostly kept my big brother attitude in check. That was probably why Pacey suggested we hang out alone for once. She trusted that I'd known him long enough not to kill him and wanted us to bond like brothers. I wasn't so sure about meeting any of those expectations.

But I'd try because she deserved to be happy.

Tilting the bottle to my lips, I drained the rest of beer number four. "You want another?" I asked him, throwing a hand up to signal Matt, one of The Dive's resident bartenders.

Guy's face was tipped down, eyes set on his phone's screen, his dark blond hair falling over his forehead, practically covering his entire face. He was a pretty boy, model type, with soft features. The hair gave him an edgier look, possibly done purposely to combat the baby face. It seemed to work for him. From what Pacey said, it was what had gotten him his fifteen minutes of fame on the reality show Beach Bum, and ultimately led to the big hundred thousand dollar jackpot. He had to do some physical challenges too, but text votes by the public played a huge role in eliminating his competition.

"Nah, I'm still good, thanks." He nodded to his half full beer without looking. After typing out another few words, he slipped his phone into his pocket and adjusted the blue polo draped on his thin shoulders. "Sorry about that. It was Edena, my stepsister. I think you met her at the engagement party. She's my acting publicist and wanted to make sure I'm not getting mobbed by any fans tonight. I have a film interview later this week, and she doesn't want any surprises."

I glanced around. The District typically saw an older demographic, so I doubted many people would recognize him, and those who did probably wouldn't care. "Doesn't seem like you have to worry around here. I'm sure you get recognized whenever you hit the beach areas, though." More if he trolled around high schools and middle schools, I wanted to say. But I promised Pay I wouldn't offend him, so I bit my tongue instead.

"Pensacola Beach can get pretty crazy since we filmed there. Panama City Beach can too," he added with a smile that didn't sit well with me. "Pacey's seen it. Everyone thinks they know you when you've been on TV. Wild stuff."

"Wild," I echoed. Matt popped the cap of my new beer and set it in front of me. "Thanks," I said, sliding him some bills then lifting the bottle to my lips to drown more sarcasm dancing on my tongue. After a long pull, I shook my head. Maybe I was being too hard on Guy. He was decent enough. Clean-cut. And he treated Pacey well. That was what really mattered. She never complained about him.

"So," he said, glancing at me briefly before looking around the bar. "Pacey told me she met the chick you're bringing to the wedding."

A shallow laugh escaped my lips. Ah, yes. He had magically found the other reason for my harsh mood. Not the fact that Pacey was playing clairvoyant with my dating life—because that was just her—but the fact that Gia had obviously ditched me before a single date. I'd texted her twice after Tuesday. With no answer, I assumed she'd given me the wrong number, which left me feeling pretty shitty. But then I took one more chance and called her. It went directly to her short and sweet voicemail message. I finally accepted she had changed her mind since she never returned my call, but it still stung like a bitch.

I took a deep breath, inhaling the fresh air mixed with perfumes and colognes from the bodies shuffling around behind us. "No, that's still undecided."

"Ouch," he muttered, obviously having heard every detail of my Gia encounter from Pacey.

Knowing that my life would forever be shared secondhand with him did not help my mood. I tipped the bottle back again for another gulp then clapped my other palm onto his shoulder, giving it a good shake. "Yup. No worries, though. I've got a couple of weeks to round up someone worthy of my little sister's wedding." The words were gritty. I released my hand and watched him adjust his shirt, instantly feeling bad. I wasn't sure why I was so twisted about Gia. Maybe it was because after only speaking to her over a busted air conditioner, a coffee, and bad puns, the thought of taking her to the wedding had actually crossed my mind.

He gave an uncomfortable laugh, evading my hostility, and said, "I don't see it being much of a problem. A few new prospects have been eyeing you tonight. Or maybe they're regulars?"

"Maybe," I replied with a grin, not even looking around. I had caught a couple of eyes earlier, but I didn't think much of it, especially since I was supposed to be brotherly bonding—at which I was failing. "Look, Guy, you should know that all I want is for Pacey to be happy. Everything else ... doesn't really matter."

"I'm hoping I can make that happen."

"Exactly what I needed to hear," I said, watching him down the rest of his beer.

He set the empty bottle on the bar and pulled his phone out of his pocket to check a message. "I've got to hit the bathroom." He was gone before I could respond.

Leaning an arm on the back of the bar stool, I spun around to face The District's circle. The music was perfect, charging the atmosphere, moving the crowd. People danced down the concrete and planked walkways to their next destination, while some leaned on the mooring posts and ropes that fenced the pond. Every couple of minutes, another person glided across the zip line suspended high above the water. Echoes from the crowd singing along with the band bounced around the buildings. Despite where my head was, it was a good night.

My eyes landed on a white sundress directly across the walkway. Light brown hair, soft looking legs. She was hot, possibly around my age—twenty-four or so—and stood out like a bright flower in the night, lit up by the lampposts and string lights around the mooring posts. Making a move during my brotherly time with Guy wasn't the best idea for obvious reasons. Also, attracting attention to him could cause unwanted recognition, and Pacey would be pissed if the night turned into a groupie gathering for her Beach Bum. Not that I thought he'd be stupid enough to flirt with anyone, especially with me around, but I wasn't about to bet on it.

On the other hand, I had no idea how long he'd be gone. Surely there was enough time to land a number. I set my beer down and looked over my T-shirt and shorts. Not my best looking clothes, but I'd go for it anyway. Gia had landed a paralyzing hit to my ego, and I wouldn't get over that until I at least spoke to another girl.

She stood alone, head tilted back some, looking above the water at the zip line stretched across the darkened sky. Moving to her side, I caught a glimpse of her smile. She beamed with amazement as she watched the people coast overhead. It made me smile in turn, but for some reason I was struck with a wave of disappointment.

I shook it off and pressed on. "Hi." A boring but classic opener.

She turned directly to me. "Hi." Her eyes were big, gorgeous, but they were hazel, not the brown I'd wanted to see.

I was losing it. This girl was beautiful and I needed to get the thought of Gia out of my head. "Are you going to watch all night or are you going to take a risk?" I tipped my chin toward the zip line but kept my eyes on her, still struggling to get my thoughts in check.

Her tongue ran over her bottom lip before she smiled and directed her focus back to the sky. "Heights aren't my thing. But my boyfriend's next in line up there."

"Ah," I sighed. The brush-off. Or was it? The silky tone of her voice hinted at something else. "So if heights are his thing, what's your risky pleasure?"

She laughed and it didn't sound nearly as sweet as I'd wanted. I wasn't exactly into taking another guy's woman, and I probably wouldn't even follow through, but this was doing a decent job of healing my ego bruises. "I'm not sure," she replied finally, still not looking at me. Her hand shot up, waving energetically to a darkened figure sliding down the line as she added, "What's your name?"

Oh yeah. "Mark," I replied, with an unavoidable cocky grin.

"Maybe you can help me find out, Mark," she said, turning to face me when her boyfriend disappeared into the shadows of the zip line's tower. There was mischief in her eyes, making me think this wasn't her first risk after all.

"I think I'm up for it."

She slipped a pen from her purse, grabbed my hand, and wrote quickly along the inside of my wrist. "Call me. This time, tomorrow night."

I nodded and watched her walk away.

"That was pretty smooth," Guy said when I returned to the bar, obviously having caught the exchange.

I laughed and took a look at the number and single initial on my wrist. "D was all right."

"Yeah," he agreed and took a drink of his new, already half-empty beer. "Look, I'm going to bail a little early. I'm crashing at my parents' place since they are closer than P-cola."

"Okay. You good to drive?" I was still slightly drunk on my own pickup skills, but when I looked past Guy's mass of hair, my eyes landed on a girl resembling Gia. Dressed in black pants and tank, dark hair in a long ponytail, her body leaned against one of the old lantern style posts along the walkway.

"Nah, Edena's actually in the area. She's picking me up. We'll be back over this way for the mini-golf tourney tomorrow anyway, so I'll just leave my jeep."

I heard him, but I wasn't paying much attention. The girl had disappeared around the corner of The Dive. "Right," I said distractedly. "The mini-golf thing." It was one of Pacey's awkward pre-wedding gatherings, a crazy attempt to prolong the festivities and promote family bonding. "You want me to walk you out?"

"Nah, man. You chill and see if you can land something more than digits for tonight. See you tomorrow."

"Yeah, later." I stood with him and gave a quick handshake before my feet took over, moving me in the direction I'd seen the brunette.

I had to be insane. What was it about this girl? I slalomed through bodies, my eyes searching all the faces, all the eyes, all the shadows.

And then she was there, staring at me from the north end of the pond, beside the zip line's launch tower. She backed up a few steps and disappeared again. I was too far to shout at her. The music was too loud, only getting louder as I rounded the curve of the pond, heading toward the stage.

I spotted her ponytail and watched her stop at the wall of people branched far out from the front of the stage. There was no way for her to move. She was trapped.

Rushing up behind her, I was prepared to tap her on the shoulder, to make sure I wasn't hallucinating. But I wasn't expecting her to flip a one-eighty and slam into my chest.

"Oomph," we both grunted. Her face slowly lifted, and the brown eyes I'd wanted to see earlier were staring at me with a frightened look that crushed any irritation I'd had about her ditching me.

"You okay?" I grabbed her arms gently, not letting her run. She looked terrified.

Her body quivered. "Oh, God, could this get any worse? I'm—I'm sorry. I really have to go."

"Hey, you don't have to run from me. If you aren't interested, it's fine. But can I have a minute to talk at least?" Why would she be scared? Did she think I was chasing her? I needed to set this straight.

"No, I can't." She twisted her arms out of my hold and glanced over her shoulder nervously. "I just have to go, okay? I promise ... I will call you—"

"Gia?" A tall guy with red hair yelled over the music, over the crowd behind her, and she blanched, pushing farther into my body, wanting to disappear right through me.

I dipped my face down and whispered, "Did he hurt you?" Her reaction had already told me that he had somehow, and I was suddenly prepared to be her henchman if that was what she needed.

"No ... unless you count breaking my heart," she answered honestly, looking straight past me, not turning in his direction. Her shoulders slumped with a long exhale.

Oh. How long ago had it been? Close enough to still affect her. "He's close. You can either stay here and follow my lead or run. Do you trust me?"

"No, I don't," she admitted in a soft but firm tone.

I stifled a laugh. She was honest, which made me want to help more. "Enough to let me help? I won't cross any lines ... I promise."

She took a deep breath and nodded silently.

"Gia?" The guy—her ex—stopped a few people away when he noticed Gia pushed up against me.

"Smile," I whispered for only her to hear over the music then placed my hands on her waist and slowly spun her around.

Gia

All of the details—Mark's hands at my waist, the fake smile burning my face, Landon's eyes staring into mine, my heart beating the same sorrow I'd felt the day he'd betrayed me—sent relentless surges of emotional burns through my body. All I'd wanted to do was duck and run, to avoid reopening the wounds. It had been several months since I'd seen Landon, but the pain was as fresh as the day I left his dorm room. And it was all because this confrontation hadn't happened sooner. I tried to walk away, to let it all go, when really I had held on tight. There was no avoiding it now.

Mark's fingers squeezed my waist, helping me focus, urging me on, and probably aiding my stability. Surely he could feel me shaking. Not knowing his plan for the conversation only made things worse. Why was I trusting a guy to handle this?

"Hi, Landon," I said, eyeing his khaki shorts and loose button-down frat boy combo, his pale face and strawberry blond hair. He looked the same. Dickhead.

He rolled out the schmoozy smile I'd fallen for, used mostly for people he didn't know. The focus this time was obviously Mark. Landon silently assessed the stranger gripping the girl he'd thrown away. Before he could utter his own greeting, a tall blonde in a white sundress breezed up beside him.

"Catch has a table open for us," she said to him, grabbing his arm. Her eyes followed his stare to us then popped as wide as mine with recognition. It was her. The one he'd cheated with. The original fun hole—OG Funhole. They were still together.

My chest and stomach heaved. I laid my hands over Mark's and squeezed a distress signal, warning him to come up with something fast or I'd break into a sprint before I either puked on Landon or started swinging. Go big then go home. No regrets.

While Landon turned his attention to Funhole with a reply, Mark's breath touched my ear. "This just got more interesting. But hang with me. We've got this."

My nails dug into his skin to confirm, and I hated myself for accepting. Letting a guy, someone I barely knew, take control of a situation I should've been handling myself was disparaging. But it was embarrassingly apparent—possibly even to the fifty people crammed around us—that Landon had become my Kryptonite, and seeing the pretty facade of such a vile heart up close again was the worst torture imaginable. Even worse than letting another guy help me.

Landon's gaze locked on Mark. "Hey, I'm Landon. This is Denise."

I dug my nails into the back of Mark's hands again. He twisted out of my hold, caught my fingers, and threaded his with them gently as he pulled my body closer. His chin lifted a greeting to Landon. "How's it goin'? I'm Mark. I take it you already know my beautiful Gia." He cuddled me affectionately, curling his body around mine, and his face dipped down beside mine, breath returning to my ear, whispering, "Keep smiling. It'll hurt him more than you think."

Landon and fun hole Denise both stared at me as the lights and music flashed around us. I kept my smile in place even though I felt like I was in a vacuum. A spine sucking vacuum.

"Yeah," Landon said, interrupting our fake-ass mushy moment. "It's good to see you, Gia."

"Can't say the same." Suddenly, I had breath again, and I felt a squeeze from Mark's fingers as he straightened up beside me.

Landon slipped an arm around Denise's waist. Denise's eyes were on Mark, though, big and wondrous. *What the shit?*

"Funny," Landon commented with a humorless laugh then looked at Mark, dismissing me. "So what is it that you do, Mark?"

Wow. He had some nerve. Seeking me out in public, rubbing my nose in what had happened again, to what, just say hi? Then to want to chat up the guy I was with? He'd upped his level of asshole.

With half my back pulled against Mark's chest, I felt his calm inhale. "There's a lot that I do. But what I do best is take care of this gorgeous woman. Right now, I'm thinking she needs a drink ... and then for me to take her to bed. So we're gonna take off."

It took a moment for me to register the words, and when it happened, my whole body ignited with a tangled mixture of embarrassment and lust. I became hyper aware of only him. His hands. His minty soap smell. The shallow breaths pushing his body into mine.

Landon was stunned silent, and Denise's eyes were still fixed on Mark, which made me smile—for real.

Mark's hands released mine and slid onto my hips, ready to guide me away. Suddenly, he stopped short. "Oh, I almost forgot ..." His hand darted out toward Landon, as if he planned to give the asshole a handshake. But instead of letting Landon grab hold, Mark twisted his forearm up. The lights around us cast a strong enough glow, revealing inked numbers and the letter D. With a quick nod to Denise, he kept his eyes on Landon. "Good luck with that."

I got to glimpse the flash of emotions in Landon's eyes just before Mark took my hand and led me through the crowd. He didn't stop until we veered off The District's main loop, rounding the corner of a closed bistro.

His hand released mine, and he watched a few people pass behind us toward the crowd before his eyes settled back on me. "How are you?"

Leaning against the brick wall, I took a relieved breath. "Okay."

"Good." His voice was its normal depth only a bit too soft, pitying.

"Thanks for that." I rubbed my shaky hands down the front of my jeans, trying to tame the rest of my emotions.

"It was no problem. Do you want to go grab a seat somewhere? Are you hungry?"

"I'm sorry, but I should actually go." I just needed to recover after my atrocious meltdown, to breathe.

He held out a hand and dropped it just as fast. "Wait. Don't ... Look I, uh ... I didn't think you were interested since you ignored my messages. That's why I ..." He twisted his forearm, showing the phone number again.

"It's okay. I get it." I waved off his reason for having Denise's number. He wasn't mine, so I had no right to be upset. I smiled, recalling what had just happened and the look on Landon's face. "It was ironically funny, though, how that worked out."

"Yeah, it was," he said with a breathy laugh.

"I have to admit, I'm kinda curious how that would've gone if she hadn't shown up."

He palmed the back of his neck with a coy smile. "Honestly?"

I narrowed my eyes in response.

"I wouldn't cross the line, like I promised—even though a little make-out session would have shut him up," he joked but quickly pressed on. "I was planning to introduce myself as your sub and call you Mistress."

A hard laugh burst from my shocked mouth as I imagined that whole scene. "What? You were not."

"I'm completely serious. Short of licking your boots, I would have sold it too. Dropped on all fours and let you sit on my back. Whatever you needed," he added with a smile.

"Well, now I'm almost sad that Funhole showed up because that would have been pretty hilarious."

His arm dropped to his side again and he slipped his hands into his pockets. "Fun hole, huh? Yikes."

I sighed. "Yeah."

"Well, hopefully the next time you see either of them it won't be as bad."

"Maybe. Maybe not. I'm pretty disappointed in myself about this time. It's been a while since I last saw him, and it just hit me harder than I thought it would."

"That's understandable."

"I should have handled it better," I admitted.

"You were fine. It happens to all of us." He shrugged his broad shoulders and looked down at his feet. "There was this girl I really wanted to talk to again, so I messaged her ... Well, she never messaged back. Then I accidentally bumped into her. Ouch, right?" he teased. "I'm not too confident about how I handled that situation."

When I met his gaze, my lips slipped into an easy smile. "I'm guessing it went really well."

"You think? I mean, I am pretty smooth."

"Let's not get carried away," I teased.

He laughed lightly, and I got caught up by the sound and everything else innately him. The symmetry of his lips, the slight bump in the bridge of his nose. The way his body leaned a little toward me, the way his eyes studied me under his low brows. Silence fell between us, the air sparking with a comfortable and enticing energy that pulled at me, willing me to move closer, wanting to feel his hands again. But I fought off the sex deprived hooker inside and pressed against the bricks behind me instead.

He cleared his throat. "So what brought you to The District tonight?"

The night had started easily enough. The Dive was the first approved location for the job, and my objective was to locate the nameless target by way of a few pictures and itinerary sent by the anonymous client. It was frustrating, but manageable. Luckily, the picture was current and the schedule was correct. When I had arrived a tad late—thanks to an avalanche of random issues that should have been a warning for the night ahead—the target was seated at the bar with a coiffed mass of hair that could make an umbrella cockatoo jealous. If I'd needed to, I could've tracked him all night by hair alone. I snapped the required itinerary pics of him, with no evidence of infidelity. At first, I didn't notice anyone interacting with him. Then Mark showed up.

I thought about his question and didn't particularly want to lie to him, especially after how nice he'd been. "I was gonna search for a new couple to stalk, and maybe buy myself one of those boring maintenance man coffees. I've heard they're pretty good."

"Really?" he asked with a grin.

"Something like that." I propped a foot behind me, settling in to get some information. "What about you? Trying to make up for that idiot girl not messaging you back?" I glanced at the arm where Funhole's number was inked.

He extended his wrist for a second, wearing a crooked smile. "Yeah, well ... Kind of. Really, I was hanging out with Guy, Pacey's fiancé."

"Guy?" Pacey's fiancé? My target was Pretty Pacey's fiancé?

"Yeah. We haven't hung out much, so Pacey wanted me to go out with him tonight. It's the start of her organized wedding activities."

"I thought her wedding wasn't for a few weeks?" I chewed my lip, thinking about the job. Someone had hired me to follow Guy. It could've been anyone. It could've even been Mark.

"Yeah, three. So the next two weekends will be filled with family and friends fun."

"That sounds ..."

"Like a blast, right? I know." His tone was so sarcastic and his smile was so dramatic that I had to laugh.

"It doesn't sound so bad." ... for him. For me, it would be insane. I had taken a job to watch a fiancé of a Silhouette client three weeks before their wedding.

"No, maybe not. We should be good as long as Guy doesn't take mini-golf as seriously as I do," he joked.

"Mini-golf?" I choked out, knowing that the family fun place down the road, Putters, was on my approved list the next day and realizing that some of the approved dates would coincide with the "family time" we were discussing.

"Yeah. You wanna come?" he asked, probably thinking I was hinting at an invite.

"Well, um ..." I shoved my jittery hands into my pockets and dropped my foot from the wall. I was trapped. Accepting his offer for a date would get me close to the target, but mixing time with him and the job wasn't the best idea. But if I declined and showed up to get the required pictures, I ran the risk of actually being seen. No one really noticed me. And yet, Mark was seeing me everywhere.

He shook his head. "I'm sorry. That was probably weird to ask. A first date shouldn't involve meeting friends and family."

I stared at him stupidly, weighing my options. "It's not that. It's just that tomorrow's Saturday. There are some final fittings scheduled and new clients coming in ... So I might have to work."

His eyebrows pulled together and his lips formed a soft smile. "How did you know it was tomorrow?"

Shit. "Oh, I just assumed ..."

"Yeah," he said, his eyes staring intently for a few more seconds. "It's probably best you're working. Not because I don't want to see you, because I really want to see you again. On purpose next time, though, not by accident."

I let out a relieved sigh. It was good that I declined the date. Watching my mouth would be a task in itself. Maybe, if I got the job done soon enough, I could actually go on a date with him. That was a big, fat maybe. At this point, I was just hoping to get through the job.

I checked my thoughts and smiled at his hopeful expression. "I would like that. But it seems like you might be busy for a little while. Maybe we can try to work something out with our schedules, or wait until after Pacey's designated family time?"

"There's no chance I'm waiting," he replied instantly. "You sure you don't want to go grab some maintenance man coffee tonight?"

I grinned at how cute he was being. "No, I'm sorry. I really should go." I already didn't trust myself around him. He was too easy to talk to, too easy to look at. If I stayed, I'd probably pull a Kass—which wouldn't be a bad thing if I hadn't found out he was connected to my target. The last two and a half grand was on the line. I could keep myself in check until the job was finished. I had to.

"Did you need to grab a cab or did you drive?"

"I drove," I answered, considering his question. "Oh ... Did you need a ride?" Giving him a ride home would make things more difficult, but there was no way I could be rude to him after what he did for me tonight.

"No, I'm good. I have a condo here. I was going to offer you a ride if you needed one."

"So you work and live on East Bay's property?" I started walking, heading toward the parking area.

He fell in step at my side, his body a little closer, his voice a little louder, as we shuffled back into the crowd. "It's not so bad. I like how it stays busy. What about you? How far do you have to drive tonight?"

I smiled to myself, pushing one foot in front of the other, afraid if I didn't get to my car fast enough I'd do something stupid like take him up on grabbing a maintenance man coffee and maybe even one of those stripped lattes or a lappuccino. "I'm closer to the boutique, at Coast Apartments. I share a two bedroom with a friend." A friend who was never home lately and who wouldn't even know if I had someone over. *Stop it, Gia.*

He kept pace beside me, bumping into me every so often as he shifted around other people. Smelling the fresh scent that had subtly surrounded me while dealing with Landon, I inhaled it again, this time noticing it fully, aware of how attractive it was, how attractive he was. His classic height. His classic build. The firm arms that had held me, calmed me, steadied me. *Seriously, stop it, Gia.*

I pushed my feet faster, hoping he wouldn't notice.

"Roommate, huh? Not Kass?" His voice quieted again as we turned away from the Main Street loop and headed toward the parking lot.

"No way." I laughed. "She and I were happy to end our Keats siblings cohabitation back when she started college. We never looked back."

"And not Viv either? Viv is your younger sister's name, right?" he asked, sounding eager for more information.

"Yeah, Viv. She's still in high school and lives with our aunt. That's all of us. The boutique crew." I weaved between a few cars before reaching the Veloster. "And is Pacey your only headache?"

Even though there were no more bodies cramming us together, he remained close as we stopped beside the car. He laughed and rested a palm on the roof. "Yeah, she's the only Foster headache."

I ran a finger over the door's auto lock and it beeped. "Well, Mark Foster ... thanks for tonight. If you hadn't chased me down, I would've ended up at home, acting badass in front of my mirror, cursing assholes and fun holes, and recalling all the witty things I should have said to them while digging into a therapeutic box of donuts and pint of pistachio."

"Wow." He shook his head with a full smile that made my insides tingle. The donuts were still on the menu, possibly the ice cream too, after a cold shower. "Maybe I made a mistake," his voice said, but there was no mistaking the gleam of excitement in his eyes.

"Maybe." I opened the door, and he stepped a tad closer.

"I think I need to find out for sure. I'm getting a message back next time, right?"

"Yes," I confirmed.

"Good." He leaned closer, staring at my lips, touching his fingers to mine on the top of the door. His face inched in then turned a bit, breath warming my cheek before his soft lips pressed against my skin. With a whisper, he said, "See you soon, Gia."

65

8

Mark

"I thought you said the parents would be here today?" I asked while stepping up to the ticket counter to pay. Pacey whipped her attention back in my direction, flinging her hair as she turned away from the gathering of her people outside the glass doors.

"No, just the wedding party today. But it seems like more people have been invited." She huffed in annoyance and turned her attention back to them.

"Thanks," I said to the young red-headed employee who rang me up. When she handed me my pink golf ball, I added, "Really?" She winked, and I shook my head.

"I just don't get it," Pacey commented in her high-pitched irritable voice, making no movement to go outside. "I asked if this day could be just us, to connect as a wedding party, before everything else starts happening—the bachelorette party, the bachelor party, the wedding. But no one really cares."

"Easy, Pay," I said, slipping an arm over her shoulder. "Are they dates for the wedding?"

"I guess." She shrugged. "Leah and Maria invited their current boyfriends, then Rick and Evin brought two chicks I've never even met." She pointed to the guys. "Looks like you and Edena are the only ones who didn't bring anyone."

"I'm not playing pairs, so don't even think about it."

She chuckled and ducked away from my arm to stare at me properly with her not-so-innocent doe eyes. "Why not? You'll never know until you give her a chance."

"Please quit trying to set me up."

"I just don't want you going to the wedding dateless. It'll be a distraction, and I'm trying to get rid of all distractions."

I let my head fall back a bit with a laugh. "Well, there's no chance at making that match, so forget it. I've already met her, remember? She's just not—"

"Your type?" she interrupted. "Please. Like you have a type besides the ones who leave after a week of boating and tanning on the beach."

"She's a hundred percent not my type. She seems all uptight."

"She's nice, and I love her look. She's perfected the sexy/messy hair, and I'd kill to have her fat lips. Just look at those things."

"I have looked at them, and I've never seen them smile." We both stared through the door at Edena and laughed at her stern expression. I immediately thought of Gia's smile instead and couldn't help my lips from turning up. Her lips were my kind of perfect. I'd wanted to feel them, taste them, the night before but held back. After seeing her reaction to her ex, I wouldn't risk any accidental emotions or motives, like heartache or revenge. Whenever it happened, no one else would be on her mind.

"Who you thinking about? Ooh. Guy said you met some blonde last night. Any luck?" She elbowed me and lifted her eyebrows.

"Not with her, no."

"Someone else? Dang, you've been busy lately, but that's good after the bridal shop chick bust. I'm really sorry about that."

I laughed. "Funny you should bring her up."

"You saw her last night too?"

"Yeah. I kind of helped her out of a situation with an ex. We talked, and she agreed to go out soon, but I'm worried she only said yes because she feels indebted."

"You're nuts. How long did you talk? You didn't drop any more stupid puns, did you?"

"Nah." I smiled again. "I guess it went well. Hopefully our schedules line up."

"Why didn't you invite her today?"

I narrowed my eyes. "I did, but I'm kinda glad she declined after you just bashed everyone out there for inviting people."

"Shut it." She elbowed me again, lighter this time, and looked out at everyone waiting on us. "You're different. And given how you're acting, you can invite her anywhere as far as I'm concerned."

I nodded at her approval. "Good to know. I'll think about it. I'm not sure I want to scare her away by bringing her around all you crazy people."

"Whatever. I've already met her, so I'm not worried."

"Ever the confident one," I teased.

"Yes, I am. And I'm confident that I'm going to kick your ass out on the mini green, so let's go."

We stepped outside into the growing crowd of chaos—parents digging into their pockets, children bouncing on their toes. Lines were already forming for kiddy rides and go-carts.

Guy introduced me to his other groomsmen, the blond chicks they'd brought, and the very grim looking Edena. I wasn't exactly happy to be there either, but I'd think she'd at least attempt to smile. Her eyes shifted around the crowd, probably on the lookout for Guy's fandom, prepared to lay the smack down on any teenagers looking for an autograph.

I laughed to myself.

"Hey, Mark," Leah and Maria said, skirting past Pacey and leaving their dates to talk with the other guys. With less than a year between the sisters, they were practically twins, and they'd been friends with Pacey since they were in high school. They were also huge flirts and knew how to work most guys over with their arsenal of assets—large tits, long legs, unrelenting innuendos, and arm touches. Their excuse was that they were friendly, expressive Italians. *Donne fatale.*

"Ladies," I replied. "Feeling better?"

"Oh, that's right," Leah said with a smile. "You filled in for the dress fitting. Yes, we're feeling better, thanks."

"And thanks for going," Maria added, grabbing my arm with her thin fingers. "Puking on her dress was not something we'd risk, even with all her angry threats."

Leah was quick to grab my other arm. These girls never stopped, but I couldn't complain. They gave everyone the same treatment, even Guy. Pacey wasn't even bothered. She knew them well enough not to worry.

"I know I'm hard to resist, but don't you think you two should ease up? I don't feel like fighting jealous boyfriends today. Pacey would probably throw more threats your way too for ruining the day," I said with a smirk.

They both laughed. "You never have to worry about that, Mark. These guys know what's up," Leah said, raising her hand with a tiny wave to the one who looked like he could shot put my one-eighty across the highway without breaking a sweat.

"Good to know."

"Don't be sad. You know we'll always"—Maria slid her hand up and down my arm—"consider you first place."

"That first-place platform must be ready to break because I'm positive you award those like participation ribbons," I joked.

"Ouch," Leah said in mock pain, pouting and grabbing her chest dramatically. "If that's the case, though, we should strip your title for refusing to play."

"It would be justified," I admitted. Even though there'd been plenty of offers during the time they'd been friends with Pacey, I didn't actually *participate* with either one of them. I knew better than to trek that road. Other, non-best friends who wouldn't make things weird after the fact, however, I couldn't say the same for.

"Here's you score card," Pacey interrupted, handing me one. "And no cheating, hookers."

"Aw, you're no fun," Maria said with a wink before she and Leah walked off toward their dates.

"All set?" Pacey asked.

I held up my pink ball and score card with a shake. "Yup. Let's do this fun thing."

9

Gia

"Anything on the IP address?" I asked, pulling my Veloster into a parking spot down a ways from the mini-golf area at Putters and looking around nervously. The pressure of being invisible today had me sweating buckets and I hadn't even stepped a foot outside my air conditioned car. My goal was to observe Guy's interactions with everyone and get some pictures, but it felt impossible knowing that Mark would be there.

"The location is designated to the Gulf Cove Resort on Miramar Beach. They usually only give Wi-Fi to customers, but it could've been anyone," Viv's voice said through the speakers of my car. "The phone was a bust too, likely a burner."

After finding out that my next target was Guy, I needed more info than what the client had given me. I'd felt like a complete idiot at The District, and I refused to deal with any more surprises. Knowing who the client was might help, so I asked Viv to trace the request from our website and do a little digging. But we'd apparently hit a wall.

"And there's no way to get beyond that on the IP?"

"Not really," she stated blandly. "Not legally without a search warrant and more equipment."

"Right. We'll just pick up with the normal info from here as soon as I get more names and faces."

"I guess now we know why they didn't disclose the names. He was on that reality show, right? Maybe they didn't want you taking the case for that reason alone."

"That's possible. It also means they are trusting my discretion and their contact's experience with us. They probably don't want any photos accidentally getting out."

"It obviously wouldn't be good publicity. But now that we know, it could also be opposite of what we're considering."

"What do you mean?" I asked, pulling on my large, undercover set of sunglasses that covered most of my face.

"Well, for celebrities, any publicity is good, right? Think of the scandalous headline. 'Weeks away from wedding bliss, Beach Bum Guy caught cheating.'"

"So maybe the client is counting on me to leak photos? I don't know about that. Why bother using a contact from someone?"

"Just a thought. Anyway, that new material you ordered for Kass with the client's dough got in this morning. Aunt Aim didn't notice. And she just finished with a client, so I've gotta go. I can do the rest of the background checks when you finish there."

"Okay. Later." The call went dead, and I sat stupefied for a few moments, considering all the possibilities as I shoved the last mini-donut into my mouth, hoping the heavenly sugar rush would take the edge off.

Putters had just opened and it was already crowded. People flooded out from the main building, heading to the mini-golf courses, go-cart tracks, or bumper cars, ready to slay their competitors cheerfully. Their numbers were good for me. It was the cover I needed to remain invisible.

Within a few minutes, I spotted the tall, sun-kissed Guy and his wave of blond hair moving toward the mini-golf area. A group of people surrounded him. One, two … maybe ten. They all looked young, like friends not family. With Pacey being at this function, I was unsure I'd get any solid cheating evidence. Either the client didn't know Pacey's schedule as well as Guy's, or they wanted me to cover all bases in the event something was happening right under Pacey's nose.

Observing from the parking lot was pointless, so I waited until they moved to the first hole then went inside to buy some tickets.

"All alone?" the teenage ticket girl said, ringing me up. "I just saw a group of hotties head out there. They'd probably let you jump in." Her eyes scanned my body. "I'd let my hair down and give it a good shake first, though. You look a little too caddie, not enough pro."

I glanced down through my undercover sunglasses at my baggie T and jean shorts then looked back at her with a brow raised.

"Not trying to be mean. You're pretty. It just may help get you noticed a bit more," she said, holding out a pink ball and score card. "Oh, and if you happen to see a guy with messy, short brown hair and a pink ball in that group, don't bother. He smelled kinda funny, like bad breath. And he looked a little crazy, too. Not boyfriend material. At all. And the hair on his face—"

"I'm not here for a date," I cut her off. "Just going to have some solitary caddie fun."

"Okay, but keep it in mind just in case."

By the time I stepped outside, Pacey's group had finished the first two holes and moved up the hill side of the large course. I grabbed a club and started my faux game. A couple of families were between us, leaving a great buffer of bodies, obstacles, and trees to hide me. I kept my phone out, camera ready to capture a few required shots and anything abnormal. The total count in their group was twelve, even split. Three girls were up front, two of which were blond and cliqued together. The other one, a brunette, hung back a bit, closer to Guy and two guys. Pacey jumped from middle to back, between Guy, two dark-haired couples, and Mark—who brought up the rear ... and what a lovely rear it was, looking all round and firm.

I shook my head and faked a putt under a small-scale boardwalk that had been tagged with graffiti art.

And so it went, hole after hole. I'd lose sight of them then encroach upon the families in front of me. I'd take a picture then duck out of sight if Pacey or Mark looked my direction. There was nothing abnormal to the group's interaction. They all just looked like friends having a good time together. Or an average time together. One of the brunettes looked miserable, while a few of the other friends were more occupied with their phones.

I stepped up beside a wishing well prop at the next hole and watched the group move through the players. The two girls that were in the back—both with black hair—had moved up closer to Guy and Pacey. Those two seemed like the most friendly of the group, touching and flirting with everyone even though they appeared to be with two guys at the back. They'd sidled closer to Guy just as the group moved around a tree. One of them looked familiar. I leaned farther as she touched his arm. *Leah.* And the other was Maria—previous client of Duplicity and name used for this job. I snapped a picture.

"Hey, lady!" screamed a squeaky voice behind me.

Startled, I fumbled with the phone, nearly dropping it into the fiberglass wishing well that was half full of water.

"Are you going to make a wish, move on, or what?" the squeaky voice spoke again.

I spun around, directly into a group of little faces looking at me like pissed off minions. "I ... uh ..."

"Just hit the ball, lady, shit," a scrawny boy with crossed arms said.

"All right, I'm going," I grumbled, flustered, then snatched my ball and cut through the small partition of trees to the next hole, which was wide open. Apparently, I'd gotten caught up in watching Guy, but that still didn't excuse those little brats' attitude.

"Mini-golf thugs," I muttered, moving closer to the base of the white lighthouse for a better view.

"Thugs, huh?" I heard Mark's voice before I saw his body step out around the lighthouse. He wore a polo with a pair of gray linen shorts—a dressier casual, more appropriate for a day on a regular course not a mini one. A set of sunglasses hid his eyes, but I could feel them boring into me from somewhere behind my own tiny reflection. "You need help getting rid of them? I have a really good thug club right here." He held out his putter with a smirk.

"No need to club baby thugs," I replied, trying to play cool by dropping my ball at the tee mat and attempting, unsuccessfully, to roll it into one of the tee holes with my flip-flop. "Designer thug purses and shoes aren't really my thing."

He laughed lightly and twisted the club a few times as he took the last steps to me. "Right. They'd likely call more attention when you're trying to stalk someone anyway."

Crap. The insinuation sounded more on the serious side. It was possible that it was, considering how we'd met. If I were him, I'd certainly think the same. There was no brushing this one off with a coincidental half-truth excuse like I'd done the night prior with "getting a coffee." What would I say this time? I like hitting a few holes to relieve some stress before work?

I put on my most charming smile, though I had a feeling it looked wonky and showcased my guilt. "I didn't end up having to work until later, so I figured I'd just come by to see if you were here ... and maybe ride the bumper cars for road rage therapy." I laughed weakly and continued rolling the ball beneath my foot.

He bent in front of me, lifted my foot, and grabbed my ball then set it into the middle hole of the tee mat. "So not only do you have an aversion to text messages and phone calls, but you'd rather stalk a person than tell them you're in the same area?"

I watched him stand, his body even closer than before. I had to tilt my head back a bit to see his face and it almost made me dizzy, my senses overloaded by his sudden proximity. My eyes focused on his jaw, watching the muscle tick under the light coating of hair as though he, too, was affected. "I ... uh ... I'm sorry about that." I breathed the words out, barely able to speak. "I saw how many people you were with and I felt bad for crashing without calling. So I was just going to wait, hoping maybe you'd be alone at some point."

"Ah," he said. "So what you're saying is you wanted to steal me for yourself?" His fingers slid across my cheek, sweeping some stray hair back to tuck behind my ear. "And now that you've accomplished that?"

Just that small touch across my skin sent a frenzy of excitement through my body. I had to get a grip. Letting a guy turn me into a pile of girlie goo—scratch that because it sounded too literal ... and eww. *A pile of damsely dew?* Anyway, allowing him to have such a strong effect on me wasn't something I needed. It was fun, and it felt good, but I still had a job to do.

"I want to apologize again," I said, forcing my legs to move me out of his gravitational field of sexiness before he felt my force field of awkward. "You should get back to them. I didn't want to interrupt ..." ... and accidentally do something stupid.

"No way," he said with a grin. "I'm invested now, and I would hate to leave you unprotected from the thugs so let's tee off."

Well, damn. My only option was to make the best of the situation. It was time to get some information.

10
Mark

"The lighthouse is a par three," I said to Gia, nodding to the pink ball at her feet. "Where's your score card?"

"I don't have one," she replied, taking her stance behind the ball. Her silver toenails pointed outward, her cute butt stuck out a little under her T-shirt, and her hands wrapped tightly around the handle of the club. From what I could see around her enormous sunglasses, there was a look of pure determination on her serious face. The fact that she'd shown up had already made my day, and it was only getting better.

I slid my scorecard out of my pocket with a chuckle. "We'll keep track from here even though there are only three holes left. You look ready, so go for it."

"Okay, don't make fun. Those last holes alone did nothing to refresh my skills." She eased the club back and forth, swinging just above her ball for a few practice strokes. "It's been a while since I've played."

"That's horrible," I replied, and she grimaced back at me. I shook my head. "I meant that you haven't been here in a while, not your swing. How long?"

"Well," she said, returning her focus to the ball at her feet, "let's see. It's been ..." She swung the club and knocked the pink ball off to the right, hitting the sweet spot of the course we called a turntable where the ball curved around in line for the hole. It dropped in with a clink and Gia hung a hand on her hip. "It's been about a month."

"Nice." I laughed and shook my head. "But you know, if you want to hustle someone, you're supposed to pretend you suck first then make a bet before blasting them with your completely refreshed skills."

She finally turned back to me with a triumphant grin. "If I wanted to hustle you, I would have."

"I'm not sure if I should find that offensive or not."

"How could that possibly be offensive? Are you saying you wanted to be hustled?"

"Well, I mean, that was a pretty decent setup, then nothing. I feel like you just wasted a great opportunity. You dropped the ball on purpose, which tells me you didn't want to invest that much effort, and that's the part that's a little upsetting. Maybe I had you pegged wrong from the beginning." I shook my head lightly, acting disappointed.

Her mouth popped open and I saw an eyebrow peek up from behind her shades. "Maybe I was just being nice so I wouldn't hurt your sensitive maintenance man feelings."

Her reaction was solid, just like all the others had been when I'd teased her. I realized it was one of the reasons I liked talking to her, playing with her. I fixed my stoic face, fighting off the smile itching to beam at her. "You see, I can't trust that. If you were honestly protecting my maintenance man feelings, you would have missed altogether. You know, to make me feel more manly."

"You think you have it all figured out, don't you?"

"I know some things." I tugged my ball from my pocket and dropped it on the mat. Gia glanced down at the ball and immediately started to laugh. "What? Now you're going to laugh at my pink ball? That's not protecting my feelings at all." I crossed my arms, waiting for her to settle down. If she thought a pink ball was funny, I honestly might have pegged her wrong from the beginning.

Bending lightly at the waist, she covered her mouth with one hand to stifle her laughter and waved the other in front of her. "I'm sorry. It's just …" She straightened up and pushed her shoulders back, regaining her composure. "I was warned about you, pink ball player."

"What?"

She giggled again, and I smiled despite my confusion. "Were you the only guy with a pink ball from your group?" Her face turned toward Pacey and the others, eyeing them.

"Yeah, why?"

Her shades pointed in that direction for another few moments then she finally returned her focus to me with a curious smile. "The ticket girl told me about you. She said I should stay away from the guy with the pink ball because he smelled like bad breath and looked a little crazy. Now that I know she was talking about you, I can see what she meant."

What? She had laughed after seeing the ball, so she thought it was funny and probably didn't think it was true. But I still felt like I had something to prove, and I was prepared to take advantage of the opportunity. I took three long strides to her, almost touching her body with mine. She gasped a little and her hand shot out to brace herself on the lighthouse beside us.

"I can get a little crazy. Maybe not crazy enough to stalk people, though. And I don't think I smell bad, but I could be wrong. What do you think?" She smelled sweet, like berries. I leaned closer and grasped the middle of her long ponytail, trying to determine the source.

She tilted her head back a little to look at me from behind her shades. Her lips parted with shallow breaths. "I think you smell … nice."

The energy between us was palpable, and I wanted more. Deciding to keep pressing her, I pushed my sunglasses to the top of my head then tipped hers back so I could finally see her gorgeous eyes. "And my breath? It's okay?"

She squinted a little, adjusting to the sunlight. Then, almost like the flip of a switch, she straightened up with a deep breath. "Well, you don't have halitosis or anything, but …"

There was a dare behind the sarcasm. "Oh really?" I looked at her lips. With only inches separating us, I could feel the heat of her breath. I wanted nothing more than to let her taste mine.

"Go get a freaking room!" a high-pitched voice yelled from behind me.

Gia laughed and ducked away from me, snatching up her own pink ball and moving down the hill to the next hole. I grunted my frustration to the lighthouse then turned to the kids with a scowl. They scowled right back. "Nice ball," one said, knocking it toward me with a smirk.

I heard Gia's laugh from down the hill and decided schooling the kids wasn't worth my time. Little cockblockers would get their own in a few years by way of puberty karma. I shook my head at them as I lowered my shades, then grabbed the ball and followed the path to Gia.

Her ball was already rolling past the iron ship anchor toward the mermaid statue. She stepped aside and cleared her throat. "She thought you were hot."

"What?" I asked, dropping my ball on the mat when hers stopped beside the rock base of the statue, close to the hole.

"The girl at the counter. She thought you were hot, so she warned me about you to keep me away." She smiled and watched me putt, eyes hidden by her sunglasses again. "She claimed you with a pink ball."

"Wow. I had no idea that was a thing," I admitted with a laugh.

"I'm guessing not many guys are man enough to accept her pink ball, so those who do are pretty special," she teased.

"I'm flattered, but why not just ask me out? I could have bought her a soda and raced her on the go-carts since she can't legally drink or drive yet."

She laughed and stepped up to her ball. "Contrary to her job, she didn't have the balls to ask." With a small putt, her ball plinked into the hole.

"Nice one," I admitted then quickly hit my ball in after hers. "That's two for both of us. Are you gonna hustle me now?"

She was focused on Pacey and the others, not far ahead. She turned back to me. "I'll let you take par on that last hole since you didn't even hit, but you're down by two with only one hole left. That means you have no chance to win. Why would I bother betting anything?"

"I'll take that, but I still think I have a chance. What do I get if I win?"

"What do you want?" she asked, holding up her club and letting it swing playfully in front of her.

I grinned and ran a hand over my mouth and chin, trying to cover my obvious excitement at those words. "Hmm."

"You don't have to think too hard about it. You're losing anyway," she teased, glancing back toward Pacey after the group had started laughing about something.

I stepped closer to Gia, wanting all of her attention. "I want a date. Soon. Like tonight soon. And this last hole is deceiving."

"Can't. I have plans with my family after work tonight."

"Then tomorrow?"

"We'll talk about it ... if you actually win." She smirked. "What do I get if I win?"

"What do you want?" I asked, moving even closer. I couldn't control myself, and I sure as hell didn't want to even if I could.

Her lips pressed together as she contemplated her prize. "I want you to kiss me."

"Done," I said, twisting my wrist up and slinging my club behind me. I wanted the date, but I'd be a damn fool if I turned down an instant kiss. I closed the space between us with two more steps, rushing up on her like a kid to an ice cream truck.

She giggled and held up a hand. Her palm greeted my chest with firm pressure, halting me. "I haven't won yet."

"You don't have to win for that," I assured, letting my dignity fall at her feet. How did that happen so easily? I couldn't get enough and wanted so much more, that was how.

"Oh yes, I do. It's the rules. So grab your pink ball, maintenance man, step around the Aerial, and take your shot."

I did as she said, catching Pacey's stare when I dropped my ball on the tee mat of the final hole. They had already finished and were either waiting on me or just talking by the club return. She smiled at me, and I turned away from her, hoping she'd give me a pass for today after seeing who I was with. "Maybe you should go first."

Gia propped the club in front of her, rested her hands on the very top, and jutted her hip out a little. "Not a chance."

I laughed. "Suit yourself. You're going down." Gripping the club with one hand, I pointed it at her, swung it around like a bat a couple of times, then settled in behind the ball knowing there wasn't a chance in hell I'd even try to win. I wanted that kiss. As soon as possible. I eased the club back then let it swing forward, connecting with the ball with tiny tap. It rolled about a foot.

"Wow, that was horrible," she admitted, dropping her ball on the mat. "Now step aside so I can show you how it's done." I backed away to give her enough space, and she took her shot. Her pink ball rolled only a few inches farther than mine.

I laughed and rubbed the back of my neck, realizing what we were both doing. "This game will never end, will it?"

"Maybe, maybe not. We'll see." Her lips tipped up and she stepped to the side so I could take my next shot. "Are they waiting for you?"

I glanced up and shook my head when Pacey looked at me again. I was being selfish, but I didn't care. Sharing Gia for whatever time left was not an option. "Nah. They'll be fine without me."

"Should I be offended you don't want to introduce me?" she asked.

"Hope not. I don't even know most of them. Today was the start of wedding party bonding or something."

"So who do you know?"

After putting another foot, I straightened up and looked toward the group. "You know Pacey, and you might have seen Guy briefly last night—with the blond wave on his head. Groomsman Evin and best man Rick are off to the left there with their dates, Kyla and Milly, I think. I don't really know them. Edena—the grumpy looking brunette near Pacey—is Guy's stepsister. And the other two chicks dressed for the beach are Leah and Maria. They've been friends with Pacey since high school. And the other two guys are their latest conquests."

"Ah," she said, switching places with me so she could take her turn. "Looks like a fun group."

"They're okay, I guess."

"How's Pacey doing about the wedding stuff? Still a little crazed?" she asked, hitting her ball a tad past mine. It edged along the bumpy blue turf then rolled into the fake water hazard.

I moved behind her, gently touching her arm as she stepped aside, wanting to be close again for a moment. "She's been a little stressed. I think I told you that she's very organized, so when things don't go exactly as planned, it gets under her skin." I whacked my ball this time, banking it off the bricks to liven things up.

Gia's smile widened. "Nice power. Looks like you're winning."

My ball stopped in the tunnel beneath the hammerhead shark. I shrugged. There was still no way I'd sink my ball purposely with a kiss at stake. "This one's pretty tricky. I'm not so sure."

She chipped her ball out of the blue turf, and it bounced a few feet. Her focus was on the group again as she stepped off the green, not even watching where her ball had stopped. "Do you like him? Guy? You're the big brother, so I'm guessing you've already threatened to end his life at least once."

I let out a breathy laugh with a small head shake. "He's okay. And no, I haven't made that threat, but I'm pretty sure it's implied. Why are you asking?"

"I was just curious what it would be like to have a protective older brother instead of a drop-dead gorgeous older sister, who unintentionally stimulates my boyfriend's body rather than threatens it harm."

"Ouch. That is a big difference. Although, I would say both would effectively weed out the assholes." Having met Kass, I understood how some guys would lose their minds around her. I could even see myself approaching her had she been hanging at The District on vacation. But, for me, compared to Gia, there was no contest.

"That is true. Did Pacey lose a fair share of bad boyfriends to your brotherly intimidation?"

"Not one," I replied. Having no way of reaching my ball upright, I lay on the turf and used the top of my club like a billiard cue stick instead. "I'm four years older, so I tried not to interfere with her life that way. But I did help pick up the pieces a few times." The ball rolled out to the other side where Gia stood.

She didn't move when I walked around except to lift her sunglasses and stare at me. I pushed mine up too, wanting another unfiltered, up close view of her eyes. They looked me over softly, traversing my face before connecting with my eyes. I was lost in her for that moment. "Sounds like you're a really great brother. I'm sure that meant a lot to her." Her voice was light, barely audible, but all the noises around us still faded. With those words, it was possible she was thinking about the previous night, possibly thanking me again for what had happened with her ex. But more than that, it felt like she was appraising me, approving me.

"Hey!" Pacey's voice cut through my thoughts and made Gia take a small step back. "Good to see you again, Gia. I don't mean to interrupt, but we're all heading over to the wooden track. You guys wanna race with us?"

I took a deep breath at her intrusion and shook my head at Gia, who was smiling nervously. "Pay, I think—"

"I actually have to get to work in a few minutes," Gia cut in. "And I'm the one who's sorry. I interrupted your day."

"Aw, no. Don't worry about it," Pacey replied to her with a grin and a "you're welcome" glance at me. "You sure you can't stay?"

"Really, I can't. Busy day for the boutique."

"Okay, well, maybe we'll see you again soon, Gia. Possibly in a couple weekends," Pacey said then eyed me again before I gave her my wide, crazy eye stare. She rolled hers and turned away.

"You do have to go?"

"Yeah, I need to go save my younger sister, Viv, before she starts hacking up the gowns with clients still in them. Her tolerance for giddy is only a tad above my own."

"Bad for business," I agreed with a nod then glanced at the two pink balls by our feet. "This is a bit of a dilemma. What should we call it? Draw?"

"Sounds fair. Should it be all or nothing?"

"Definitely all."

The small grin told me she agreed. I dropped my club and closed the gap between us, reaching up to hold her jaw, feeling the softness of her skin a little more than the night before. My eyes wandered over her face, studying her. The curl in her long lashes. The shades of brown in her wanting eyes. The smooth look of her lips. I cupped her face and watched her eyelids flutter closed then closed my own and pressed my lips to hers, feeling her hands navigate my arms and grip gently. As good as it felt, I knew I wouldn't be satisfied until I tasted her. I shifted my head, my lips, testing her response. She accepted, opening with me and waiting for more. I inhaled her, elated, and slipped my tongue in to meet hers. It was blissful, heady. It made my heart kick a couple notches and my head dial 911 on my dick's level of excitement. The last thing I wanted to do was break away from her. I needed more. But this was the first kiss, to show her what could be, what would be. What if.

I pressed my lips to hers two more times and eased away. The relaxed look of her face as she cracked her eyes open said it all. My impression was a good one. *Yes.*

"Holy shit, dude," a squeaky voice said beside us, causing Gia's eyes to widen and her body to stiffen.

"Are you going to return my messages now?" I asked, not bothering to look at the little thugs I was mentally preparing to club.

"Yes," she replied as I reluctantly released her face. "I'll text you back."

"Glad to hear it."

11

Gia

I trailed my fingers across my lips, thinking of how Mark's had felt against mine. Their tenderness, their control. I was lucky to have gotten out alive. If I had stayed, I would have surely suffocated. Because a kiss like his steals all reason to breathe, and I was a greedy bitch.

Ding. Ding. Ding. "Excuse me!" a voice called as the reception desk's bell chimed loudly, cutting through the white noise music playing in the boutique.

I dropped my fingers, tore my blank stare away from the front window, and turned toward the massive scowl standing in front of me. "I'm sorry. Can I help you?"

An older blonde with beautiful eyes and flared nostrils relaxed her pressed lips and let out an irritated breath. "I'm hoping so. Do you host trunk shows here?"

"No, sorry, we don't. But if the bride is interested in a specific dress from any of our designers' latest lines, we can compare other styles and fits then special order."

She turned away silently and moved toward the back display racks where a younger version of her faced a mirror with a dress pressed against her body.

I ran my fingers across my lips again, smiling at my lack of concentration despite what it really meant: I was too focused on Mark. He was a distraction that could cost me. If I hadn't already taken the required photos before seeing him at Putters, it could have cost me the job.

"Gia, did you inventory the latest order? Looks like a lot of fabric back there." Aunt Aimee asked, stepping in front of the desk's high countertop and straightening a hair accessory display. There were chips along the tips of her nails, which had only been painted beige for a couple days.

"Yeah, I looked when I got in. It's right." Since I'd paid for the extra material separately, the bank account that she tracked diligently hadn't been touched. Luckily, she didn't watch the actual inventory as closely. In this case, what she didn't know wouldn't hurt her.

She turned, shifting her focus toward the back of the store where the mother and daughter inspected another dress. "Okay, good. I also need you to look up the Cavelli order and cut the A-line cowl necks."

"All sizes? There were four if I remember correctly."

"Yes. That style isn't selling, and we can't afford to let them collect dust and deodorant stains for the whole year."

"Anything I should worry about?"

"No, just adjusting to match the demand." She turned to face me, her gray eyes holding less of their usual joy. "I'll be in the back office."

A few minutes later, Viv sidled up beside me. "Hey," she said, setting up her laptop.

"Hey. Did you get the info?"

Her fingers paused on the keys and she side-eyed me. "Of course."

I'd sent her pictures and names of everyone who had been with Guy and Pacey as soon as I'd gotten into my car at Putters. When I arrived at the boutique, she left to take a late lunch, which entailed driving somewhere to intercept some free Wi-Fi, digging for background information, and apparently eating something heavy on the onions.

I waved my hand in front of my face. "You are in serious need of a mint." The words made my thoughts jump to Mark again and how his breath was nowhere near bad. Simply recalling the minty taste of his mouth had me licking my lips. My mind had officially betrayed me, so I scolded myself with a swift smack to the spot I'd just licked.

Viv chuckled while she pulled up the info. "I know that smack wasn't for my breath or some pesky fly. You gonna tell me what happened?"

"Not a chance," I replied, leaning toward her screen for a closer look. "Find anything good?"

"Well, Leah and Maria are definitely from the other job. But you knew that."

"So this new client knows Maria personally enough to give Duplicity a recommendation."

"Or it's Maria again," Viv noted. "She could know something and is afraid to ruin another relationship."

I stared at the pictures she had pulled up, considering the info. "True. Maria and Leah were flirting with Guy, not really caring. If it is her hiring us again, though, she wouldn't be the one cheating with Guy. I mean, if she wanted to out herself to Pacey, she could just set up a rendezvous where Pacey would catch her and Guy in the act."

"Right. Still, she could be hiring us knowing about someone else. Maybe even her sister, Leah?"

"We can't rule her out of anything. Either of them. Leah knows of us from our direct messages exposing her ex, but there's also a chance that Maria told her she'd hired us for the job." I pointed to Viv's keyboard. "I can't really worry about the client right now, though. I need to focus on who Guy might be hooking up with. So who's next?"

She scrolled through the pictures and profiles she'd expertly put together. "I found the usual. Schools, birth places, and social media profiles. Most are enrolled at the University of West Florida. Here's the groomsmen and their dates. The blondes both work at a coffee shop called Perky near their dorms. Both are also psych majors. Only Milly is nailing a prof, though," she added, clearly proud to have found that bit of info. "Pretty much the same with the groomsmen. They share a place closer to downtown, not far from Pacey and Guy. Best man Rick was another contestant on that reality show Beach Bum with Guy. Evin's an outfielder, but he'll lose his spot if he doesn't bring his GPA up this term. When Guy isn't with Pacey, he's usually with them. How did the guys interact together? Maybe he's bi or a closet case?"

"Those three goofed off a bit, but I didn't catch any long junk gazes or playful butt slaps. Not that that means much. What about the others?"

"The stepsister, Edena, is a twenty-two-year-old unsuccessful entrepreneur with a few abandoned websites. She also tends bar at her dad's restaurant in Gulf Breeze. Her dad married Guy's mom about five years ago, and her listed address is still their place. Our old client, Maria, is an unemployed junior like Pacey. Sister Leah dropped out of school and now works at a resort on Pensacola Beach. They share a condo their parents own, not far from that resort. The only thing I found on their dates was that they compete as amateur bodybuilders and are based at a gym near the girls' condo."

"That's a good amount of info, Viv. Great job."

"Thanks," she murmured, eyes still on the screen, though her usual resting-bitch lips tipped up a tad.

I nudged my shoulder against hers. "So we've got some basic backgrounds in case we need them. Now it's all about the watching."

"Which might be a problem for you now," she stated in a playful whisper.

"It shouldn't be." I straightened up, hoping to counteract the desire to go all gooey at the thought of Mark.

She shrugged with a head tilt. "It shouldn't be, but it might. Then again, it also might be useful. He could get you around Guy more, just like today."

"I thought that would be a good thing too, but I don't see Guy trying to mess around on Pacey while her brother's hanging out. That would be moronic."

"Like we haven't encountered morons before."

I giggled with her. "True. For now, I'll follow the schedule and deal with Mark on my off time. He'll understand."

"Sure he will. As long as he doesn't catch you watching his sister's fiancé."

"Or find out that I might ruin her wedding." He was her protector, her confidant. When he'd talked at Putters about helping to heal her heartaches … my own heart skipped a few beats. How could I have resisted a kiss after that? That's right, I couldn't. Because like some deprived love addict, I needed to taste someone with that kind of devotion. My mistake was thinking one taste would be harmless. I should have known it'd be more like buying a box of tarts with a plan to only eat a few—a damn lie. There was no way I'd want to walk away, and that was the problem. There had been a fleeting moment, just before the kiss, that telling him had crossed my mind. And that was bad. That risked everything. The job. Duplicity. The boutique. My life and my family's. I had to remember that my feelings were not important. The Duplicity job was. Finding what Guy might be doing behind Pacey's back, *who* Guy might be doing behind Pacey's back, was the only important thing.

Viv nodded just a tad and tucked a golden lock of hair behind her ear. "I'll help you manage the schedule, and maybe I'll look into his to prevent possible run-ins. You just try not to tell him what you're doing when you see him."

"Sounds easy, but I already know he's pretty intuitive."

"Do you want to know more about him to get a leg up? You didn't ask about his details."

Do I want to know? Viv probably had a good background base on him already, and all I had to do was say the word. But it didn't feel right. I actually wanted to hear it all from him, sooner or later. Besides, if he was a psycho with a record or an avid toenail collector, she would surely tell me. "Thanks, but I'll find out from him."

She nodded. "He is squeaky. And as far as your convos with him, just don't ask too many questions about Pacey. And if you happen to go with him to another family thing, just don't get too close to Guy."

"Right," I agreed, looking out the store windows, watching more people exit Fresh Brewed next door with cups of life fuel, thinking my next cup might be a maintenance man. I shook my head. "What was the next location?"

"Well, we turned down the brunch he's attending tomorrow, so it'll be Wednesday night. He's supposed to be at Evin and Rick's place to watch a baseball game."

"Right. The friends' place could be prime for something to happen, especially if it's just the guys hanging out. Not easy to see what's happening inside, though. Is it ground level?"

"No, second floor," she answered.

"Did you happen to check the satellite maps?"

"Yeah, it looks like a pretty standard apartment with a balcony. Some tree cover behind the building."

"Hmm. I hope they're the 'open all the windows and doors' type." There was a part of me, beyond the usual need to catch the target, that just wanted to catch Guy in the act so the job would end sooner rather than later. "Is it bad that I want it to be true so it'll all be over?"

Viv turned to me, looking at me with a deep, knowing stare. "This has to do with Mark. You really like him, huh?"

"I think so."

"You want to be happy. That's not a bad thing."

"But it is. I'm pretty much hoping for Pacey's heart to break. That makes me pretty horrible."

"You're hoping for resolution. It's what you are always hoping for with these jobs. And the suspicions usually end up being true, so chances are that her heart will break. There's just another reason for you to want it to end quickly this time."

I shrugged and looked away from her sympathetic eyes. My selfishness didn't deserve kindness. I wanted an end, to be around Mark with nothing between us. I'd be able to see him without looking past him, to touch him without feeling guilty, to taste him without tasting lies.

I ran my fingers across my lips at the thought.

And I wanted it all so badly that I was ready to crush his sister's heart.

$$12$$

Mark

Tonight, I texted Gia, hiding my phone under the table like a teenager so Pacey didn't catch me ignoring her wedding ramblings. I wouldn't have had to worry about extra attention had Guy shown up this morning instead of bailing on this family brunch to attend some last-minute promotional interview for Beach Bum.

After my phone call had gone unanswered the night before, I'd finally gotten a text response from Gia. She was still dodging my attempts to set up a date, but I had no idea why. I knew that kiss at Putters had made as much of an impression on her as it had on me. So she was either second-guessing it all or playing hard to get. My only option was to push forward. There was something between us that was worth it, and I wouldn't let up until we had at least one real date. After that, if she told me to go to hell, I'd go with a smile.

My phone vibrated. I shifted my gaze away from the chatter around the table down to my thigh.

I don't know. She was not giving in easily.

Dinner out? Dinner in? I make a mean cobbler.

Dessert?

I grinned at the screen. *Got something against dessert?*

Another quick reply. *Sounds fancy for a man who likes his coffee so boring.*

Hey now. My coffee might be boring, but I can assure you not much else is. That kiss definitely wasn't. I wondered if she was thinking of it too. Again and again. Her lips—

A sharp kick to the shin snapped my eyes back up to the table where they met Pacey's glare. I raised a brow in question, and she smirked in response.

"So have you?" my mom asked. The dark blue eyes I'd inherited narrowed when my own shifted to her, deepening the feathered wrinkles at their corners, and glinted with an unnerving amount of curiosity—a look that momentarily hid the vigor and determination that had taken root since Pacey had announced her wedding.

"Have I …?" I felt my phone vibrate again, but I fought the urge to look as I held my mother's scrutinizing gaze, which was still far more welcoming than Pacey's at the moment.

My father cleared his throat and arched his brows with the patent "I'm staying out of this" look before he turned his silver-streaked head away, raising a hand to the waitress for the check.

"Invited your plus-one," Pacey answered my question with a teasing tone.

"Pacey said you were seeing someone. You haven't mentioned her." Mom's words were her usual soft tone, but there was an edge, demanding more information.

It was my turn to shoot a glare at Pacey, and she quickly looked away with a huge smile on her face. She knew this was not a topic I liked to discuss with our mom. It usually led to follow-ups about my last girlfriend, and then how "book club friend number twelve" had a single daughter who'd be absolutely perfect for me.

What I hated more than those conversations, though, was the hint of sorrow I'd see in her eyes every time I had to tell her another relationship—actually the latest vacation bang—was over. She understood my reasons—that I was still young, that I needed to test the market, and above all that, I wouldn't just settle—but I knew it still hurt her overly romantic heart.

I nodded with a small grin, thinking of Gia as I tapped my phone to my thigh. There was no fighting the conversation or the fact that I'd end up inviting Gia. I could already tell she'd be able to handle a crazy family function without getting weird or clingy. At this point, she seemed more cling-free than I did. But I had my doubts she'd even accept. A response to a simple dinner invite was proving difficult enough.

"I see what you meant," Mom murmured to Pacey, jarring me out of my daze.

Pacey's eyebrows were the ones quirked at me this time, keeping her grin firmly set in place.

I shook my head. "And what was it that Pacey meant?"

"That Miss Gia has you staring into space," Pacey admitted with a shrug.

"Not that unusual."

"The goofy expressions you make when you do it are," she retorted.

"So ..." Mom cut into our exchange with a more serious tone as she removed the napkin from her lap and placed it on her finished plate. "So tell me about the girl who finally has my boy daydreaming for longer than a single weekend."

The waitress brought the check with a polite smile. Dad slid some bills into the folder and handed it back before she could leave. "Thanks," he said to her, then turned back to our conversation as he stood. "Your inquisition will have to wait, Julie. Our East Bay tee-time's in a half hour."

I gratefully followed his lead, standing quickly, and Mom grabbed her things without argument. As she fell in step with Pacey behind Dad, a phone dropped from her purse. I snatched it from the floor and trailed behind, dodging a cluster of people at the entrance of the café. The harbor walkway had filled up with the chatter of hungry seagulls and tourists out enjoying the mild temps of mid-morning and unwittingly blocking my mom's quest for more information during our walk to the lot.

When we reached their car, Mom risked one more question as Dad ushered her into the passenger seat. "Will we meet her before the wedding? That might be too hectic of a day for an introduction."

"Maybe," I answered truthfully then leaned in to kiss her on the cheek. Remembering what I held in my hand, I glanced down at the clunky black phone and extended it to her. "This fell out of your purse. I thought your phone and case had full warranties. Why the change?"

"Oh, thanks. No, no. It's not a replacement. I thought I'd lost mine the other day, so I decided to start carrying a backup for emergencies." She smiled. "I better get to meet Gia soon, okay? Love ya's!" My dad closed the door before anything more could be added.

"Thanks for covering for me in there," I said to him as we walked around the front end of the car.

He clapped a hand on my shoulder and nodded with a grin, then gave Pacey a swift hug. "Worry about your day and leave your brother alone, all right? Us Foster men take time to consider things. We don't rush."

Pacey pursed her lips at him with a playful head shake. "Yeah, yeah."

As we watched their car pull away, I said, "And thank *you* for hanging me out to dry. I'm so glad Guy bailed on you today so you could talk about all my shit."

Pacey headed farther down the lot toward her dinged up coupe, not waiting for me to follow. "Just like Dad said, you men are slow. You needed a good truth slap, and I'm always happy to help with those."

I stared at all the dents in her front fender, smirking at their direct reflection of her pushy personality. "A truth slap is totally different than a shove off Mom's guilt cliff."

She opened her door and swung around to face me. "Look, I get it. But that look you've got says it all. I just want to make sure you won't blow your chance by waiting too long."

"Believe me, I'm not. The ball is more in her court than mine." She tipped her head in question. "That's why I was texting inside. I asked her to dinner, but despite what happened at Putters, she's holding back."

She chucked her purse to the passenger seat then hooked her hands on the top of the doorframe. "Okay, I believe you. Do you think it has anything to do with her sister working on my dress?"

"That's a stretch. You already bought the dress. The wedding's almost here. I don't see how that connection would matter much."

"Maybe she's just not sure about you yet. So you'll have to convince her that you're not a douche ... which might be tricky." She punched my shoulder playfully.

"Ha. Funny."

"Oh!" she said suddenly. "Back to the wedding ... about the dress. I forgot to mention this while we were eating since Mom was busy talking about the guest list."

"You? Forget to tell us something? That's actually funny."

"Shut it. Anyway, I submitted a picture of my dress to Destination Bride magazine last week and got an email response yesterday requesting more info—me, the venue, the dress, and the designer."

"Sounds great."

"It could be more than great! They might show more interest because of Guy and his Beach Bum thing, but the dress is what got their attention. It could mean good exposure for Kass and their boutique."

"Is that something Kass wants?"

"I didn't actually tell her," she said, and I couldn't help but scowl. "But we chatted about publicity during my appointments. She mentioned wanting more work, more visibility. It's her passion. This could really make her a household name."

"You need to tell her."

"Maybe it's best to wait. They might not even follow up."

I sighed. "Pushing me about relationships is big, but this is on a different level, Pay. You can't mess with someone's life that way without them knowing."

"I know, I know." She lifted her elbow onto her roof and looked toward the road with a head shake. "I just want to help."

I smiled. Her intentions were always good even though they were often chaotic. "I hope the news is good all around then."

"Me too." She nodded and let her elbow slide off the roof's edge. "That goes for your news with Gia too. You shouldn't wait around for that answer."

"Yeah," I said, slipping the phone out of my pocket and holding it up. The thought of Gia's unread text added an unsettling amount of weight to the phone ... and my stomach. What if her answer was no?

"Better get to it then. Talk to you later."

I waved and headed toward my Charger, tapping the phone a few nervous times before swiping the screen.

Hope not, because boring cobbler sounds really depressing.

"Yes!" I yelled, shocking myself and drawing several confused and anxious stares from across the parking lot. Unabashed, I smiled and slid behind the wheel of my car, knowing I'd willingly become a fool for this girl.

So, tonight? Dinner out then non-boring cobbler.

She let me sweat the whole ride home, waiting for my phone to beep. After I stepped through my door, the notification finally came.

What time?

13
Gia

Being early was essential for Duplicity. I never knew what to expect when I arrived somewhere to bust a cheater. The thing that was almost always certain, though, was that nothing happened on schedule. Late. Early. I'd caught my fair share of picture-worthy evidence—targets crawling through windows, hookups at bars—long after and way before the times I was given. It was a good reason to show up ahead of time. Luckily, I was good with punctuality most of the time.

Even for my own dates.

The Sunday night crowd at The District was a good combination of locals and late summer vacationers enjoying the open atmosphere, watching people wander in and out of shops, bars, and restaurants. I was no exception. With my first beer already in hand, I had been people watching from my high swivel chair for a couple of minutes. Glancing at the bar clock hanging between a scuba tank and a mounted marlin, I noted there were still twenty eavesdropping minutes before my date with Mark. Arriving early and pounding a beer was a strategic start. Both would help me relax and prevent me from backing out. I knew I should have just said no, avoided the whole situation, but like a fool, I couldn't resist him ... or dessert.

Over the last few days, my thoughts kept shifting to him, struggling with how to handle it all. My job could possibly kill his sister's wedding, but there was no way I could tell him that. Duplicity was a secret that I wanted to keep. And there was also the fact that I was practically a stranger. A nobody. Even if I had proof of Guy's cheating to show him right away, which I didn't, he'd be suspicious of my involvement and he'd have every right to be.

A low cough drew my attention down to the end of the bar. A guy. Mid-thirties. Shaved head. His eyes focused on the TV overhead while his left hand twisted the beer bottle in front of him, his wedding band catching the light with every turn. No matching ring at his side.

I downed a long gulp of beer and turned toward Main Street, spotting Mark a few moments later as he rounded the corner of a closed jewelry store. My eyes flickered back to the clock. Eighteen minutes early. Maybe he was feeling the same? Well, feeling the same about everything but the "ruining his sister's marriage and killing all hope for a relationship" thing.

His tapered hair was a tad shorter at the sides than it had been the day before, but the long, messy spikes in front were the same. He wore a plain white T-shirt and a dark blue pair of cargo shorts, looking relaxed and unbelievably sexy. I gripped my beer bottle and took another long drink to calm the excitement pulsing through me, anxious to be close again. My body clearly needed sedation to be near him. Maybe the date wasn't a good idea after all. How could I trust my actions around him, my words. Questions would be asked, answers expected. Did I really want to lie? Wasn't that what I was trying to protect people from, really? Infidelity was the main infraction, sure, but the lies behind it were just as bad.

Was I just a big, fat hypocrite, lying to someone I wanted to start a relationship with?

He said hi to a few people in passing and waved at someone calling his name from a table outside a café.

My nervousness forced my eyes away, glancing down the bar again to lessen my worry. A tall blonde edged up beside the married guy with the shaved head. She smiled at him then called the bartender over with a toss of her hair. The beer bottle in front of him stopped turning. The blonde's attention was back on him, and words exchanged between them. When the bottle started turning again, there was no ring glinting under the light.

I shook my head at another doomed marriage and turned away, my eyes zeroing in on Mark again. I could have been getting ahead of myself. I barely knew him. He could be a hardcore player. After all, he'd landed Denise's number the other night while she was with Landon. And, as he moved through The District, a few women reacted with hair touches and alluring smiles. Did they know him? Then there was the fact that he invited me to his place, which we all know is pretty much asking for a run at all the bases. The cobbler offer was pretty specific and unique, though, so there was a chance he could be one of those rare guys who was undoubtedly thinking about the home run but fully prepared for a few practice swings before stepping to the plate.

Okay, enough with the baseball analogies. I don't even like baseball.

My mind spun. I couldn't decide what I even wanted. Did I want to take the Kass route and get him out of my system? Or did I want this to be more? Try to trust someone again? At least he hadn't used the line "Netflix and chill." That alone would have earned a "nope" even with the cobbler. Regardless, the decision was imminent. If there was a chance I wanted more, it would be better to take the cautious route and keep my distance until the Duplicity job was over. So essentially, I'd have to cross my legs and hold my tongue. That didn't sound difficult at all.

I took another long, tense drink from the bottle, watching him approach the bar. When his eyes finally landed on me, he quirked a bemused, happy looking smile. It was the same look he'd had after our kiss at Putters, and the memory instantly made my whole body sigh. That included an audible one. Unfortunately, I forgot to tilt the bottle down before I released the air from my lips, which spilled cool beer down my chin, my neck, pouring between the V of my mustard-colored shirt, and channeling into my cleavage before I could even drop my arm.

Great. I twisted back toward the bar, grabbing the thin drink napkin to wipe the trail as the last bit darkened the Victorian patterns of my skirt. At least I hadn't chosen the white linen.

"Hey, Matt!" Mark's deep voice called from my side. "Towel?"

I continued to wipe nervously, hiding my face for as long as possible. The saturated napkin disintegrated in my fingers, leaving little wads of tissue down my neck and shirt. Accepting my millionth loss to the gods of humiliation, I looked up to face my embarrassment with an exasperated huff.

Mark had one hand on the back of my chair, the other splayed on the bar, leaning in close, his face inches from mine. I inhaled a nervous breath and was surprised with the tangy smell of berries. "You're early." It was a mere whisper, just loud enough to hear over the bar's music.

"And clumsy," I admitted, glancing at the clock. "You're early, too."

"And thirsty," he replied with a cute grin. "Looks like we got the 'What's your fake dwarf name?' first-date question out of the way. Though, I guess I knew yours when we met at the air conditioner."

Heat rose up my neck and spread across my face, erasing whatever coolness the beer had left behind. Clumsy was a much better adjective choice for a dwarf name than what I had really been on the air conditioner that day. Horny. Horny the dwarf. Probably Snow White's favorite in the adult film parody. *Hi ho, hi ho.* I swallowed the nervous lump in my throat and locked the thoughts of the air conditioner away. "I suppose you did. I'd like to say that's better than Sneezy, but I'm not so sure."

"I'd choose Clumsy any day," he said. Matt passed by quickly, sliding a small towel across the bar. Mark grabbed it and tilted his chin with a quick thanks before turning back to me. "I'm hoping this doesn't mean the date's over before it was supposed to begin." He placed the towel in my hand and straightened back up. He was worried I'd take off after a beer spill? That gave me an automatic out if I wanted one, if I had the sense to take one.

I swiped away the remnants of the first napkin then blotted, taking in the wreckage of my clothes ... and confidence. Overall, the wetness wasn't so bad, but the air was pretty humid. "This won't dry for a while." Not that I cared. In an easier life, I'd walk around completely soaked just to stay there with him. I couldn't convince myself otherwise.

His head turned, looking across the water. "Our reservation is for seven-fifteen over at Catch. We could sit here for the half hour and hope it dries some, or we could walk the short distance to my place and either wait there or toss your stuff into the dryer."

Oh. So much for the dinner and drinks delaying the dessert. I could sit and let my skin marinate in summer ale, or I could risk getting naked at his place. I trusted him, but should I trust myself? "I ... uh ..."

"I have clothes you can wear while we wait if that's what you're worried about. Nothing fancy. Just comfy, boring maintenance-man wear." The corners of his lips pulled up into an easy grin.

I laughed softly, letting my concerns slip away along with thoughts of being offered clothes some other girl had left at his place. "Why did I just imagine trying on your evening wear?"

"Well, I don't have any gowns, but I do have a few suits. Or if artistic is more your style, I have a tablecloth or some beach towels."

"Boring sounds perfect," I admitted with a smile.

"Okay, good." He slipped a few bills onto the bar to cover my tab with tip, not caring whether I'd already paid or not, then grasped my hand.

I hooked my purse in my other arm and let him lead me away. His hand was rough but warm, with a light, welcoming grip. Even though The District wasn't as packed as it had been Friday, Mark pinned our hands to his side, keeping my body close while we navigated the walkways. The music and bright lights faded, darkness and quiet settling around us with each new step. I inhaled the night air, smelling the beer on my shirt but also catching another whiff of berries and the same minty soap scent I'd smelled when Mark's arms had wrapped around me on Friday night, supporting me as I'd faced my Kryptonite.

A few people walked by, chatting about drinks and dinner as they hurried toward the busy streets at our backs. My eyes took in the changes around us—cement turned to brick walkways and small gardens, shops turned into townhouses enclosed behind decorative iron gates. They were different than the townhouses where I'd met Mark on Monday, positioned closer together, more primped and pricey.

"I'm glad you decided to come tonight," Mark said, glancing at me and squeezing my hand, "despite having to work tomorrow."

"I never turn down dessert." I pressed my lips together in a smile and turned my eyes to a beautiful gated pool area, practically deserted under the dark sky. Only a few people could be seen, couples pressed closely together, in the dim light from the surrounding lantern posts.

"Really? I'll have to remember that," he replied then pointed at a set of stairs beside us. "This is me. Anchor House."

My eyes traveled the short path and up the exterior of the four-story white and gray building. At first glance it could have been deemed plain compared to the alternating color schemes of the shops and bars just a hundred yards away, but in no way was the architecture plain, with varied sized balconies, paneled windows, and lofty pillar accents.

Mark tugged my hand, pulling me forward. "It's the oldest condo building here, but it's still in really good shape."

"It's nice," I admitted, my eyes continuing to roam as we entered and he led me to the elevators. "I've never been over in this area before."

The doors opened and he let me enter first, his fingers still loosely threaded with mine. I glanced down at our hands and bit my lower lip as the doors closed us inside the small space. Alone.

His thumb moved across mine lightly. "So, about what I texted you earlier ..."

That had my full attention. I jerked my chin up so I could look into his eyes. "Please don't tell me you lied about the cobbler because I will leave and never talk to you again. I'm very serious." The berry scent still lingered on him, so I was pretty sure he hadn't lied, but I had to let him know the severity of using dessert against me.

A low chuckle escaped his smiling lips, pushing his cheeks high, humor and happiness causing his eyes to squint as they stared at me. It was a look I'd already seen, and it sure was enamoring. The elevator released us and we moved toward the back of the building. "No, I didn't lie about the cobbler. I said not much else was boring about me, but there is something I left out."

"Oh? Well, now I really should just leave," I joked, twisting my body back toward the elevator.

His fingers tightened around mine and tugged me back. The motion wasn't harsh, but I surrendered my body to it so much I ended up smacking into him. Within a second and without hesitation, his free arm wrapped around me, pressing a hand to the middle of my back while the other remained locked with mine at our sides. "You'll regret it."

The words whispered close to my ear. I tipped my head back to look at him as a rush of heat flashed through my skin. My body had gone rogue. It had its very own plans near him, and it surely wasn't listening to my brain's prudence. The internal fight tied my tongue, leaving only shallow breaths to pass my lips.

"That sounded too serial killer, didn't it?" he asked, dropping his arm and backing up a step, allowing air to flow between us and my brain to take control again, stabilizing my thoughts.

A laugh burst from me, relieved he decided to joke instead of kiss me. There would have been no turning back then. "Yeah, a bit."

"Good to know. C'mon. I promise only the victims turned me down." His hand pulled mine again, leading us down to the end of the hallway. He slid his key into the door to unlock it then paused. "The boring part I left out was about my place. It's kinda plain. Only a couple corpses. Nothing on a real serial level."

"Shut up and open the door," I said, shoving his shoulder playfully.

He chuckled and pushed the door wide.

The first thing to hit me was the sight. Basic. Gray couch along the opposite wall. Black recliner to its side and a wooden coffee table in front. Decent sized design. But most importantly, clean. Next to hit me was the smell. Berries! Sugar! The heavenly pastry scents surrounded me like I'd just stepped into a bakery, drowning the smell of the beer clinging to the front of my shirt.

I smiled and inhaled again. Ecstasy.

G ia nudged past me, sniffing the air. "My God, it smells amazing in here." Possessed by her nose, she dropped her purse on the dinette chair and moved into the kitchen where I'd left the cobblers on the glass stove.

"I was going to wait to bake them, but I thought it best to have them finished to mask the dead body smell."

She leaned close, closing her eyes and grinning. "I'm so glad you did." After a long moment of praising the dishes, she spun around and took in the rest of my place. "It's nice here, definitely not boring, especially with the constant change of vacationers, I assume."

"Part of the original appeal. Plus being close to work. I can walk or snatch a golf cart when I need to." I tossed my keys onto the kitchen counter and watched her walk around. "The bedroom is over here. I can grab you something to change into if you want."

"Yes, please," she agreed, following me past the guest bathroom back into the bedroom suite. "It's a tad smaller than my apartment, but I have a two-bedroom with a roommate. She's in a serious relationship, though, so she's never home." Her eyes moved around and stopped on the bed.

There was no way to curb my thoughts with her standing there at the foot, gazing down at the comforter. Yes, my thoughts definitely went there, and I wondered if hers had too—her wrapped in my sheets, in my arms, the feel of her skin, of her mouth. I peeled my eyes away and gritted my teeth to focus on the reason we were there. After searching my dresser, I snatched a pair of drawstring sweatpants and a T-shirt then turned and handed them to her. "Um. You can change in here or the guest bathroom. Whichever. I'll just ..." I hitched a thumb over my shoulder and backed away. "I'll be in the kitchen."

A month. It had been a full month since a woman was in my room, naked. Like most of the dates I'd had over the past year, she was a renter. Lexi was her name. A tall brunette from Tennessee, vacationing with her best friend for a week long girls' getaway. She was fun, and like the rest, had no strings. But she had nothing on who was currently shedding her clothes in there. The thought of her peeling the beer soaked shirt off her body made me bite my lip and white-knuckle the edge of the kitchen counter.

I shook my head, trying my damnedest to think about anything else before she exited my bedroom and saw exactly what I'd been thinking with a single glance at my waist. Not that I was ashamed for her to see, I just didn't want to give the impression that sex was the only reason I was into her. The goal was more than that, and I'd known before the kiss at Putters. The connection between us felt different, more distinct than I'd ever experienced after a week of knowing someone. Even in my head, that sounded ridiculous enough to laugh at, but there was no other way to describe it. At least Pacey would probably understand. Well, even if she didn't, she would at least pretend simply to ensure I had a date to her wedding. So there was that at least.

Gia stepped tentatively around the corner from the hallway, completely engulfed by my clothes. Her thumbs hooked into the top of the gray sweats to show off how she'd rolled them and wrapped the tie string around her entire waist before looping it into a knot. I laughed, a real gut laugh, unable to hold back. It was a funny sight. The legs still pooled over her ankles, making her look shorter than she actually was. And the T-shirt sagged, its neckline wide enough to show off as much as her V-neck shirt had plus one of her bra straps. Maybe it wasn't funny. It was sexy. I took a deep breath, my laugh instantly disappearing.

"Funny?" she asked, smiling.

"Yeah, I'm sorry. I just grabbed what I usually lounge in. There might be something smaller if you want."

"So you did this on purpose, huh?" She moved toward me, appearing to glide across the floor the way the sweats swayed loosely around her legs.

I swallowed as my eyes roamed up her body, taking in the soft look of her neck, on full display with her hair twisted and pinned up. Her lips curved up slightly and her eyes narrowed, creating a soft crinkle in her mousy nose. "All part of the plan to make you look like a halfling."

"That makes sense," she said, passing me and turning to the dishes on the stove for another whiff. "I mean, you've already ensnared me with food. So what's the next step in hobbit role play? A full pint and an adventure to Mordor?"

I laughed again, mentally checking off another pro as she turned back to me laughing too. *Lord of the Rings* banter was not always well received or understood. I opened the fridge beside me, grabbed a Corona, and held it up. "A pint, or rather three quarters of one, if you're interested."

She nodded. "I'll try to refrain from spilling again."

After I opened her bottle and watched her take a drink, I said, "I forgot to ask what you wanted to do with your clothes."

"I hung them in your bathroom. I don't really want to toss them in the dryer."

"We might miss the dinner reservation if they air dry."

"I don't mind if you don't."

"Not at all," I said, taking a long drink as she looked around the room. "I have to be honest. I don't have anything to make a decent meal here. I can always order something for delivery or something from Catch and go grab it."

She tapped the rim of her bottle to her lips with a grin. "I have to be honest, too. I don't really want dinner."

I coughed, almost choking as thoughts of her mouth around something else flashed to mind.

"I want dessert," she added, ignoring my cough and turning toward the covered cobbler. "This smells like blackberry. Mmm. And why a second one?"

"I didn't know what kind you'd like," I said, recovering more civil thoughts and grabbing plates and spoons. "The other one's peach."

"That has to be the most thoughtful thing anyone has ever done for me."

Stepping beside her, I slid the plates near the dish. "That's a joke, right?"

Her eyes lifted to me, big and brown and flecked with light. "Well, there was this one time that Viv bought me a blueberry scone and a maple." Her eyes shifted up to the ceiling, as if she were replaying the memory. "No, maybe the maple one was for her, but Kass ate it instead." Her shoulders shrugged and her teeth bit down on her bottom lip dramatically. "Honestly, though, not far from the truth."

"Sisters. I understand that." I wasn't about to comment on the obvious implication: that no other guy had done anything nice for her. Idiots. "So you're serious about all pastries then, not just desserts." I dug a serving spoon into the cobbler and dished some onto a plate for her.

"It's true. I can't resist any of them." Her eyes widened as she took the plate in one hand and dug a spoon in. "Oh, this looks so delicious." She slipped the spoon into her mouth, closed her eyes, and moaned softly.

The velvety sound sent pulses through my body, causing me to force out a cough/laugh combo, trying hard to ignore my thoughts again. I dished my own serving and took a quick bite. The sweet and tangy taste barely registered while I watched her eyes open to me. "Good?"

"You have my absolute attention. God! Where have you been all my life?" she asked the plate, making me laugh again. After another bite and a stifled moan, she looked back at me. "This is amazing. The maintenance man has a secret skill. And it is definitely not as boring as his coffee. Is this a hobby or a passion?"

"A mixture of both." I watched her mouth ready the next question and held up my spoon. "Yes. The answer to your next question is that I do have plans. For right now, though, I'm happy where I am, working toward a possible goal." I took another bite and waited for her to finish chewing on her last.

"That's not what I was going to ask at all, actually."

"Really?" I mumbled around my food, a little shocked.

"I was going to ask if you planned to cut into the peach tonight too." She giggled. "Kidding. Well, kind of."

"Absolutely. There's no way I'd let it sit when you're fully prepared to eat it all."

"Ha! I am, seriously. Judging by the taste of this, if you open a business, it'll be a hit. I'll buy something from you every day. I wouldn't even care where you were located. If you had to bake in jail after the police found all the dead bodies, I would still find a way."

"Not sure if I should be frightened by that or not," I joked.

"I told you, I am very serious," she said, then ate the last bite on her plate with an audible "Mmm."

"More?"

"Give me a minute and I'll be all over it. It's a good thing my skirt has more room than these restrictive sweats of yours," she joked then took a drink of her beer. "Did you know about this talent before working at East Bay?"

"Not that I wanted to pursue it further, no. I landed the job at East Bay after high school, took some basic courses while working, but never got a degree. I've always liked baking, though. I have Pacey to thank for putting the business idea in my head."

"She seems like a great sister."

"She is. This wedding has her a bit rattled, but overall, she's a mild headache," I said, recalling how she had referred to her sisters.

"Is it the usual wedding rattled or something more?" she asked, backing against the counter across from me and taking another drink.

I took another long drink too. "Normal stuff, I suppose. I'm not exactly an expert with the wedding thing."

"How are you feeling about it all? I mean, you said you were kind of protective but that you trust Guy. Is their relationship pretty solid?"

I shrugged. "As solid as anyone's can be. She doesn't really tell me about any problems. And I'm not one to ask questions unless she looks upset, which she really hasn't been."

"He was on that reality show, right? Beach Bum? I never watched it."

"Neither did I, but I heard a lot of underage girls did," I joked.

"I'm pretty sure Kass watched. But she'll watch anything as long as it has one hot guy in it, even if there are twenty some girls fighting to date him."

"If Beach Bum had been Beach Bachelor, I would have killed Guy before he tried to give Pacey a rose or STD. But she said the show was more about sporty challenges. Jet skiing, volleyball, stuff like that."

"That doesn't sound too bad."

"No, but they had the house drama too. I'm not a fan."

"Same. I wouldn't be able to have that many roommates, even for a week." She eyed me as I took another drink, her fingers twisting the tie string knot at her waist. "So does Guy still talk to any of those people? Even though there's drama, living together is bound to make both enemies and friendships."

"I guess. Well, he's close to Rick, his best man, but they grew up together and both made it on the show."

"Oh. That's cool."

Not liking that the conversation had become a discussion about Guy and his reality fame, I asked, "Now you. I know the bridal place is a family thing, but whenever you've talked about weddings, it doesn't sound like you're that invested. So does the bridal chick have a secret skill too?"

She nodded toward the dish of peach cobbler. "Can I?"

"Yeah, let me," I replied, stepping close to her to dish more for both of us.

She kept her spot, leaning against the counter, watching my progress. "I'm not a total fan of weddings, no, or the way brides go mental over a single day. I try my best not to let that affect the way I do my job, though. Helping my aunt keep her and my mom's dream alive matters more to me than anything else right now, so that's where I am."

"That's understandable," I replied, handing her plate over and serving some for myself. "But is there anything else you're passionate about? Something you want for yourself eventually?"

Her eyes closed as she wrapped her lips around a spoon, humming her appreciation again. I watched, transfixed, studying her movements, her sounds. Without thought, I set my plate onto the counter, no longer hungry for food.

She cracked her eyes open, smiling as her mouth finished chewing the bite. "What?" Her eyes narrowed playfully. "The peach tastes just as good. Sorry. I told you I'm serious about this. It could be considered a passion. Eating pastries. Maybe I should go into the taste testing business. Would you hire me?"

"Absolutely," I said, but I knew there was no way I'd be able to control myself if I had to watch her beautiful mouth every day, hear her euphoric sounds. I could barely keep it together right now. "Can I tell you something?"

"Sure." Her smile dropped a bit, responding to my serious tone.

I reached up and pinched a shorter strand of her hair hanging loose at her temple. "I made the blackberry because that's what your hair smelled like."

"Oh," she responded. "Shampoo. Good thing I don't just like the smell."

I smiled and let my fingers trail down her cheek. "Exactly why I made the peach too."

"Oh, right," she whispered as I leaned a little closer. Her chin tipped up to adjust her gaze.

I took her plate and slid it onto the counter, leaving nothing left between us except soft, anticipated breaths. She sucked her bottom lip between her teeth, eyes glancing at my mouth, showing her thoughts were exactly the same.

My gut twisted, not wanting to blow it. Having her there at my place, kissing her there, was totally different than the instant, uncalculated kiss at Putters. Sure there had been a lot at stake there too, but this was … final. If I screwed it up, I probably wouldn't get a second chance. And that had never mattered to me before. With nothing to lose but the time it took to meet the next renter, I was completely confident and careless. But not this time.

I grinned and watched her lips tip up like mine, relaxing at the sight of her, sharing the anxious moment.

"Are you trying to torture me?" she asked, making me chuckle.

"Is that what I'm doing?" I replied, backing off a hair and sliding my hand from the counter to her waist. Not too high, not too low. The roll in the sweats was thick, so I gripped firmly to let her know I was there.

"You took my plate away," she teased.

I laughed again and shook my head, thoroughly burnt by her sarcasm. "Consider it a lesson learned. Is there anything else I should know? I would hate to—"

My phone rang in my cargo pocket, the slasher ringtone slicing through the room, effectively killing the moment. I groaned a little, and Gia quirked an eyebrow before saying, "Okay now I'm worried you might really want to torture me and hide my body."

I smirked. "It's Pacey. She can leave a message or just text like everyone else." More high-pitched serial killing tones sounded off loud and clear.

"You should get it. I'm going to check my clothes."

I grabbed the phone and waited for Gia to disappear around the corner then answered, "You're dead."

"Hey! How's it going?" Pacey asked, sounding cheerful and ready for a conversation. She was probably bored.

"Is this important, Pay? Because if not, I've got to go."

"Hmm. Well, that depends on your definition of—"

"Pay," I grumbled.

"Okay, not important. But why are you so angry?"

"I'm on a da—"

"Date!" she finished the word, acting as if she hadn't already come to that conclusion the moment I told her I had to go. "Okay, I'm hanging up. Good luck. Remember to invite her to—"

I hit the end call icon a tad too late. She just had to squeeze that reminder in. The wedding was approaching fast, but it still seemed far too early to ask Gia to go, especially after our discussion about weddings. Maybe I was over thinking it all. She might be willing to go for me, for Pacey. I slid my phone onto the counter and stepped into the living room to wait.

It didn't take her long to return with her own clothes on, still not fully dry. I wasn't thrilled about her changing again so soon. Having her in my clothes felt comfortable, removing all awkwardness, as if we'd been on a hundred dates already and she was already mine. Her tentative movements almost suggested she was feeling the same, unsure about where to go, what to do.

"Are you still hungry at all? I can order something, or we can go out again if you want."

"No, that's okay. I left your clothes on the bed. I wasn't sure where your washer was."

"That's fine, thanks," I said, moving toward the kitchen. "Let me grab our drinks. Have a seat."

"Actually, I think I should probably go," she replied as I turned, bottles in hand. Unable to stop it, my smile disappeared, my disappointment on full display. In response, she quickly added,

"I've had a great time. It's not that. I just think that with a full day tomorrow, I should get going."

Before we go further. I didn't need to read her mind to see the battle in her eyes. I nodded, understanding.

When I didn't respond, she added, "My aunt seems to think I scare more brides to the crazy cat lady life when I haven't had enough sleep." She laughed lightly.

I set the beers down and returned to the living room, stopping only inches from her, needing to be that close again. "I've never wanted to ruin anyone's wedding, but I'm almost positive it'd be worth it."

Her eyebrows rose and she pinched her lips together with a nod. "You have *no idea* how real that struggle is."

The tone of those words sounded heavy with a double meaning. But I only focused on the affirmation of her wanting to stay and let my instincts kick in, lifting my hands to her cheeks, finding her shocked yet welcome gaze. Her lips parted to speak but nothing came, so I pushed mine to hers before either of us could object, before anything could interrupt. She relaxed against me, surrendering, sliding her hands around my back to hold on. Gently, I cradled her head, easing my fingers into her twisted hair. Our tongues met, exploring, tasting. The difference from the first kiss was intoxicating. No one was here to take the focus away. No Pacey or waiting wedding party. No little punk ass kids mouthing off behind us. This time was undisturbed. Clear. Hotter—as we both knew it would be and the reason she was planning to leave. Also the reason I should've backed away. She didn't want to rush, and even though I wanted nothing more than to take her to my bed, I respected that.

But she was also a grown woman. A grown, sexy-as-hell woman, digging her fingers into my back, pulling me closer, biting my lip.

Goddamn.

I bit hers back and pushed her up against the front door, attacking her mouth as if I really were heading to jail and she was my last taste of freedom. And freedom tasted so damn good. Blackberry. Peach. Lust. My body was burning.

She sighed into my assaulting mouth, and I skimmed my hands down the sides of her body, stopping only to pull her ass away from the door, squeezing it greedily. I wanted to taste more of her, to lick the trail the beer had left earlier in the night. My lips moved without restraint, unlocking from hers and kissing down her jaw to her neck. There was no stopping.

Her breaths quickened as my lips skipped down her throat, stopping at the hollow dip at the base. Fingers raked up my body, slipping into my hair and pinching the strands. I took in all her cues, all her blatant tells, savoring them, devouring them, then squeezed her ass harder and lifted her up. Her legs cinched tightly above my hips and I pushed against her, letting her feel how much I wanted her. Her grip tightened in my hair and she tugged my head back, prying my lips from her neck so she could kiss me again.

A ringtone sounded somewhere far off, muffled. I was surprised it even registered in my mind over the thrumming of my heartbeat and Gia's wild breaths. The tone chimed again, some sweet melody, and as much as I wanted to ignore it and everything else in the room, I couldn't ignore the relaxation disappearing from Gia's body.

"I ... uhh ..." she breathed. I swept my tongue over the ridge of her collarbone. She released a sigh and straightened her back. "I should probably ..." Her fingers released their grasp on my hair and slipped away.

"Answer," I acknowledged, releasing my hold and letting her body slide down mine then taking a step away.

She nodded and hurried to her purse to answer. "Hey, what's up? ... No, yeah." I chewed on my lip as she spoke, letting my eyes roam her back, appreciative of the view but missing her body already. I rubbed the back of my neck and walked past her to the counter.

"Yeah, I'll be in early," she continued.

I stared at her as I dipped a spoon directly into the dish of blackberry cobbler. Her eyes popped wide with a grin, tracking my movements.

"Listen, Viv, I'll ... yeah. Bye."

"I hate to kick you out, but I don't think I want to share any more of this," I said then took a bite. "Mmm."

She dropped the phone into her purse then shouldered the straps with a laugh. "I know what you're doing."

I smirked and pushed the dish away protectively when she got too close. "What am I doing?"

"Trying to tempt me, of course. But you chose the wrong weapon this time." She backed toward the door, mirroring my smirk. "Had you kissed me again, though, I would have been buying cats tomorrow for my aunt's new business."

I laughed and grabbed the cobbler, covering it with a towel as I walked toward her. "Can I walk you out to the parking lot at least?"

"Better not," she admitted.

"I'm okay with that. But you have to take this with you. If I keep both, bad things will happen."

"In that case ..." Her hands took the dish and I opened the door for her to step outside. "I'd hate to add to the body count."

"Would it be weird for me to ask you to call or text when you get home?" My hand gripped the doorframe, squeezing almost painfully with restraint. I wanted to kiss her again. And again.

"So weird," she quipped, shaking her head before she leaned in quickly and pressed a soft kiss to my cheek. "Thanks for tonight. I'll definitely text you."

15

Gia

The backside of Evin and Rick's apartment building bordered a dead-end road, in a less than stellar part of downtown Pensacola with rundown houses, busted street lights, and apparently one of the best hole-in-the-wall cafés that served beignets from a to-go window a block away.

What? I was hungry, and stakeouts were unpredictable.

Traffic and work put me an hour behind the estimated time of Guy's arrival—I was seriously slipping—but after a few drive-bys, I knew all the guys' vehicles were accounted for. Despite the area's lack of mid-week activity, I decided not to stage my stealthy self directly in front of the building. The sun hadn't quite set yet, and I wouldn't risk drawing attention from usual residents to my unfamiliar car. Instead, I parked the Velostar along the curb in front of a mostly vacant and partially boarded-up strip mall across the street. The only doors with actual business signs were for a psychic reader and an adult store. The latter was the only one with an open sign lit up on the glass door ... and a vinyl blow-up sheep in the display window beside a set of neon boob lights.

The area was also still too quiet to stalk the apartment up close. I was good at being invisible, sure, but the place was dead. That meant I had to wait for the cover of darkness to peek in any windows. It also meant I could miss anything that would happen until then, but at least I'd get the required location picture one way or another.

I wasn't letting the job slip because of the guaranteed cash either. Caution was a top priority if I didn't want jail time. Also, there was the issue with knowing the target and dating his soon-to-be brother-in-law. The weight of it had gotten worse following my date with Mark on Sunday. I'd kept communication with him short since then. Small texts and very little talk time. It had been enough to confirm he wouldn't be one of the guys watching the game inside. I also had excuses to end the conversations, mostly related to the boutique, lying about an influx of crazed brides demanding special ordered gowns and ridiculous alterations. The lies were stressing me out, too, making me eat any pastry in sight. I hated it. Well, not that last part.

I bit down on the beignet, holding my breath so the powdered sugar didn't spray all over the wheel and dash like the first one had. The taste was incredible. And yet, it had nothing on the cobbler Mark had made for me. Though, my senses could be biased, mixing together from the whole experience. The feel of him, the taste of him, all of it blending in a frenzy that left one hell of an impression on my entire body. I let my eyes close for a second, recalling the touch of his lips on my neck. If I had ignored Viv's call Sunday, it would have been game over. Since I was on the fence about everything, I couldn't let that happen. But, holy shit, it had been hard to pry myself away.

A figure walked around the building, stepping out into the street and the final rays of the setting sun. I ducked my head a little lower. It was a dude with long wavy hair, not Guy or the others. He continued along the road until the stop sign and disappeared around the corner. My phone buzzed in the passenger seat and I picked it up. "What's up?"

"Any news?" Viv asked in a low voice that matched mine.

"No. And you do know that you aren't the one who has to be quiet, right?"

"Duh. Aunt Aimee is wandering the house, though."

"It's only seven. It's not like you need to be in bed."

"I'm supposed to be studying. SAT prep crap. Anyway, what's the deal?"

I stared at the back of the building, looking at the second floor balcony I knew from Viv's research to be Evin and Rick's. "I've been here half an hour. I have a view of Guy's car in a spot alongside the building. Blinds are still closed. No signs of movement, but I won't leave until he does, or I see something go down." I took another bite of the beignet.

"You aren't planning to climb some balconies tonight, are you?"

It was possible. *Gia undercover, double O … eight? Balcony badass and spy extraordinaire.*

"If so," she continued, "try not to land on your head."

"Ye ov lil faiff," I replied around the remainder of fluffy goodness in my mouth. "Anything else?"

"Nothing new has come up. No new emails. Everything's on schedule."

"Okay, then I'll talk to you later. The sun's down. I need to start snooping."

"Be careful. Bye."

I sat for another minute, studying the area before hopping out of the car. After one step into the road, the balcony's vertical blinds retracted and then the sliding glass door opened with a whoosh, letting noise from a TV filter out into the twilight. I jumped back against the car door, hoping there were enough shadows to camouflage me. Two people stepped outside, the light from the apartment turning them into silhouettes. One had long hair, the other short and a bit spiky. I couldn't make out their features, but one resembled best man Rick and the other, possibly his date from mini-golf. I watched them smoke and then make out for a couple minutes, ideas of balcony climbing dying away as pains splintered through my crouched legs. Another person stepped out just as they went in. All I needed to see was the top swoop of silhouetted hair to recognize Guy. He leaned on the corner of the railing, talking on a phone.

As much as I strained my ears, there was no way to hear his convo. And there was no way to move closer without being spotted from his vantage point. I snapped a few dark pics with the burner. At least it was something. He retreated into the apartment after a minute, and I jumped upright and stretched my legs with a relieved groan. Getting evidence on the second floor would be virtually impossible. I had to try something, though.

I got on the sidewalk first, to observe the building from across the street, just as headlights turned down the road. With no time to get back into the car, I walked slowly and mumbled, "Please keep driving. Please keep driving." When the car slowed, like an idiot, I turned.

"Gia?" Mark's voice called from the window as the car—his Charger—stopped beside me. "What are you doing here?"

My throat tightened with panic and launched me into a coughing fit, choking on saliva and all my fears.

He pulled over in front of my car then jumped out. "Whoa, are you okay?" His hand soothed my back while I doubled over.

I slowed the coughing fit but continued to breathe deep and slow, trying to find some kind of excuse, some ridiculous reason for being outside of Evin and Rick's place at eight o'clock on a

Wednesday night. There was nothing. Nothing logical. Nothing reasonable. My gas tank was full, and there was no other reason to pull down this road, except to spy on Guy. Or ... I side-eyed the empty strip mall, cringing at my only real option since Madame Emilia's neon all-seeing eye didn't see at night. *Porn shop it is.*

His hand remained on my back as I stood, rubbing gently and lowering to the back of my waist. "Easy," he said calmly until he looked at my face. His eyebrows lifted then quickly scrunched in question while his hand fell away from my back. "Are you ... high?"

"What?" I choked out. Why would he even ...?

He stepped closer, and I immediately stiffened, feeling like I'd already gotten caught with a fat bag of lies and also because of his absurd question. He thought I was on drugs? His nose brushed my cheek and he let out an airy laugh. "Sugar."

At first, I thought he was calling me sugar. Until he kissed the corner of my mouth then backed away and ran his tongue over his bottom lip. *Oh, God.*

"Beignet," I admitted sheepishly, wiping more powdered sugar off my face with my palm.

"Ah. Beignet high." He grinned then tilted his head. "So you just happen to be all the way over in Pensacola tonight ... scouting beignet dealers?" His eyes shifted around, twinkling with the reflection of the neon boob light behind me while he obviously looked for the café located a block away.

"Well, no, not exactly." I cleared my throat and put on my serious face, preparing to pull more lies from my fat bag of bullshit. "I ... uh ... Well, there's really no way to say this without it sounding really strange." He shoved his hands into the pockets of his shorts, listening. "So, as I texted to you earlier, I had to work pretty late. Anyway, Kass was invited to this bachelorette party Friday night and she, um ... made this party order a while back and turned down delivery…" I jerked my head and watched his eyes take in the adult store. "She kept forgetting and begged me to pick it up for her. I decided to come tonight since we didn't have plans. Plus, I got to stop at my favorite beignet place up the street, so it wasn't all bad. And now you're here too, so it's definitely not bad … or embarrassing … in the least bit." I giggled, attempting to settle my nerves. "What are you doing here?"

He stared at the shop for a few contemplative moments, wiping a hand across his mouth then shoving both hands into his front pockets before shifting his attention back to me. Sweat lined my palms, worried that he wouldn't buy my bullshit. I wasn't sure if I'd buy it myself. He took a deep breath and flashed me a tiny grin. I stared openly at him, my anxiety slowly dissolving as my enamored eyes focused on the sexy five o'clock scruff covering his jaw and the messy waves in his hair.

"I'm running a sister errand too, actually," he said with a nod. "Guy's watching a game over at Rick's place. That building right there, I think." He turned in the direction, pointed, then reached into his pocket and held a phone up at eye level. "I was over visiting Pacey, and she asked me to drop off Guy's phone on my way home since he forgot it. He'll be home later, but she seemed to think he needed it before then."

His phone! If he was cheating, it could have information. But Pacey had access to it. So if there was any info in there, chances were she would know and there'd be no reason for anyone to hire me. Unless she didn't check his phone, and maybe whoever hired me knew she was too trusting. The next thought in my mind was finding a way to see it without Mark catching me. Or maybe it wasn't even worth it. It was a huge risk. Curiosity nudged at me, though, begging for me to find a way. The case was black like my current burner, around the same size …

"You never know what can happen in a couple of hours," I agreed with Pacey's reason, watching Mark stash the phone in his front pocket again. Guy had to have borrowed the phone he'd been using on the balcony. Who had he called?

"I suppose," he replied, glancing back at the store behind me. "Do you need help with this?"

"Oh, no. I'll be fine." Sensing his unease—or possibly distrust—from his tense posture, I leaned in and planted a chaste kiss on his lips, hoping that would convince him to leave. "I'll talk to you later, okay?"

He grasped my arm, stopping me from turning. "I don't really like the look of this place. I'm going in with you."

"Okay ... thanks." There was no way I could have argued without coming off like a total bitch or lunatic. I just had to go with it, let this perfectly chivalrous guy escort me into the adult store after only half a date, a mountain worth of my lies, and enough sexual tension to melt all the edible panties we'd pass inside. *Fuck.*

16

Mark

Unlike the building's outside, the sex shop was pristine. Cluttered, but clean and brightly lit, with rows of fluorescents, reflecting all kinds of shiny metal goods. I released Gia's hand and followed her to the counter on the side. A video area was at the back, sectioned with bookcases. All the toys were at the front—boxes, bins, and shelves filled with everything from dildos to anal beads. Bondage items took up a good section of the side and hung from the ceiling or along the wall, ropes and chains dangling alone or from pieces of leather. I'd been to a couple similar places, mostly to buy pranks for friends with friends. Birthdays. April Fool's. It had been a while, though.

I pinched the lacy fabric on a pair of pink panties displayed by the counter, admitting to myself that there was still a certain appeal to physically touching some things before buying. There was no stopping my eyes from moving to Gia as she leaned over the glass counter to ring the call bell, which seemed to be purposely pushed back close to the register. She glanced back at me with a timid look then grinned and turned away when she saw what I was touching. As much as I wanted to think about her wearing the panties and nothing else, I had to turn my thoughts back to where we were and why. Outside of Rick and Evin's place was the absolute last place I would have imagined running into her. The odds were off the charts. And yet, it still happened. I wanted to believe her, to believe this entire freaky coincidence, but I could only think about the week before when I'd spotted her at The District too. Her ex had been there, and I helped her get out of that situation, but she never said why she'd been there to begin with. I wasn't sure what to believe. Aside from ensuring her safety, trust was the other reason I chose to stay with her. I wanted more time with her, to make sure it was the coincidence I wanted it to be and not some psycho scenario.

A dark-haired bull of a guy came out of a back office, wearing a pair of pink suspenders to hold his jeans up and a wide, contagious smile. He looked like a biker turned hipster. "What can I help ya folks with tonight?" His eyes took Gia in a bit longer than I would have liked, but he turned to me and nodded with understanding before I had to throw a hard glare his way.

Gia cleared her throat with a little cough. "I'm here to pick up an order for Kass Keats."

"Order, huh?" he mumbled, then bent over and looked beneath the counter beside the register. "I don't see an order for any Kass."

Gia smiled sweetly. "Hmm. Maybe I got the wrong place. Or maybe Kass mixed up the bachelorette date or something. It's no big deal. I'll straighten it out with her later."

I didn't want the doubt to creep in, but the mix-up certainly wasn't helping. She also hadn't even made a motion to grab her phone to contact Kass.

"Hang on a second. Sometimes these things get left in the office," the guy said and took off toward the back of the store again, a few chains and feathered toys swaying on the racks in his wake.

I stepped directly next to Gia. "Can't you text Kass to sort it out?"

Her head shook as she looked around the room. "She was closing tonight and then passing out ... probably in someone else's bed, but I still won't bother her. If she has to come grab this stuff herself, then oh well. She was stupid enough not to order online like every other person this century." Her eyes finally returned to me and she trailed her fingers down my arm. "I'm sorry that this is really weird. I'm glad we ran into each other, though."

"I am too," I admitted, leaning in closer, still smelling powdered sugar. Her eyes were wide and held a longing that called to every part of me, my body willing me to make out with her right next to the five-dollar impulse buy bins filled with cock rings, lubes, and condoms. I smiled at the thought then reached up and twisted her ponytail lightly in my fingers. Not the time or the place.

The guy returned, toting a medium-sized box under one arm. "I found it. My assistant probably took the order and left it back there."

"You found it?" Gia's voice cracked a little with a giggle. "Terrific." She waited for him to drop the box then she dug inside, pulling out a pink penis lollipop. Her eyebrows rose.

The guy scooted around the counter. "Give me a second and I'll grab the rest from the front here."

"The rest?" she squeaked.

I leaned closer to her again, looking into the box as she began lifting other things to inspect. "Didn't she tell you what she ordered?"

"Nope. That's Kass. Full of surprises." She fished a ball gag out followed by a pair of feathered cuffs.

"The cuffs are nice," I stated with a grin, unable to keep my thoughts in check.

She laughed, and I could see a pinkish tinge creep up her neck. "They are. Comfy too."

"Okay, this should be all of it," the guy said, moving toward the counter again with a black and purple leather flogger gripped in his hand along with a fully inflated male blowup doll, the long leather strips slapping against the doll's ass with every step.

I looked at Gia, watching her eyes pop and mouth drop. The entire situation was hilarious enough alone, but watching the shock register on her face was what made a loud laugh rip through me.

Gia's laugh, on the other hand, was soft and uneasy. She kept her attention on the items and straightened her back, staving off more humor. "I'm not sure it was necessary to have him ... inflated."

"He's the last of his model," the guy replied, tapping a hand over the doll's open mouth. "I'll discount since he was on display."

"Okay," she replied, wiping a hand across her forehead. "What's the damage?"

Biker geek punched the numbers on the register, and I stepped away, giving her room to handle business.

"Thanks a bunch," Gia said with a tight smile when he handed her the receipt.

"Welcome. Come back anytime," he replied with a gruff chuckle and took off toward the back.

Gia unwrapped one of the lollipops and popped it into her mouth. "Not bad."

"There is so much I can do with that, but I'll spare you," I joked, snatching the box from the counter, letting her handle the doll and flogger.

"Please, don't hold back. I really need a good laugh after the money I just spent." Her arm hooked the doll around the waist and she grabbed the flogger with her other hand, smacking the doll's face for show as we moved toward the door.

"She didn't give you money to buy this stuff either?"

We stepped outside, and she looked around quickly, making sure no one was out front watching, then picked up her pace. "I forgot to grab it from her before I left."

"Ouch."

"Yeah."

"No, I mean ouch," I said, watching her bite on the lollipop.

"Ha!" She smiled wide around the stick. "Thanks for that. And carrying. And coming in with me. Just ... thanks. For being so sweet."

"No problem," I said while she unlocked her trunk and packed everything inside.

The doll wouldn't fold right, so she relented and stuck him in the passenger seat. She backed up, assessing the doll's rigid diagonal position—feet under the dash, face to the ceiling, dick toward the windshield. "At least my windows are tinted. People might just assume my passenger is pointing at something."

"Just don't get pulled over," I joked, closing the door. "You're not going to this thing Friday night, right? Just Kass?"

"Only her. A client of hers."

"Pacey's having hers this weekend too. A Saturday spa thing with a few close friends to relax before the wedding next weekend."

"Wow. That came up fast."

"Yeah, it did. Guy's bachelor party is also Saturday. I'm supposed to go."

"Fun." She wrinkled her nose and swept the lollipop stick to the other side of her mouth. "I'm guessing that's not a spa thing."

"No, probably not." I chuckled. "The only details I've gotten is to meet them at Guy and Pacey's place that night. But I want to see you again before that. Friday? After work?"

"Sure," she agreed, "that sounds good."

"Okay, good." I pinched the edge of her lollipop stick and slowly pulled it from her grinning mouth. Her lips looked wet and inviting, glistening from the candy. I tipped her chin with my other fingers and pressed my lips to hers, dying for a taste. With a slow sweep of my tongue, the sweet candy flavor filled my mouth. After days of wanting to kiss her fully again, I groaned at the pleasure.

Her hands snaked around my back, but she broke our lips apart for a moment. "Who would have thought a dickpop was so delicious, huh?"

I took her lips again with a laugh then walked her a few steps over to my car. "I certainly wouldn't have," I said, bending to kiss her neck while grabbing my car door to unlock it. "Stay with me for a little while. I want to kiss you some more."

"Yes, please."

17

Gia

My head spun with one word on constant repeat: Liar. Liar. Liar. *I am the biggest fucking liar.* My skin crawled with every lie I had to tell Mark. All the little lies spread like wildfire from that first big one of the evening—the reason I had been outside Rick and Evin's building when he'd shown up. I hadn't come out unscathed, though. The adult store owner wrung me out like a sex addict. Sneaky bastard. He either had a bachelorette party order without a name and decided it was mine, or he totally knew something was up and threw together some merch he wanted to unload. So not only was I feeling guilty for my dishonesty, I was roughly two hundred in the hole with an inflatable love doll, some other miscellaneous kink, and almost a lifetime supply of tasty dickpops.

Oh, God! I bit my lip as ripples of pleasure tingled through my neck.

And Mark. I also had Mark. Beneath me. Reclined all the way in the passenger seat of his Charger. One hand pressed against my back, pinning me down on him, while the other hand hooked the back of my neck as his lips continued to kiss and suck the front. My mind blanked again, everything fading away with the euphoric rush coursing through my entire body. My brain refused to operate around him. Once again, it was the reason I couldn't tell him goodbye and just leave like a good liar wanting to keep the secrets from spilling. No, I had to torture myself. I needed to be near him, needed to feel him as much as he was wanting to feel me. And, oh, were those feelings so good.

With my legs bent, knees at his sides, my keys dug deeply into my jean pockets, the burner phone and slim wallet too—the only things remotely making this experience physically uncomfortable. I pushed away, sitting back to dig them out. He stared up at me, thick, full lips parted and panting. He quickly followed my lead, possibly experiencing the same discomfort. Only he tossed two phones onto his driver seat beside mine. The second phone was Guy's. I closed my eyes as curiosity struck again, awakening my mind to tonight's job once more.

I hadn't been watching. Guy could have been nailing some chick into Rick's balcony railing like a jackhammer and I wouldn't have seen or heard. Possibly not even cared.

Mark's body shifted upright and I cracked my eyes open in time to see him peel his shirt over his head. My eyes followed the lines of his bare chest, the smooth ridges and indents from relaxed muscles, down to the grooves of his abs. I inhaled and laid my hands on him, caressing, exploring. He dug his fingers into my hips, pulling me forward to capture my lips. His tongue plunged into my mouth, more forceful this time, showing me how much he wanted me. I palmed his chest and pushed him down, flat into the seat. It was my turn. I peeled my shirt up, ducking slightly to get it over my head. His hands slid up my body, exploring the same way I'd done to him. Despite the heat between us, which had already fogged the windows, chills erupted from his touch, splintering deliciously throughout my skin. I unhooked my bra and let it slip off my arms and into the driver's seat.

Switching places in the front of a car was not an easy task, but Mark had me under him in no time flat. "I'm pretty thankful I have tinted windows too," he said, pushing me high into the seat. "I would have to kill anyone else for seeing what I'm seeing right now, including that blow up doll. You're gorgeous." His rough hand skimmed up my body and gently cradled my breast.

"Don't make me blush," I teased, fanning myself.

"I am completely serious. It's not just because your breasts are in my face, either."

"Shut up." I pinched his shoulder.

"Ooh, a little pain play. I have to say that when you held that flogger in your hand, I was a little turned on. It's not usually my thing, but like I already told you, I'm prepared to be your sub." He dipped his face into the side of my neck then continued south. The scruffy hairs on his chin led down, tickling my skin before planting small kisses along an unobstructed path.

I laughed, recalling what he'd said the night he helped me deal with Landon at The District. "Maybe I'll keep it then. Ahh," I breathed as the flat of his tongue bathed my nipple, shooting pulses right between my thighs.

"Christ," he mumbled between kisses. "I've never been happier inside my car."

"I guess you've never eaten takeout in your car before," I joked, threading my fingers into his hair and arching my back to show him what I liked.

Light bursts of warm air blew over my skin with his chuckle, then he nipped at the soft flesh of my breast. "Not this delicious."

"I have to be honest with you. That beignet I had earlier might be hard to top, unless you drive me to New Orleans." I felt his smile against my skin and then another soft nip.

"Whatever you want to call it. But know that I'm just getting started." His hand found the top button of my jeans and made quick work of getting inside while keeping his mouth busy.

I tugged at his hair and bit my lip, fully expecting to feel his able fingers any moment. But my expectation was cut off when he sat back, lifted my butt, and slid my jeans and panties down with a swift tug instead. I jerked my head up, unsure about the turn we were taking. Foreplay in the car, I anticipated. Full-on sex, I'd rather our first time together be tangled in bed sheets. Or simply somewhere with more leg room ... and head room. Just more room altogether.

He smirked wickedly, tugging my jeans farther down to my shins. "I shocked you. That's good." After he checked that the seat was all the way back and positioned himself, he ducked his head and threaded the space between my bare thighs, hooking my knees over his shoulders and supporting me from below. As his determined motions sank in, anxiety and eagerness set my body ablaze. It had been too long. I squirmed on the smooth leather upholstery, staring at the ceiling, my emotions manic, waiting for his next move.

His hands slid higher on the outside of my thighs, digging his thumbs in underneath. I glanced down and met his eyes just as he leaned in and kissed my lips. My heart knocked so hard he could probably feel my pulse through his lips. *His soft lips.* Slowly, they traveled over the sensitive skin, planting tiny, adoring kisses. I felt—and heard—a breathy, appeased hum before his tongue licked swiftly up my line. My hips jolted from the sudden pleasure and his fingers tightened their hold of my thighs in response. I moaned and let my head roll back, gripping the sides of the chair so hard my fingers numbed. His tongue circled around and around, massaging some before it traveled down to my opening and entered. I cried out and grabbed his hair with one hand, unable to control myself.

One of the phones chimed a notification from beneath our shirts on the driver's seat. The alert wasn't mine, so it had to be Mark's or Guy's. Mark didn't even pause. He fell into a hypnotic rhythm for a while then released one hand from my thigh and slid a finger inside me. There was no question in my mind how good he was. He worked me at an expert level, bringing me to the edge in such a short time it was almost embarrassing. He slipped another finger inside and curled them against my spot, pushing and pulling. I moved with him, grabbing my breast, tugging his hair. Building higher and higher. Until the world fell away beneath me, my body bursting in the most glorious way. I quivered and panted, coming back down to his watching eyes and endearing grin.

He ducked his head and helped pull my pants up before flipping our positions again, laying me sideways against him. I felt like a limp noodle, tucked into him, not wanting to move while my nerves continued to pulse with aftershocks. His erection pressed hard against my thigh. It had to be aching for some attention, but he made no movements to go further tonight. As much as I wanted to wrap my hand around him, even return the oral favor, I was actually glad he wasn't quick to push for more inside this confined space. I wanted more room to fully explore him.

His hands roamed across my back and my arm as he cradled me. "So, let's talk about boring for a second."

I smiled against his shoulder. Oh, he was happy with himself. "Boring? What's that?" Indeed. Car cunnilingus. Definitely not boring. I glanced up at him through my lashes.

He raised a cocky brow and licked his lips. "That's what I thought. And the beignet?" He scooted me higher and burrowed his face into the crook of my neck.

"Hmm. Well ..."

His mouth opened, licking my skin for a moment before his teeth clamped down hard enough to make me whimper with delight.

"You are absolutely better than a beignet."

"Mmm. Good." His arms tightened around me. "I'm glad you stayed longer."

"I'm glad you asked." I really was, even if it hindered my job catching Guy in a compromising position. I glanced over at our shirts, thoughts drifting back to the phone. Sneaking a peek at his screen seemed impossible. The risk of trying far outweighed what I'd be able to see within a few seconds anyway, so there really wasn't a point. Still, that nagging curiosity ...

He gently placed a hand on my cheek, turning my face to his for a light kiss. "I should probably get Guy's phone to him so Pacey doesn't flip." He leaned us both forward and grabbed my bra, happily assisting me with breast placement and hooking the back clasps. After helping me with my shirt also, he pulled his own over his head.

My mind raced as I stared down at the phones. The only chance I'd get was staring right back at me. Two black cases, relatively the same size. Would Mark even know if I grabbed Guy's instead of mine? As soon as Mark's face popped through his shirt, I snatched the phone with my wallet and keys and squelched all rational thought.

"You want to wait for me?" he asked, grabbing the rest of the items on his seat. "I can follow you back to Destin."

"Sure."

He tilted his head. "You okay? Did I do something?"

"What? No. It's very sweet of you to offer that, thanks. I'm just thinking about work. I'm sorry." The phone felt hot, burning inside my guilty palm.

His blue eyes squinted, silently assessing me. "I get it. I promise, Friday night, I'll take your mind off work."

I smiled as he opened the door. We both climbed out and walked to my car.

"Give me a few," he said as I slid into my seat. "Don't let this guy take advantage of you." He nodded to the blow up doll with a laugh then shut the door.

I watched him jog toward Rick and Evin's building and glanced up at their empty balcony. Hurrying was essential. Given the apartment was on the second floor, I probably had two minutes, tops. Less if Mark realized it was the wrong phone before handing it over to Guy.

I pushed the menu button and a picture of the Beach Bum logo popped up as the lock screen—title text under a beach umbrella. No empty passcode boxes blocked the picture. At least Guy wasn't a secure freak. I glanced up for a Mark-check then swiped the screen to a wallpaper picture of Pacey and Guy underneath several app icons. Social media would take too long to peruse. Text history was the safest bet for a short time. I touched the envelope icon and traced the names. Pacey was the latest from a few minutes ago, expecting it had already been dropped off, not that Mark had made a pit stop in my pants first.

I glanced up again for a quick Mark-check. The side area of the building was still dark and quiet. No people. I left Pacey's message unread and scrolled. "Mom" was next followed by Rick. Both threads appeared clean, with pictures of cats or poop memes. The latter were from Rick, not Mom, thankfully. My mouth popped open at the next name. Leah. I opened the thread, noting messages from the same afternoon. Most talked about Pacey and the wedding. But there were noticeable gaps, especially around a message from him that said, *Saturday, 6pm.* His bachelor party was later that same evening.

Mark-check. Window clear.

The next name was Edena. I skimmed quickly, noting Beach Bum publicity information and dinner with family at home as the most frequent messages. Evin's name followed with mostly link attachments to baseball info and videos.

Mark-check—walking through the last bit of grass, almost to the road.

I fumbled the phone between my fingers, desperately trying to exit the app and darken the screen while silently thanking whoever invented tinted windows for the third time in one evening. As soon as the screen went black, I opened the door with a smile and stepped out to meet him. "Sorry. I didn't realize it wasn't mine until you disappeared around the building." And there went another lie. I cringed inwardly.

"No problem." He swapped the phones with me and held onto my hand, pulling me against him for a quick kiss before jogging away again.

I slinked back into the car, my conscience gnawing holes inside to escape my rotting soul. Had I let everything go too far? I was being so selfish, wanting to be around him, to start this relationship when all I could do was lie to him. But in my mind, my reason was solid. The job was important. The money would not only help me but my family too. Then there was the heart of Duplicity, the reason I had started it all to begin with: to catch someone unfaithful. No matter how much I hated the thought of actually ruining Pacey's wedding, I knew I would do it if it was the right thing to do. Pacey would want to know. Even Mark would want her to know … right?

Mark returned quickly and came over to talk through my window. "I'll follow you to make sure you get home, but I wanted to say goodbye here."

"Yes," I agreed, relieved he was being the voice of reason because I wasn't sure I'd be able to say no if his sexy ass was standing on my welcome mat. "Good idea."

He hooked his hands on the doorframe and leaned into the open window for a kiss that made me want to change my mind. When he backed up a bit, he ran a hand through his hair and looked down at his feet. "There's something else I wanted to ask you. It's not exactly the best time, but there's really no good time … so I'm just gonna ask."

What? My thoughts scrambled. Did he see something? Hear something? Look at my burner? But it had a passcode so that couldn't be it …

"Will you go to the wedding with me?" His eyes were focused on mine for only a few moments before he dropped them to his feet again and shook his head. "I would love for you to go, but if it's not something you want to do, I understand. You don't have to answer now. If you don't go, Pacey'll have to live with me going alone. So you can even wait until the day before if—"

"I'd love to." The words slipped out with an honest smile. The urge to slap myself followed, but I held off by digging my fingers deep into my thighs instead. *Feel the pain, you idiot.*

He looked back at me. His eyes widened then his expression softened with an easy smile. "Good. Okay. Well, we should probably get out of here. I'll follow you and call you tomorrow."

"Okay," I agreed and watched him walk toward his car.

Well, shit. I accepted an invite to a wedding I planned to demolish. I dropped my forehead to the wheel again then twisted my face to see the beige man-balloon in the passenger seat, his gaping mouth filled with derision. I slapped an arm across his ribbed abs. "Don't think I won't pop you, Air Boy."

18

Mark

"For the last time, no," I said, hopping out of the golf cart. "You'll have to get Charlie to help. He can use the extra hours anyway."

"Charlie can't tell the time on a standard clock," John said with a grunt as he fell in step beside me, moving toward the maintenance building door. His head pivoted on its stack of muscles to watch a red bikini walk by on the way to the clubhouse pool.

I pulled the door open and didn't wait for him to follow. As soon as I stepped over the threshold, I heard a loud smack and turned to see him rubbing his bearded face. "Ouch. Dick."

I laughed and kept moving toward my locker. "Well, you and Charlie will work well together tonight then. You can tell him the time and he can hold the doors for you."

"Funny," he replied with a grimace. "C'mon, no-life having son of a bitch, you never pass on overtime. What gives?"

I smiled into my locker and dropped the tool belt inside with a clank. "None of your damn business."

"Oh shit. You're hooking it up. Who is she? A new renter? Is she here with friends? Or a sister maybe?"

I shook my head, shut the locker, and moved around him.

"A mother?"

"Dude, no. On all counts," I added before he could ask then walked to the door and pushed through.

"Psssh," he called from behind me.

I waved a hand over my head, not bothering to look back. "Have a good night!"

To his disappointment, we'd never hung out to "chase tail" despite working together off and on at East Bay for about four years. He knew by now that his bromance wasn't the only one I'd rejected. The only time the guys from work saw me off duty was if they happened to show up at The District while I was there. I'd always been more of a loner, never really latching onto the idea of having anyone around all the time. A couple girlfriends out of high school I'd been serious enough with, sure. But there still was nothing that pushed me for something else, made me consider that person on a deeper level, want a more intuitive connection. To not only know them, but to understand them. Their habits. Their choices. Their desires.

Over the last few days, though, I'd found myself wondering those things about Gia.

Our texts and calls continued to be short despite seeing her on Wednesday night, which had me a bit concerned. I didn't want to bother her, and certainly not come off as needy, so I had to hope her excuse about being busy with work was true and it had nothing to do with my invite to Pacey's wedding. Wednesday had been such a rush that I decided it was the best time to pull that plus-one trigger. Maybe I'd just shot myself. I hadn't even expected to see her that night anyway, but she was there. And the next thing I knew, her almost completely bare body was lying in my passenger seat and I was making her forget all about her beignet high.

All the more reason that seeing her trumped overtime. I had to sort through the phone silence, see if there was something—or someone—else on her mind, holding her back. One way or another, I had every intention to make her forget more than beignets, make her crave only me.

I entered my condo and double-checked the time before heading for the shower. After she'd refused my suggestion to pick her up, Gia offered to meet at my place. With lack of communication, and her work concerns and excuses, that was all the info we'd worked out.

My phone rang a default tone while I was still rinsing the soap from my body. Not wanting to miss the call if it was her, I leaned out of the shower, dried my hand, and answered the phone on speaker. "Hello?"

"Hey, Mar—Oh! Is that water? The shower? Oh my God, Gia, he's in the shower right now," someone giddy said with a laugh.

From somewhere in the background, I heard Gia's scream. "Kass! What the shit? You did not seriously call him."

I stifled a laugh.

"What?" Kass asked, her voice a little muffled, possibly from covering the phone mic. She came back clearer. "Hey, Mark. Sorry 'bout that. I hijacked Gia's phone because she's refusing to leave work right now even though I told her I'm closing shop no matter what amount of work she thinks still needs to get done. And, out of curiosity, how hot is that water right now? Ow!" she said with a giggle. "It's not nice to throw things, Gia."

"She's refusing to leave work?" I asked. Had that invite really spooked her?

"Uh-huh. And she knows that—Ow!—I've got to go soon. I've got plans tonight."

Images of the sex shop flashed to mind. I knew her plans. "To your client's bachelorette party."

"My client's bachelorette party ..." It sounded like a question. I heard the phone drop and Kass cough when her voice returned. "Shoot, sorry. Yeah, I've got to get to this party. So please tell her that work is not as important as spending time with your fine ass."

I laughed again. "If you're sure work is the only thing holding her back."

"One hundred percent."

"Tell her I'll be at her place in twenty. If she's not there, well, I guess I'll need to reevaluate how fine my ass really is."

Coast Apartments sat midway between the bay and the ocean, less than a mile from Destin's executive airport. Ungated. Unguarded. The property's lot design had buildings positioned in the shape of an oval, completely surrounded by single family homes. Gia's building was the farthest north, identical to the rest—two-story with facades of white siding and brick. Not seeing her car where she'd parked on Wednesday, I pulled my car into the adjacent open spot and got out to wait. Before I could dwell too much on her absence, her car rolled up.

"Hey," she said with a tight smile, juggling her purse and keys as she closed her car door.

"Hey," I replied, pushing away from my car door and sliding my hands into my front pockets. The vibe between us certainly had shifted during the two days apart. I had to find out the reason. "Can I help?"

She moved toward the outside staircase, not bothering to wait for me to follow. "I'm okay, thanks. I'm sorry about that phone call. I was planning to call you, but Kass decided to butt in."

"You don't need to apologize. I'm actually sorry for inviting myself over."

She unlocked her door and moved inside, glancing over her shoulder. "It's okay. Come on in."

I stepped inside cautiously, still unsure if she really wanted me there. This was the first time I was seeing this side of her. I'd seen several of her other emotions, including unease or fear when she had to face her ex, but I hadn't really seen irritation.

She set her purse on the round dining table as she passed by, heading into the narrow kitchen. "Do you want something to drink?"

"I'm good, thanks," I said, glancing around the space. It was a combined plan, much like mine but a tad bigger to accommodate two bedrooms at opposite sides of the open living area. She'd said as much when she'd been at my place.

A bottle hissed and a cap clinked onto the counter, drawing my attention back to the kitchen. "You sure?" she asked before taking a long sip from her beer.

I moved closer and placed a hand on the breakfast bar. Clearly it was an invite to stay a little while at least. I'd take it. "Okay."

She grabbed another from the fridge. "Look, I'm sorry that I'm in a jacked mood. I shouldn't take it out on you. Work has just been crazier than I thought it would be. Things aren't … working out as easily as I'd like and it's really affecting me more than it should." The words spilled out as she opened the beer and handed it to me.

"That really sucks. Sorry. I gotta admit that I was a little worried my invite to Pacey's wedding may have freaked you."

She looked down at the floor and shook her head, her long, loose hair sweeping over her shoulders in ripples. "No, it's not that. I've just been generally overwhelmed lately." She stepped out of her high heels and sighed when her bare feet flattened on the linoleum.

I took a sip from the beer, considering her words and forming a conclusion. "And adding a relationship has only amplified things."

"A bit," she admitted, looking up into my eyes. "But I don't want you to think that I want to stop this. Us. I just need things to sync up."

"I understand. Maybe slow things down a bit?" She'd been doing that all week as it was. I was just too excited or too worried to understand. "And I just fucked that up tonight."

"It wasn't you. I should've never agreed if I wanted to slow down. Plus, Kass is a pushy bitch."

"I can see that," I said with a light laugh then stepped closer to take her hand in mine. "I don't want you to feel like you can't tell me something, okay? If you need a night off, or more, I'll be perfectly fine with that." Her lips pulled into a smile. It was a start. I only wanted to make her feel good, not overwhelmed. "I might make you a variety of enticing pastries to temp you anyway, but ..."

A giggle escaped her lips and her smile grew wider. "You would." It was a statement because she already knew. I would take care of her, no matter the situation.

"I would, absolutely. The most delicious things in my arsenal." I smirked at her and swept her hair away from her face. "If it would make you feel better."

"You're too good." Her hand lifted between us, pressing gently against my chest, fingers skimming over my heart. She stared at them, and I stared down at her, knowing that while the compliment was sweet at face value, the underlying insinuation about herself was not.

"And so are you," I stressed, hooking her chin and pulling up so she'd lift her eyes.

They stared into mine as if she were searching for something inside, maybe for that intuitive connection that had been on my mind lately.

As much as I wanted to kiss her, I decided to hold back. She had been prepared to cancel earlier, needing to slow things down. I didn't want the spark between us burning out before our fuse had a chance to catch.

"Maybe I should—"

"Stay," she interrupted, grasping my face and pulling me down to meet her lips.

The kiss was desperate, urgent, begging me, coaxing me. I broke away—my conscience sounding off an asshole alarm somewhere in my head—and placed my hands at her waist. "Gia, I don't want this to be something—"

"I've been agonizing about this, beating myself up"—her fingers popped the top buttons of her shirt—"thinking far too much. I don't want to think anymore." She opened the rest of the silky blue fabric, dropped it to the floor, then slipped her skirt to her ankles with one quick motion. "I know what I need, and I've been trying to stay away because it all scares me. Starting over. Trusting someone." She stood in front of me in only a sheer pink bra and panties and that asshole alarm instantly died. Her fingers reached to the hem of my shirt and tugged it up. I leaned over to help her pull it fully off. "But when I look into your eyes, I'm not scared. I'm done fighting this."

And I was done too.

I grabbed her, pawing at her like I was sixteen again, aching to feel every part of her on me and afraid it was all a fucking dream. Her lips were on mine again and I thrust my tongue into her mouth roughly, the need inside too demanding to be gentle.

She whimpered and dug her fingers into the back of my neck. I slid my hands down around her ass, lifted her into the air, and started to move while her legs cinched around my waist.

"Bed?" I mumbled through hard breaths and rushed kisses.

"Left."

I stumbled my way to her master bedroom suite, bumping a few corners that neither of us acknowledged. With one more step to the bed, I let Gia slide down my body, setting her feet on the floor. She continued farther down, taking a seat on the edge of the bed and pulling me forward, taking the lead. Her fingers worked deftly, unfastening and yanking my jeans down. I kicked them off with my shoes as her hands slid into the elastic of my boxers, working to remove them too. With a long slide of her hands down my thighs, they fell the remaining way to the floor. Her eyes widened like she'd just unwrapped a present.

She licked her lips and eased her hands around me. "My turn."

I tipped my head back and let out a moan at the feeling of her firm grip gliding over my skin.

"God, Mark, you are so gorgeous. And I'm not just saying that because your dick is in my face either," she whispered, imitating my words from Wednesday night.

I laughed hard, tipping my head back. *This girl.* I looked down as she pulled me into her smiling mouth. "Fuck." The word escaped as a strangled whisper. I combed her hair back with one hand, watching as she continued to control me. Her mouth was unbelievable. After a single minute, she had me biting my lip in an attempt to redirect my focus, dull the intense sensation begging for release. She twirled her tongue and gripped my thighs, and I nearly lost my mind.

Air hissed through my teeth and I backed out of her mouth. "Too good," I whispered to her questioning eyes. There was no way to hold back if she continued. I had to slow this down. Hooking her under her arms, I lifted and laid her back onto the bed. She sat up to remove her bra, and I kissed her briefly before moving down her neck, her chest. I slid a hand between her legs and palmed her, feeling her warmth.

"Mark," she said reverently, eyes closed to the ceiling while I twirled my tongue around a hardened nipple and slipped a finger past her panties. She uttered a soft, breathy moan.

My head buzzed from the sensory overload. I was at odds with myself. Out of a million things I wanted to do to her, there was no way to choose just one. Taking my time, showing her how much this meant—that was the goal.

"I want you," she panted and my entire body responded, pulsing with approval.

Decision made.

Everything else could wait. We had time. She was more than a single week, so much more. She had me hooked. Everything about her.

I backed off with my eyes still on her, reaching for my jeans on the floor, for my wallet, the condom inside. Biting her lip, she slipped her panties down past her knees. My eyes tracked their movement while my arm and body stretched long, feeling the jeans beneath my fingers. *Almost.* And then I shifted past the balance point, rolling off the edge of the bed and landing with a thud flat on my back.

"Shit," I mumbled to the ceiling as my fingers finally felt the leather of my wallet.

The maniacal laughter that followed didn't crush my ego as much as I thought it would.

She peered over the edge of the bed with an adorable smile. "Nine point four," she teased. "I had to deduct because that landing was atrocious."

I slipped the condom out of my wallet and knelt up beside the bed, eye level and only a breath away from her mouth. "I think I may have broken something, so that might be my final score of the night."

Her eyes popped open at my joke and she pursed her lips. "Real competitors push through their pain."

I smirked and ripped open the condom, making a show of rolling it on. "Good thing I can handle the pain. But this competition is definitely going uncontested." I climbed onto the bed and attacked her body with my mouth.

She giggled and ran her fingers through my hair.

When I skimmed my lips up to her neck, I stopped and backed off to admire the view. Passion had taken over the air again, erasing all the humor, leaving her lips parted and a look of pure desire in her dreamy eyes. "So sexy."

She tugged my hair, pulling my lips down to hers. I kneed her legs wider and eased myself inside her. Even though I wanted badly to close my eyes around the sensation, the need to see Gia's face, to watch her erotic expressions, was far greater. She sighed and closed her eyes for a moment then opened them back up to me as I started to move. Her heady gaze turned me on even more. After a few of the most insanely provocative and stimulating minutes, I backed onto my knees to see and feel even more of her body.

As I grasped her hips to control my rhythm, her hands glided over her own skin. She felt her breast with one hand and slid the other down lower to play. She was the sexiest thing I'd ever seen.

She panted, "Harder."

There was no holding back from there. I tightened my grasp and worked her hips. Sustaining the tempo while watching her wouldn't be possible for very long. I was too turned on, too close. She started to release pleasured cries, telling me she was just as close. Every muscle in her body tensed and her eyes found mine again as she cried out one more time.

Within a minute, I was there too, coming completely unhinged on top of her.

The pounding of our hearts, the hard pants of our breaths, tangling together ... it was melodic and sublime.

Her eyes closed and she bit her lip. "Oh, that was ..."

"Yeah," I agreed, knowing words would fail to describe the feeling. I leaned in for another kiss as our bodies stilled and our breaths slowed, the high drifting.

When I crashed onto my side, she smiled fully. "That was the hottest boring I've ever had."

19

Gia

"Do it," Mark mumbled into my hair, pressing his hand into my stomach, pulling my body tighter against him as we lay beneath the blankets in bed. "Tell me."

"No way. I can't believe you're asking me that. It's so personal. And such a hard decision." I traced circles over his hand, staring at the glow of the alarm clock in my darkened room as the harsh reality of my current situation pressed in like an ocean around me, ready to drown me in waves of my lies and deceit.

Aside from a quick bathroom trip, we'd been tangled together in bed in the minutes following our blazing hot hookup. I wished I could say it had been just okay. Even though it would still be difficult, mediocrity would at least make the idea of kicking him out a little easier. But the truth was, it was extraordinary. *He* was extraordinary. And I was a piece of shit for enjoying him. I was supposed to ditch the date, avoid him until I ended the job, not end up comfy in his arms with his contented breath blowing into my hair. Stupid Kass. Stupid me. I should have told him to leave. Come up with some excuse. Seeing him when I'd gotten home, though, leaning against his car like some eighties movie hottie, there was no way I could have refused. He was just too damn sexy for his own good, with all the perfect moves too. I thought

Wednesday night would have been hard to top. I was so wrong. He was hotter and sweeter than I could have ever imagined.

"C'mon, just answer," he breathed. "It's something I need to know."

"One of those essential questions, huh? Like the seven dwarfs thing."

"Yes. And for the record, I'm still Thirsty, even more for you now than then."

I smiled and closed my eyes to the clock, needing to shut out reality for at least another minute. "I'm pretty sure we switched names tonight, though, after that bed dismount, Clumsy."

His breathy laugh rocked both of our bodies. "Quit changing the subject."

"Fine. I can't believe I'm going to tell you this," I joked with a sigh. "If I were stranded on a deserted island with a lifetime supply of only one dessert, that dessert would have to be cannoli."

"Cannoli? Really? Besides the fact that it's lacking some serious survival nutrients, you'd have some serious temperature issues. And it's kinda boring."

My foot *accidentally* heeled his shin. "Let's just say I'd die happy then, either from a nutritional deficiency or a bacterial infection. And also, I'm learning that boring may just be the best thing for me." His soft lips smiled against the back of my neck. "Okay, now you have to answer something for me, since we're nailing down the essential questions."

"Anything, I'm open."

I squeezed my eyelids tighter, wishing I could be as transparent. I couldn't even ask him what I really wanted to know—if he'd forgive me once he knew—because there was no doubt I'd have to say goodbye to the best thing that had happened to me in a long time. I'd lose him. If I told him the truth right now, I'd also risk losing the job. And with Pacey as a client, there was even a chance it would all blow back to the boutique.

"What's your biggest regret?"

"Wow. And I thought we were only asking essentials," he teased. "Hmm. I'm not sure, really. Would it be too cliché for me to say that I don't have any?"

"No, not at all," I admitted, understanding where his thoughts were probably headed—I'm here because of and despite it all. Fate.

"I've learned a lot from some stupid stupid mistakes," he added.

"I have too." I shifted my body, turning to face him. "Do you think it's possible to regret something you haven't done yet?"

The hand that had started roaming the base of my spine stopped and the small grin in his lips flattened in a serious line as he considered my question. "Not sure I want to answer that one or hear where it's leading."

I smoothed my hand up his chest and neck, skimming the prickly hairs along his jaw before touching his parted lips. "As much as I'm enjoying this, I don't think it's a good idea for you to stay the night."

His lips kissed the pads of my fingers. "I wasn't assuming anything. Do you want me to leave now?"

I glanced toward my cracked open closet, partly to avoid looking at him when I lied again and partly thinking about all the adult store items stashed inside, thanking God that Air Boy wasn't filled with helium. "It would probably be best."

He nodded before leaning in and kissing my lips sweetly. "Work tomorrow?"

"Yeah," I acknowledged, knowing that my work tomorrow would also involve avoiding him at the next location: Guy's bachelor party. The starting location for it, at least.

He sat up and moved to the edge of the bed, grabbing his boxers and pants from the floor. "I was free during the day, but if you have to work, I'm going to see if I can pick up an extra shift before the bachelor party tomorrow night."

I stared at the curve of his butt when he stood, at the muscles in his back, flexing as he pulled his clothes on, then finally climbed out of bed myself to grab a pair of sweats.

"Are you busy Sunday? We've been avoiding real food for too long—shit." He shook his head after slipping on his other shoe. "No, never mind. Pacey has something planned for Sunday. Some afternoon thing at the beach, I think. Interested in going with me?"

Sunday at the beach was another location I'd signed up for. I'd be there, with or without his invite.

"I know your game. You just want me to fan you and apply your sunscreen." I chuckled, somewhat uneasily, walking past him to grab a drink from the kitchen. Brushing off an invite from him was no longer easy.

He stepped up close behind me, waiting for me to take a drink of water before scooping my hair off my neck and dipping his face to the same area. His breath and lips brushed my skin, shooting the good shivers all the way to my toes. "Sun protection is important. And I definitely wouldn't object to you fanning me."

I bit my lip. "Can I get back to you?"

He turned my body and eyed me with a smile. "Sure. We can talk about it later."

"Okay."

His kiss wasn't nearly long enough, but I couldn't complain. All I could do was promise myself that once the job was over, I'd let him stay overnight, for as many nights as he wanted, and kiss him until my lips hurt. That was if he still wanted me by the time it was all over.

"Thanks so much for taking that weekend tutoring position at school. I was stuck alone for our clearance sale with Aunt Aim and a never-ending stampede of ravenous brides all day because you were gone and Kass called in sick from a yacht somewhere off the coast of Miami. Don't ask me how she got there. I swear, she'll be on the other side of the Duplicity binoculars one day, without my permission," I said into the phone, keeping my eyes on Guy and Pacey's apartment building in Pensacola. Guy's beater jeep had sat untouched since I'd arrived twenty minutes before.

"Hello to you too," Viv replied. "I take it your date went well last night."

I let out a pathetic whimper, like a dog begging for another bone because the first had been so unbelievably good.

"That amazing, huh?" she asked. "Does he have a younger brother?"

"You already know the answer to that question."

She chuckled. "What's the deal with today again?"

"Well, the original plan was to be at Guy's later so I could follow the bachelor party wherever they end up going. But after seeing the text on Guy's phone from Leah about a meeting at six o'clock, I knew I had to start the night early."

"So you're at Guy's?"

"Yeah. According to Mark, Pacey had a bachelorette spa day today. That's why the meet up with Leah was intriguing. Shouldn't she be with Pacey?"

"Unless the spa stuff ends before then."

"True. But then she would be with her, or be back at home when the guys left."

"So, Mark will be at the bachelor party tonight," she stated, digging in another direction.

"Your point?"

"You'll have to be extra cautious."

"Tell me something I don't know ... like more info about the beach gathering tomorrow. It's on the list, but Mark invited me to go too."

"You're going to go with him? I thought you were trying to keep things separate?"

"I was ..." But not hard enough. "I just want this to be over—the job. I need it to be over so I don't have to lie to him anymore."

"Wow. Things are getting serious then."

"He asked me what my favorite dessert is."

"Wow, that is serious. Okay, well let me pull up the info and—"

"Hang on," I interrupted, watching the blond swoop of hair trot down the apartment's outdoor stairs. "Text me the info. I've got to go."

"Okay, be safe."

"Bye." The call ended as Guy opened his jeep door and jumped inside. "Here we go," I mumbled to myself, grabbing one of the dickpops I'd stashed in my glove box, slipping it into my mouth, then pushing my car's ignition.

He had to be leaving to meet Leah since the bachelor party gang wasn't due to arrive for a few hours. Anything could happen during that time. Hotel hookup, beach hookup, dinner hookup, dessert hookup ... My thoughts drifted to Mark and the way his hands had controlled and comforted me so thoroughly and all at once.

I shook my head and cranked my radio, focusing on the jeep driving onto the bridge leading to Pensacola beach. It wasn't long before we pulled into a condo complex. I circled around in a separate parking area, keeping within sight as Guy jumped out and made his way to a door. A dark-haired and tanned Leah answered and moved aside so Guy could enter.

All Duplicity jobs up to this point had been standard. When I was given a location and a target, it was spot-on. I knew all cases wouldn't end up the same. But overall, most people knew or at least had an idea of what was happening and where. This time was different. I had no idea if Guy was there to grab something for Pacey or to grab something for himself. There was no telling how long he'd be inside.

Before I could get into my stealth mode mindset and go full-on window peeper, Guy and Leah walked out to the jeep. Their meeting had lasted two minutes, tops. The area was too busy to hear what they were saying, but I noticed a box tucked under Guy's arm as his other wrapped around Leah for a side "goodbye" hug. I zoomed in and took the clearest pic I could given the distance.

Another minute later and we were back on the road. We didn't go back to the apartment, though. Guy's jeep led us to a house at the end of a crowded residential street in Gulf Breeze. I pulled close to a neighborhood playground, keeping some distance while I tried to recall all the contact info Viv had given me. When Guy got out of his jeep carrying the box and, using one hand, jumped into a basketball game with a group of boys in the street, I realized the area was home. His family lived there. Dinner with family was one of the frequent messages on his phone. He visited often.

"Well, shit." I crunched down the remainder of my dickpop and settled in for a while. Leaving wasn't an option in the off chance he'd go somewhere else before the bachelor party, so I got comfortable.

He stayed until just before eight—the set time for the guys to meet at his apartment—and left the box behind. Whatever Leah had given him, it had to be something he didn't want Pacey to see. There was a possibility that it was a surprise for her, for the wedding. The short time he was with Leah, and the side hug he'd given her, none of it looked friendly enough to be anything more.

Even though the sun had set, I parked two buildings away from his apartment, barely able to see when each of the guys arrived. They piled into the stretched Hummer a little while later. I groaned and started my car, scolding myself internally for agreeing to spy on a bachelor party. The night might turn out to be the best ever for some of them, but I had a feeling mine might be the shittiest.

20

Mark

The booths and seats at Club Vixen were all filled with guys, eyes focused on the main stage or on the current girl straddling them. We navigated the dark walkway along the edge of the room, passing the bar and heading toward one of the raised VIP sections that Rick had secured for Guy's bachelor party. I was glad we weren't close to the stage. The last thing I wanted to do was defend a chair from horny drunks fighting for attention with handfuls of bills.

I really wasn't feeling the whole night anyway. The only thing I had on my mind was Gia and how her amazing breasts were the only ones I wanted in my face. The fact that she hadn't returned my texts all day didn't help. I would have been concerned if I hadn't driven past the boutique earlier and seen so many women in the parking lot. The place looked swamped, so I knew she was busy. Probably frustrated too. I smiled, thinking about her pursing those sexy lips, preparing to fight all the crazy brides.

We stepped up into one of the VIP sections with its own mini stage and spread out around the huge semi-circle booth. A few of Guy's non-groomsmen friends looked across at the main stage, watching the dancer spin around to the tempo of the song blaring through the stack of speakers mounted behind us. I guessed hearing was not an option in the VIP area, but I couldn't complain. It was still better than brawling for a chair.

"What can I get you to drink?" a short blonde screamed over the music, wearing a blue latex outfit and a peacock feather mask covering half her face. Odd. I glanced around, noticing some of the other girls wore masks too.

"Shots all around to start," Rick yelled then he leaned closer to her ear for specifics.

I put on a smile when the eyes behind the feathers landed on me. "What's with the masks?"

"Oh," she said, touching the feathers at her cheeks. "It's Saturday."

When she didn't elaborate further, I shouted, "Ah! Okay. I'll have an IPA."

She smiled and set off for the drinks. Rick and Evin joined the other guys at the railing to watch the stage, and Guy hung back with me.

"If you're worried, don't be. None of this interests me," Guy shouted beside me. "I just wanted to go to the bar, but these guys wouldn't take no for an answer."

I nodded. "Rite of passage."

"I guess," he replied. "You don't seem too interested either. The girl Pacey mentioned?"

"Gia," I confirmed.

The small blonde returned with a tiger-faced friend, both carrying drink trays.

"I know where that dumbstruck look leads," Guy said, handing me a shot and lifting his own as the other guys pushed around to grab theirs.

I smiled and tossed the shot back with all of them, my thoughts escaping to somewhere else and planning to stay there all night.

21
Gia

I sat in the crowded parking lot of Club Vixen for a while, debating my next move. Part of me knew the evidence I'd get from inside wouldn't count for much. Most grooms still went to lap dance heaven for their last flight of freedom before the shackles of monogamy confined them forever. Or until the honeymoon was over, anyway, and they went off to find a fun hole. So lap dance pictures wouldn't technically count, unless Guy took several trips to heaven with one frequent flier. None of our information indicated that but without knowing who the client was, lots of information could be missing, and there were things I wouldn't risk Viv hacking.

The fluorescent sign above the entrance blinked erratically, flashing on my dashboard from across the lot. I watched the chaotic battle between light and dark, biting my nails as my own battle warred inside. Was going in even worth the risk? As soon as my thoughts shifted to Mark, someone else grinding in his lap, the decision was made. My feet moved without another thought, without a plan. It was careless and reckless and completely insane, but I couldn't sit outside and let those thoughts consume me. I hoped Mark was different. He'd felt different from the start, with his attentiveness and tenderness. But then again, we hadn't even discussed what we'd wanted, where we stood. And that was mostly my fault. I'd been keeping him at arm's length in an attempt to hide Duplicity. Considering all of that, and that it had only been a couple weeks since we'd met, how could I expect him to think about commitment?

I paced the edge of the parking lot, back and forth like a lunatic.

A few seconds. That would be all I needed. Just enough time to shut down the idiot side of my brain and focus on what I needed to accomplish.

I rubbed the sweat of my nervous hands on my ripped jeans then straightened my tank top and pulled the door open. A skinny guy sitting behind a desk looked at me from behind his phone. The sign behind his head read "No Cover for Ladies." I flashed my ID and his attention returned to his phone without a word.

When I wrenched the next door open, my senses were immediately bombarded. The wail of a guitar hit my ears as I inhaled a lungful of perfume and blinked at the colored lights slicing the air toward the stage. As my eyes adjusted, I stepped cautiously toward the bar. The room was packed, but it wasn't hard to spot the guys in a raised section close to the stage. A few of them leaned over the railing, tossing bills to the girl on the main stage while the others reclined in a curved booth.

"What can I get ya?" the bartender yelled to me as she punched the keys on her register.

"Oh. Nothing, thanks," I replied, my eyes moving from her cat eyes and hot pink wig to the stage where a girl was ending her routine.

"Do I need to grab my doorman?" she asked, slapping some change in front of a bald guy then moving back to the end of the bar. "Because you look like you're here to throw a brick at someone."

I should have known I wasn't the biggest lunatic this place had seen. "No, not at all. I'm just interested."

"In what? Girls? Guys? A job?"

"A job, maybe." Never too early to prepare my backup plan. Mark may have been right with his jokes when we first technically spoke at Fresh Brewed. Maybe my watching habits were destined to have me in a gentleman's club. Or I could always apply back at the adult store and make some cash while indulging my new dickpop habit.

"Why don't you come back and talk to the manager tomorrow. I'm sure you'll make him happy." Her eyes looked me over before turning to grab some glasses to dry.

She wasn't having any of it, so I knew coming partly clean was probably a better strategy. "Look," I said, moving in close to the bar. "You're right. I'm here for another reason, but it's more of a research job than a breakup job."

"I knew it. So, what do you want?"

"Would it be possible to get me closer to the VIP area?"

"Jazz," a waitress wearing a peacock mask called to the bartender from the other end of the bar. "I need another round for the top."

The bartender eyed her then looked back at me with a smirk. "Jewel is waiting on them tonight." She waved her down to our end.

Jewel tilted her head a bit, the feathers waving around her face, then she moved down to us. "Are you going to make me walk them from here? I'd rather not add more ass grabs to the carry."

"Is Mare coming out to dance for them now?" the bartender, Jazz, asked her, pouring the first beer.

"Yeah, that's why I need to be up there."

"You mind letting this one help with their drinks?" Jazz asked her, a slow, diabolical smile overtaking her face.

What? "I'm not sure I should get that close," I cut in, the threat of exposure activating my flight response.

"Sure! Misty went on break, so I was going to make two trips anyway," Jewel said, ignoring me. "She'll need a mask. Not that that will help with the clothes, though."

"True, but there's no time to change."

"Won't this be an issue with the manager?" I asked, trying to duck out of an impossible situation.

"Nah," Jazz said. "I'm manager tonight and I'm allowed to test potential employees." She reached under the bar then tossed a long blond wig and gorgeous wire and lace butterfly mask on top. "I'll prep the drinks down the end."

Shit. Shit. Shit.

I tried to turn around, but Jewel snatched the wig off the bar and pulled it over my head, securing my own hair in no time at all. I glanced at the mask as she tugged it onto my face, hoping it covered enough.

"Don't sweat it," she said as I pulled the corners of the mask. "You look fab and completely different. Let's go." She grabbed my arm and pulled me toward the end of the bar.

I watched from behind the darkened mask as we passed guys on stools, my body swaying away from their hands instinctively, my focus remaining on the VIP area growing closer and closer. Mark's soft spikes were visible over the top of the booth's backing, but I couldn't see any more of him. The music changed to a louder rock song when we reached the end, hard beats and a faster tempo.

"You take the shots. If the guys don't grab from the tray, just drop them on the table. Mare's walking up to dance on the private stage now, so they probably won't even look at us anyway."

My right pocket vibrated. *Left pocket burner. Right pocket personal.*

"Let's go," she said, handing me the shot tray and grabbing the beers before I could check my phone. I should have left it in the car, but I never planned I'd end up staying longer than a minute, let alone walking directly up to Mark and Guy.

"Good luck," Jazz yelled with a laugh as we stepped away.

I kept my eyes straight ahead as my heart pounded a death march. There was an out of body experience happening that I couldn't break free from. Usually, I was invisible, able to keep out of the light to get the answers I needed. But this time, I was shoving myself directly into the spotlight, hiding beneath a curtain of wire, lace, and ten pounds of hair.

Mare beat us up to the guys' stage, red ponytail swinging like a helicopter to the beat as she spun around the pole. She had their attention all right. A couple of the guys I didn't recognize leaned closer to the stage while the others lounged back. I took a deep breath, following Jewel's skin-tight pink boy shorts up the last step. She placed the beers around the table then backed up. I moved in and held the tray out, scanning the faces.

"Next round!" one of the guys yelled. With his surfer boy shaggy hair and his spot beside Guy, I immediately recognized him as Rick. Arms came at me from below and above as the guys swarmed the tray. When the bodies cleared, turning focus back to Mare, who was inverted on the pole—*wow, that takes some serious strength*—I noticed two shots left. Guy took his with a wink and a smile then clinked glasses with Rick and downed the clear liquid. Mark finally leaned forward and took his glass, glancing up at me.

The look was so heavy, I nearly fell over. Or maybe it was just the wig hair that was heavy. My body swayed back against Jewel, fear and embarrassment hitting me with a dizzy stick. She grabbed hold of my waist, and Mark jumped up and grabbed my arm to steady me.

"Whoa," he yelled loudly over the music. Then leaned in closer to my ear. "You okay?"

Jewel's hands squeezed my waist and her boobs jiggled with a giggle at my back. I straightened up and nodded at Mark, not daring to speak. If he didn't know yet, he would surely know then. His eyes narrowed with a head tilt as he scanned me up and down. Even with jeans and a tank top covering a good 70 percent of my skin, I felt stripped bare.

"She's new," Jewel piped in, watching it all unfold. "She has the body to dance, though, doesn't she?"

Mark's eyes cut to her and his lips eased into a small grin. He looked back at me. "Good luck to you, new girl. I really like that mask."

I smiled in response, and he narrowed his eyes again. That was my cue to bolt. Jewel let me back away without restraint, and I hustled down the few steps, peeling off my disguise closer to the end of the bar.

"Get enough research info?" Jazz called to me, crossing her tattooed arms. "Mare might be willing to include you in her dance if you want some more."

The attention that would garner would crush a far better disguise. And by my reaction to Mark up there, I bet she knew it.

"Thanks for the offer," I called back, tossing the mask and wig around some guy's head onto the bar, "but I think I have plenty to go on."

She nodded with a satisfied smirk, and I kept moving for the door.

When I got back to the car and checked my phone, I saw the text had been from Mark.

Wanting to see only you right now.

After another hour or so, the guys stumbled outside and loaded up for a longer drive. Category Five nightclub sat right on the beach in Destin. With a dressy indoor setup that bled out onto a boardwalk connected to restaurants and shops, it was a vacationer and local favorite.

I parked in the jammed lot and waited a minute before blending in with a group. The bouncer looked over my ID, narrowed his eyes at my black tank and jeans, and waved me off. Because he was the size of a small vehicle and way more intimidating than the doorman at the strip club, I almost left. But I knew if anything would happen during the bachelor party, this club would be where it went down. Plenty of people. Plenty of places for Guy to sneak away.

I stepped aside with a huff, flipped my hair out with a shake, and quickly threaded the front hem of my tank through my cleavage, transforming it into a halter ... of sorts.

The bouncer grinned and let me pass, his judgy eyes twinkling with mirth. I stepped through the arched entrance and felt a little semblance of nostalgia. I'd been to Category Five numerous times with Landon after turning twenty-one. Funny how a place can turn rotten, tainted by the memory of a single person, no matter how many good times were had there.

Catching sight of the guys in the cut-out VIP lounge closest to the back beach entrance, I moved away from the dance floor and headed toward the bathroom hallway to regroup. Plus, my bladder had decided it had had enough after hours of sitting in the car.

I splashed some water on my face, preparing for the second stretch of the night. A group of girls swarmed around the sinks and mirrors, laughing and checking makeup.

Another trotted in, heels clicking a haphazard, drunken beat. "Y'all won't believe who's here in the VIP area tonight."

"Who?" the chorus asked.

Oh, shit.

"It's Guy Pernell and Rick Newton. From Beach Bum."

The high-pitched screams that followed took me by surprise. I plugged my ears from the vocal assault and exited the area as fast as I could, ducking out to the bar, realizing my escape placed me at the end closer to the VIP lounge. The girls rushed out within seconds, pushing all around for a closer view. I inched myself as far back to the bar as I could while they shoved toward the half wall that sectioned off the lounge, calling Guy's and Rick's names to get their attention. Mark turned too and my brain went on instant strike. Seeing him in the dance club's lights compared to the dark strip club had me reeling. His spiked hair reminded me of how he'd looked in my bed, which made my body recall every touch, every taste, in one huge flash of heat. An easy grin formed on his lips while he looked at the girls babbling in front of them. Then a different kind of heat flashed through me. Anger. Jealousy. Maybe it was the best place to spy. And maybe Guy wouldn't be the only one I'd catch with his hands on off-limit goodies.

My next immediate emotion was embarrassment again. How could I think the worst right away? I'd seen him so calm inside a strip club, bare boobs bouncing all around him ... and he'd texted me. I wanted to believe the honest parts, the good parts, the inherent parts that were monogamous without having to define the new relationship, that were simply a given. Duplicity made me think about the odds, though. Not everyone wanted that, and not everyone wanted to be honest.

I wanted to be honest. And I felt like a coward because I wasn't.

Guy and Rick didn't hesitate greeting the girls, letting them take selfies like good reality stars enjoying their fame. From the edge of the bar, I watched a few bouncers position around the VIP area, preparing for anything—fights, pantie throwing, busted eardrums. With whispers spreading through the club, more girls migrated toward the action. The bouncers were about to have their hands full of frenzied fans and pissed off dates. I stepped on my tiptoes to snap a picture then scanned the area for Mark. The other guys still stood among the chaos, but there was no sign of him. I spun back toward the bathroom hallway, my heart speeding up, worried he could've seen me, and turned directly into a solid, button-down wall of chest that smelled of mint, sweat, and the sweet perfume from the strip club.

"Hey." His deep voice was calm, but that did absolutely nothing to soothe the panic attack ripping my chest apart. Especially when he added, "So you're the one."

As soon as I saw Gia standing at the bar with the girls pushing to see Guy and Rick, I thought my eyes were playing tricks on me again. I'd been thinking of her all night, even seeing her gorgeous eyes behind the mask of a Club Vixen waitress. She had me losing my mind. I'd had a decent amount of drinks, but there was no way this was a drunken hallucination. I wiped my face and shook my head, and she was still there, holding close to the bar as the mayhem started unfurling around the guys. I hopped over the VIP's half wall and cut around the crowd, watching her eyes track Guy and Rick.

Millions of thoughts played in my head, trying to find a reason she was staring at them with that same transfixed look as all the others. Could her attendance have been a coincidence? Maybe. But then why not find me? Was she here with someone else? As infuriating as that thought was, it was possible. But then the memories started popping up of the other coincidences. She was at The District the night I was hanging out with Guy, and she never gave a real reason for being there. And the next day at Putters. She was just watching until I'd approached her. Had she been watching Guy? Pacey was a client of her boutique ...

And the other night ... I cringed at the thought. She had been outside of Rick's place. That bachelorette purchase for Kass seemed so asinine now. *Fuck!* And I'd been falling all over myself for her. How could I have not seen that things weren't adding up, that something was wrong? Was she just some stalker fan girl? Was this all some sick fucking game to get closer to him? To them? The thought made me sick, made me ache, and pissed me off beyond belief.

I ran a shaky hand through my hair and moved closer, anger building, raging inside. Deep breaths wouldn't help. Ideas for potential reasons and excuses couldn't slow my movements as I unapologetically pushed through the bodies around me. I stopped behind her and clenched my fists at my sides, furious with myself for wanting nothing more than to sweep her hair back and kiss her neck until she whimpered. I gritted my teeth, unable to speak, unable to make the first contact.

She turned right into me, hitting my body with hers. Her eyes popped wide-open as she realized who she'd hit.

"Hey," I said as calmly as I could. "So you're the one?"

"Wha—what?" she asked, not bothering to say hi and play stupid.

I kept my hands pinned to my sides, afraid to get lost with a single touch. Closing my eyes, letting the buzz wrap around my emotions, I repeated, "So you're the one. The one my mom warned me about when I was younger. That one girl who would come out of nowhere, grab hold, make me feel something I never had before, then rip me apart with some unfathomable truth. Maybe I'm completely insane for even reacting this way since I've only known you for a couple of weeks, but if you find someone you think you've truly connected with, it really fucking sucks when you find out they probably couldn't care less. That they have some secret agenda and you were just some convenient detour to the real destination.”

“Mark, I—” she started, but I wasn't ready to hear the excuses yet.

“No.” I wiped my hand over my face, my body so amped with anger that sweat lined my brow. “I'm not sure what the hell you're going to say, but I'm almost positive it's going to be a lie of some kind. Some ‘I just happened to be at the club tonight’ bullshit. Fuck, Gia!” I slammed my hand down on the bar, frustration getting the best of me. *Holy shit.* Maybe I was insane and drunk. But I couldn't help but spill it out there like a lovesick asshole.

“I'm sorry,” she said, resting a hand over mine.

I glanced at her. The way her brows drew together as if she truly was sorry made me welcome her touch. I scowled at her, at my own weakness, pulled my hand away, and shifted my eyes down her body to escape her gaze.

“Mark, I just ... I have to tell you some things.” Her top was pulled up and tucked between her breasts, exposing most of her upper body, the soft stomach I'd had my hands and lips on the night before. Her black jeans had rips at the thigh and ...

“You were at the strip club, too,” I blurted, recognizing the pants. *The waitress.* The eyes beneath the wired butterfly. The long blond wig. “Are you a stalker? Are you some Beach Bum groupie like those girls, just waiting to get some time with Guy? That's pretty fucking low, Gia. Wait ...” I shook my head as thoughts rushed in. “You were watching someone else at East Bay the day we met too. Who the fuck are you?”

“No! No!” she cried out, shaking her head and touching my bicep. “It's not that. I'm not a stalker. I've never even seen Beach Bum. Please, if you just listen, I will tell you everything. Everything. Please, Mark. Can we go somewhere?”

The entire situation was like a jacked up dream. I'd thought I'd finally found someone worth taking a chance on, to find more of a connection with than a usual vacation fuck, and it was all blowing up in my face. But I couldn't just shut it down either, couldn't be a dick and walk away without hearing what she had to say. Clenching my jaw, I nodded. "Outside." I placed a hand on her back, leading her around the people in the side hall and out the front doors. Unable to take the feel of her skin beneath my fingertips any longer, I pulled my hand away and jammed both into my pockets. I couldn't trust myself while touching her, especially with the alcohol haze doing even more to kick my emotions around.

In silence, we dodged the people moving toward the club and walked toward the corner edge of the parking lot. She stopped where the sand spilled onto the pavement and turned, her hands tugging her shirt down then smoothing it out. "I can't really say that I never meant to lie to you because that's actually not true."

I shook my head and took a deep breath, not thrilled with the way the conversation had started.

"See, I don't just work at the boutique. I started another side business a while back, and it isn't exactly traditional."

I rubbed my face again and looked around. "I'm not even sure I want to know. Are you paparazzi or something?"

"Well, no. There really isn't a good way to say this. I need you to keep an open mind, though, because I don't want you to hate me. I really care about you and I never wanted to hurt you."

"Is it seriously worse than what I was thinking inside there? If so, I'm not sure I want to keep an open mind." While part of me thought she was full of shit, preparing to write her off and just walk away, most of me still wanted her to have a good excuse, one I could forgive so I wouldn't have to say goodbye. I hated that. I hated that

I felt so goddamn weak around her, unable to push away what had the potential to rip me apart.

"I run a for-hire business called Duplicity. Viv helps me. Sometimes Kass too. It's a word of mouth entry, not open to the public. I catch cheaters."

"Cheaters?"

"Guys or girls who step out on their relationships. Most of the time I'm hired by friends who suspect something or who have evidence of their friend's boyfriend cheating. Sometimes it's even a friend of the cheater. They don't want to be the bad guys."

"A private investigator?"

"Not licensed, but basically. It's also another way to help the boutique with some extra cash."

It all sounded ridiculous, but was it the truth? I looked into her eyes, watching them glisten under the lights around the lot, trying to determine what was real. "So, then ..."

"It's Guy." She bit her lip. "He's my current target."

"Guy?" I scrunched my face in disbelief. "He's not cheating on Pay. I would know."

"Would you?" she asked softly. "You're Pacey's brother, and Guy doesn't seem that stupid."

I ran a hand through my hair, the information slamming me fiercer than I could have imagined. Everything had switched gears, stealing most of my buzz and making me question everything. "So you don't know if he is cheating, but you're trying to find out?"

"Right."

"Who hired you? You said your business, Du ..."

"Duplicity," she filled in.

"Duplicity," I continued, "is word of mouth. So who hired you to watch Guy?"

"I'm not exactly sure this time. I've been trying to—"

"You were hired by an unknown person to watch the winner of Beach Bum in order to possibly break up his wedding?"

She pressed her lips together. "I know that sounds bad. We usually know who the client is, but we made an exception this time. And it's not like we don't take precautions. In order for someone to even contact us, the client has to have a referral name from a previous client and a codeword to access our website."

My mind refused to comprehend what was happening. I inhaled a deep, uneasy breath of gulf air, the smell of salt and shore doing nothing to settle all the shit in my head. Pacing, I threaded my fingers and pressed my palms to the top of my head, hoping to relieve the slow throbbing that continued to build inside. "I can't deal with this right now." The words ground out through my teeth so I wouldn't scream them. It was all too much. The lies. The truth. Her job could split Pacey's world apart.

My focus drifted back down to her, taking in her worried eyes, still wanting to comfort her even though she'd been lying to me the whole time we'd been together. *Fuck me.* I let my hands fall to my sides and squeezed them into fists as my emotions warred inside, ripping me in two very different directions, my body fighting itself to gain some semblance of control and coming up with nothing but pain. Nothing but a hollow ache in my chest.

"Go home, Gia." I turned to walk away and her hand grabbed my wrist.

"Mark, wait. I'm sorry. Can I just—"

I twisted my arm from her grasp and kept moving, unable to meet her eyes again.

23

Gia

Silhouette

Hangover? I wished. What I had was worse. The night before had been a nightmare. Pure and simple. And only I was to blame for first stuffing my monster bag of lies in the closet then letting it out to wreak havoc on my relationship with Mark. I deserved every tear I'd shed on the drive back to my apartment, every unanswered message, every snotty tissue I'd blown straight through.

I deserved it all.

But I still wouldn't give up. On him. On the job. If he loved his sister as much as I thought he did, he would understand that her finding out about Guy now was better than finding out later. He had to realize that. Knowing was worth the burden of canceling a wedding, feeling the heartbreak now instead of years down the road. If he didn't understand that, maybe he wasn't who I thought he was.

The beach side of East Bay resort was the next location I'd signed up for. Mark had invited me on Friday night, and I'd never given him an answer. I could almost guarantee I was uninvited, which was a good reason to stay far out of sight.

But I wouldn't.

I needed to clear things up with him. Since he wasn't returning my texts, the best way to get his attention was to confront him, set it all straight as soon as possible. If he had told Pacey about me and about the chance that Guy was cheating, the job would likely be over anyway, so it really didn't matter if I showed. A piece of Duplicity's anonymity was gone either way. No matter what, being honest with Mark was worth it. I didn't want to lose him.

I ate the last tough bite of a stale donut I hadn't had the stomach to finish at breakfast, shouldered my small beach bag, then left my car in the parking lot and headed toward the beach entrance beside the towering hotel high-rise. People milled around, some toting luggage for check-out or check-in, while others lugged umbrellas and coolers to enjoy the gorgeous day on the water.

As soon as I walked around the side lot and decks, passing an outdoor pool bar and small retail shop, I noticed Pacey sitting on the edge of the walkway wrapping her hair into a bun with her feet dipped into the sand. The section of the beach was relatively deserted, far enough away from the main building and pier. The volleyball nets, however, had some people gathered at the end sitting in chairs and four players in motion on the court. *The rest of her party. And Mark.*

He moved inside the court with the other guys, shirtless, his back to me. I suddenly wished I hadn't eaten that donut. My mouth dried and my stomach churned, flashing me back to my teen years where I was barely able to look at a guy so gorgeous without turning into a complete fool—a fear-induced illusion. Now, though, I absolutely was a fool. Not for falling all over myself, but for possibly ruining a connection that had the potential to be everything. I could only hope apologizing profusely would work ... or begging. I wasn't above getting on my knees. For him especially.

I shoved all the feelings deep down and gritted my teeth as I started moving toward Pacey. Worst case, I'd be leveled and thrown out. I'd survive. I'd get over it. Maybe.

"Hi," I said with a small, nervous wave, watching Pacey stand and adjust the cover skirt over her string bikini.

"Hey!" she replied after her eyes lifted to me. "Mark didn't tell me you were coming today. This is great!"

Phew.

"I'm so happy you're here." She hooked her arm with mine and pulled me toward the beach. "And thrilled you agreed to come to the wedding too. Mark actually seems excited. Well, except today. He's grumpy, but I'm sure that'll change when he sees you. I'm sorry. I'm babbling. How are you?" She turned her huge sunglasses toward me while we continued to walk, her slim nose and beaming smile the only things I could see besides the dark lenses.

I was glad I'd worn my face blocker shades too. Being so close had me even more nervous, almost positive she could spot my blotchy skin and puffy eyes. "I'm okay. I've just been busy."

"I bet! Kass told me that the boutique has been jumpin'. I'm picking up my dress tomorrow."

"That's always exciting," I replied with a grin then finally braved a look in front of us. The guys had stopped playing, and Mark had moved off the court to get a drink. Sweat glistened on his profiled face, his biceps, the slopes of his back. The temperature seemed to rise around me with no warning at all, causing me to suck air like a suffocating fish.

"They're sweating off their hangovers," Pacey said, noticing they'd stolen my attention.

"Rough night, huh?" I reeled in my lustful thoughts and steeled myself. Focus was what I needed if I wanted to stay and get Mark to even speak to me. After that, there was no guarantee.

They started their game again, and I let my eyes move to the sidelines. Three girls lounged—the rest of the wedding party.

"I'm sure you heard it was the bachelor party. The night was wrecked by some crazy Beach Bum fans, though. They had to ride around in the limo for a while to shake the tails."

"Wow. Must be rough." I pictured Mark having to endure the ride and cringed. It was probably the icing after my shitty news.

"Meh. They had to realize it would happen going to Category Five." We got closer to the courts and the girls' sunglasses tilted up in our direction. "Ladies, this is Gia. Gia, this is Leah, Maria, and Edena," Pacey introduced, and we exchanged waves and hellos. "We went to the spa yesterday. The guys probably should have done the same."

"Yeah, they should have. I've been dealing with the aftermath all morning," Edena said, her voice as deep and sultry as her lips advertised.

"Edena is Guy and Rick's publicist, so she gets to deal with the headaches associated with the screaming fangirls and boys," Pacey noted.

As if on cue, Edena's phone rang, and she stood and walked off to answer. Leah and Maria appraised me with silent smiles, their bronzed skin glinting under the sun's rays.

I looked around and caught Mark's eye on the court. His stare was penetrating, pinning me to the spot even with sunglasses on. I could feel the intensity all the way to my toes.

"The bachelorette spa day"—Pacey's voice sliced through Mark's invisible hold on me, drawing my focus back to her—"went much better. I'd take massages and facials over a club—"

"Hey," Mark's stern voice interrupted, pulling my eyes back to him as he walked the last couple of steps, grabbed his water, and gulped some down.

"Hey," I replied, unprepared for the closeness, the tension, the heat.

"Can we talk?" he asked, but I knew it wasn't a request, even without looking at the hardened line of his lips.

"Sure." I smiled to the girls, not knowing if I'd be back to chat.

He started walking but slowed his stride so I could keep up. There were no words spoken as we moved toward the hotel. The crunch of sand beneath our feet, the calm waves breaking in the distance, the worried beat of my heart—those were the only sounds of the trek toward the hotel, possibly back to my car even though I had no intention of actually leaving. I needed a picture.

We stepped onto the solid walkway and continued toward the pool bar. I was convinced he had no intention to talk at all until he finally stopped and wiped the sweat from his brow.

"You couldn't even give me a day alone to sort this out?"

"I would have been here anyway, watching. It's on my list. But I didn't want to hide from you anymore."

His hands hooked on his waist, resting on the V indent above the board shorts he wore, and he looked down at our feet. "What happens if you don't find anything? Do you still divulge everything? Will Pacey hear about it?"

"This whole job is different than what I've dealt with before. I don't even have another number, just the client's. But if there's no evidence, no, I don't usually inform the target's significant other. I wouldn't want to hurt her unnecessarily."

"What about me?" he asked pointedly, his eyes lifting to mine with a dark gaze hardened with emotion.

I sighed. "I didn't want to hurt you."

"Was I a perk? Just some convenient part of this job?" His arms dropped to his sides and he stepped closer to me, crowding me.

My body hummed, reacting to the current sparking between us with the memory of Friday night. "I never saw you that way."

"How did you see me?"

"At first? Like a bad distraction I shouldn't get involved with," I replied honestly and eased my hand up his forearm. "Then, like someone I didn't want to lose."

He inhaled deeply then reached up and lifted my sunglasses. "You look exhausted." I nodded, confirming the reason he already knew. "I am too."

"I'm sorry," I whispered.

"So am I." He slid my glasses back into place. "But that doesn't mean I can let you do this, Gia."

"What?" I took a step back.

"I can't let you do this. My mind was all over the place last night. I kept thinking about you, but I also couldn't stop thinking about Pacey and how much this could crush her. And I watched Guy last night. Even with all those girls throwing themselves at him, he showed no interest."

I laughed. I couldn't help it. "You were right next to him, Mark. Of course he won't let you see anything."

He shook his head. "This entire thing could be set up by anyone. Someone looking to end them, or even throw a wrench in his career. Who knows."

"It's not."

"How can you be so sure? You can't."

"They had to get the info from a previous client to find us." It wasn't infallible, but it meant a lot.

His hands shot back to his hips. "So who was it? Who was the previous client?"

I bit the inside of my cheek. "Maria."

"Maria? Maria Soriano?"

"Yes," I replied, glancing over in their direction. "She hired us a while back for Leah's boyfriend."

"Wait, so she knows who you are? Did she hire you for this job too?"

"No, she doesn't know who I am, just knows about Duplicity. But it is possible that she's hiring us again. Or it could be Leah. We disclosed our info to her when we sent the evidence of her boyfriend. But she wouldn't have known it was Maria who hired us—to use her name and the codeword—unless they talked afterward, which is possible. And if not them, then it could be any of their friends."

"They aren't exactly quiet," he said, glancing in their direction too. "And they have a lot of mutual friends, but Pacey is the closest. They've been friends since high school. They spent so much time at our house, my parents consider them daughters."

I smiled, feeling a little happiness from learning more about him, his family. "Sounds crowded."

He nodded a bit and peered at me with a side glance until he turned fully to face me again. "Yeah." For a moment, through a single look, he'd torn down his wall. Within a second, it was back up. "Look, Gia. Maybe I'm asking too much here, but it is what it is. I want to spend more time with you. I do. Lots more time. But I also want you to ditch this job."

He was laying it on thick. He was also thickheaded, and that was beyond frustrating.

"I want to spend more time with you, too." I touched him again, this time running a few fingers over his stomach. "A lot more time." His muscles tensed beneath my fingers and I bit my lip while watching his part with a heavy breath. "But I'm not ditching this job."

His jaw clenched and his lips pursed. "Why can't you let this one go? Can't you help wreck someone else's life?"

I huffed and backed away. "No, Mark, I can't. I thought you'd be a little more understanding about this considering it involves the sister you want to protect. Wouldn't you want to know, without any doubt, that her fiancé wasn't cheating on her before she walked down the aisle next week? Or would you rather she find out a few years from now when she's pregnant with his kid?"

"How much do people pay you to be the bearer of bad news? That's what this is about, right?"

"You want more details? Five thousand. Someone is paying five thousand for this job. We've already gotten half up front, which I used to purchase more material for Kass to make client dresses and show pieces for promo ads. I gave Viv the rest for new equipment. When I get the remainder, after either finding solid evidence or meeting the necessary locations, I'll use it for my PI classes or whatever else the boutique needs."

"I find it ironic that this money is helping your aunt's bridal store. Does she even know about this?"

I cringed a bit, knowing that Aunt Aimee probably wouldn't be thrilled if she found out about this job, maybe even about Duplicity in general. "She'd understand my motives." *Eventually.* I'd wanted this conversation to be amicable. And by amicable, I meant him totally understanding and agreeing with me. Apparently, that wouldn't happen. I mimicked his stance, hooking my hands on my hips. "I'm in this for good reasons, not just for money. It's too bad if you don't want to be sure your sister's being treated right."

When his cold silence stretched on, I took one more look into his shaded eyes and scrunched my brows defiantly. If he couldn't see my anger, he'd surely feel the heat. "I don't want to be rude to your sister, so I'm heading back to chat."

24
Mark

I should have known convincing Gia to drop the job was a long shot. She was adamant and determined to see it through to the end. Bringing up the money had been a last-ditch effort in my frustration, and it brought out an angry, tenacious side of her I hadn't seen before. What the hell was I supposed to do? I understood her reasons and contrary to what she probably thought, I would rather my sister find out earlier than later. But the thought of her hurting in any way crippled the desire to push for the truth. Gia's involvement didn't help matters either.

There was no easy answer to the problem and there'd be no easy outcome. I knew two things for certain. One, the entire situation had the potential to blow the hell up, shrapnel from the emotional explosion hitting everyone involved, including Gia and me. And two, I wanted Gia.

Badly.

I couldn't hide that fact. My anger had nearly extinguished when she'd first arrived. Short cotton shorts high on her thighs. Thin gray tank covering very little of a lime green bikini. My body betrayed my mind, needing the sight of her, the elation she brought with a simple glance, craving the feel of her, the sedation she brought with a simple touch.

As I watched her stalk away through the sand, I knew I had to fix it all somehow. So I bit back all my worry and convinced myself it could work out if I just went with it. I'd help her. There was a definite chance that Guy wasn't doing anything wrong. And I could try to find out who was behind hiring Gia to begin with.

I caught up with her halfway to the court. "The wedding is next week."

"And?" she replied, continuing her determined steps.

"So you either prove it true, or you have to show up to the locations for it to end, right?"

"Yes."

"How many locations can you possibly have left to watch him?"

"Does it matter?"

"It does. I want to know since I'm gonna help you."

She stopped and turned toward me. "I know what you're doing. There's no way I'm letting you help."

"What? You just practically called me an ass back there for not wanting to protect my sister and now you won't let me help you?"

"You won't help me. You'll distract me."

"You think I'd come along to distract you? Why in the hell would I do that? Not wanting to get involved in the mess is entirely different than purposely distracting you from finding out if my sister's being cheated on."

Her shoulders relaxed, tension dissipating a little. "So maybe not purposely. But you're too close. You could slip up. Tell her, or tell him."

"I'm helping," I said, finalizing my plans. "There's no way I'd make this situation worse."

"No, you're not because yes, you could. I can handle this myself."

She turned to walk again, but I grasped her wrist to stop her. "I'm sure you can handle this yourself." I slid my hand up her arm. "But I want to help you."

She side-eyed the group—not far off now—the girls all staring in our direction from their chairs. "No," she whispered, smiling sweetly for our audience.

I unleashed a cocky smile back with a laugh, putting on a show with her, and moved my hands to her waist. "Yes."

"No." Her hands moved too, to my stomach, feeling my abs softly, making me tense up and ache for more.

"Yes," I whispered, pulling her closer and leaning toward her neck. "I think your aunt would want me to help too."

Her body stilled and her breath caught. "You wouldn't tell her."

"Oh, yes, I would," I breathed with a laugh.

"That's pretty low."

"Yeah? Well, it's not good to keep secrets from people, Gia, especially people who care about you." The insinuation wasn't subtle. I needed to remind her that her lies had hurt, so I wasn't taking no for an answer about this. "I think you already know that."

Her hands snaked around to my back, allowing the small space between us to disappear. "Yeah, I know." Her fingers fidgeted with the top of my shorts at my back.

"Okay," I said, gently pressing my lips to her neck. It took all the restraint I had not to start a make-up make-out session right there, witnesses and all. But evidently she had business to take care of, and I had a game to get back to.

"I hope you know what you're getting yourself into," she said, smirking again as she pulled away from me and started walking toward Pacey and the girls—who were all still staring at us, grinning like vultures.

I laughed at her statement. "Oh, I do. I hope you're ready." I walked backward a few steps, watching the girls mob her with chatter. As much as I wanted to enjoy the moment—rekindling things with Gia, watching her interact with Pacey—my thoughts immediately shot to my sister's wedding day and its possible destruction.

"Damn, you've been holding out. Where'd you find her?" Rick said, tearing my eyes from the girls.

As soon as I turned around, the ball flew at my face. I caught it and spun it in my hand.

"That's what I wanna know," Evin agreed, wiping a palm from his sweaty forehead up through his buzz cut.

I smirked, acknowledging their appreciation but not happy about the thoughts obviously running through their heads. "She works at the store where Pacey got her wedding dress." She also catches cheats. And she kisses me ... kisses me like she needs nothing else. Like I'm life. The same way I kiss her.

Evin and Rick looked at Guy for confirmation, and he nodded with a smile. "Yup, she does," he said to them. "She is smokin', Mark. Better keep her close so these assholes don't get any ideas."

I spun the ball in my hands again and glanced at Gia, catching her eyes peering at me over her lowered sunglasses as she talked to Pacey. "That's the plan."

25

Gia

"Where have you been? Why haven't you returned my calls? And why are you calling me now? Shouldn't you be in class?" I fired off the questions into the phone, then took a long drink of the tall black coffee I'd ordered moments before I'd arrived outside Guy and Pacey's apartment. I swallowed thickly and smacked my lips as the potency attacked my taste buds. "Oh, shit, that's strong."

"School's been crazy," Viv replied. "Tutoring plus reports. Aunt Aim wouldn't let me take work shifts this week so I had a chance to get ahead. Since I have some free time before trig, I figured I'd call you back. Were you able to talk Aunt Aim into a later shift today so you could make the location?"

I reached into my glove box, grabbed and unwrapped a pink dickpop, and stirred its sugary goodness into the coffee. "Yeah, Kass had to come in early to cover for me, but she owed me for ditching Saturday's sale. I'm outside Guy's place now. Pacey just left. I think she has a couple classes this morning."

"If she's following her usual class schedule, yes. Did she get her dress on Monday?"

"Yes, after I'd already left for the day. What was Guy's appointment again today? A new interview or something?" I kept stirring as I watched his jeep, thinking about Sunday again.

There had been absolutely no hint of any wrongdoing at the beach. He'd been the perfect fiancé to Pacey—loving, attentive, flirty. They had nearly made me barf on a few occasions. They probably thought the same about Mark and me a few times, too. And although it added a level of awkwardness, the hidden agenda behind our actions only made things hotter between us. I wasn't complaining in the least because I was thrilled he had changed his mind about the job, but I also wasn't planning to let him jump completely into it either. Which was why he wasn't sitting beside me drinking his own tall black swizzled with a dickpop.

"The interview's with a local magazine. Can't remember the name. The client info didn't mention anything else on his schedule today."

"I'll tail him for as long as I can, but I'm starting to think that Mark was right about this one being a falsie of some kind. I just hope it's not someone trying to smear Guy in the tabloids."

"We've sent the client a few shots of him pretty close to other girls. If that was the case, wouldn't they have already used them?"

"Maybe they're saving up."

"At least none have been bad enough to land the headline 'Beach Bum caught impregnating secret alien visitor.'"

"Ha! Truth," I replied, thinking of how busy his publicist stepsister, Edena, had been at the beach and wondering how she'd handle the alien baby news.

"How did Sunday go, by the way? Did you get the beach pic?"

"I sent a single shot of Guy with Pacey. Maybe that'll make the client think a little bit. Pacey's been at most of the locations. It doesn't make sense."

"Maybe they wanted to cover all the bases just in case. Or maybe—like we thought before, since Maria's name was used—they're closer to Pacey and know more about her schedule than his."

"I suppose it doesn't matter too much. I'm just ready for this to end."

"Hmm. I'm wondering if that has to do with Mark," she said with a laugh. "Did you end up talking to him like you mentioned in our Sunday morning hazy phone call or did you keep your distance to get the picture?"

I groaned. "No, I charged it head-on. He was completely set on me dropping the job at first. In the end, I'm guessing he had to accept that I wasn't the bad guy. But the kicker is that he wants to help."

"Really?"

"Yeah, I—hang on," I said, noticing movement. A little boy exited a downstairs apartment to throw out a trash bag then disappeared inside again. "Sorry, just a kid. Anyway, yes, Mark threatened to tell Aunt Aim about Duplicity if I didn't let him come with me on the rest of the locations."

"No!"

"I told him about the rehearsal dinner on Friday. We've been texting the past couple of days but I haven't seen him since Sunday."

"And today?"

"He didn't need to know. It's the last time I can trail Guy by himself. I couldn't risk the distraction. I need to be focused, serious ..." I pulled the dissolved dickpop out of the coffee and took a sip. "Better."

"At least he's agreeing with you. Could be worse. He could've ditched you."

And I thought he had at the club, even at the beach. Letting him walk away would have been difficult, but I knew things wouldn't have worked between us if he had. Duplicity was mine. It was part of my life. And if he didn't understand my reasons for creating it, he wouldn't understand me.

"I'm glad he didn't," I admitted. "I just need to figure out what to do about him—" My phone beeped, so I put Viv on speaker to read the text. "Hang a sec. Have a message."

What are you doing?

"Crap. Mark messaged me. I don't want to lie to him."

"You should have thought about that before you decided not to tell him about today's location."

I rolled my eyes. "I know, I know. Gah!"

You gonna answer? I know you aren't busy.

What? I told him I'd be at work. "Viv. I'll call—"

Click. I turned my head toward my passenger door as it swung wide open. "What the hell?" It was a frantic scream, one fueled with the terror of the unknown, the horror of a carjacking.

A familiar face and body quickly dropped into the seat beside me and closed the door. My eyes blinked at the messy brown hair and stormy eyes with recognition. Terror faded quickly, morphing into humiliation and then into the achy kind of fear that was usually a precursor to an inevitable loss.

I had lied. He caught me.

"Gia! What the hell is happening? Are you okay?" Viv's scream was identical to my own, helpless and haunting.

Mark laughed. "Hey, person on the phone. It's Mark. She's okay, I promise. She's just really excited to see me."

My mouth hung open as I watched him open his own to mock me. He was here. In my car. Watching Guy and Pacey's place.

"Shit." Viv's voice said the exact word I was too stunned to vocalize, drawing it out as if she were speaking for me. "Well, I guess I'll let you go. Have fun."

The line went dead but not before I heard a little chuckle.

"You know, you really should lock your doors if you're sitting in your car. Anybody could just jump right in and accost you ... or give you a bad tongue-lashing."

"I'm sorry." The apology was out before I could register his final words. As soon as they sank in, my whole body went up in flames, thinking about our time in his car. "I ... uh ..."

He grinned and lifted the paper bag he was carrying in front of him. "Not gonna lie. I'm pretty pissed you didn't tell me about this. But I bought cookies anyway." He dug into the bag and handed me a golden brown cookie.

I still couldn't process what exactly was happening. He was mad ... but he brought me cookies? I smiled uneasily at him, watching as he took a bite of his own.

"Mmm," he hummed as he chewed. "So Friday is absolutely the last date, right? No more lying to me, Gia."

"Yes. That's the last date, promise," I said then took a bite of cookie, watching the tips of his lips curve up again into a wicked, sexy grin. I knew the reason for that sinister look as soon as I chomped down and my taste buds absorbed the bland substance.

"I should have mentioned that one was sugar and dairy free."

"Ahh," I mumbled around the bite then took a long gulp of my coffee and scowled because it did nothing to fill the sugar void. "Well, that didn't help."

Mark eyed the cup and grabbed it to read the order on the side. "You decided to try the maintenance man? Delicious, right?"

"Too strong."

"Like that's a bad thing."

I shook my head with a laugh then glanced out the windshield. After a silent moment, I said, "I am really sorry. I never wanted to hurt you. This is important to me for many reasons and I wanted to be focused."

"I invaded your job. I get it. But I still don't want to deal with lies whether they're about this job or not." He lifted a new cookie to my mouth. "The rest are the real deal."

I opened my mouth and took a bite. "Mmm. Thank you."

He nodded, and I knew he understood my thanks was for much more than the cookie. "Pacey told me about Guy's meeting, so I changed my shift. We gonna tail him?"

"That's the plan. Though, in the spirit of honesty, I have my doubts that this job is completely warranted. Someone could have simply wanted to check his faithfulness before Pacey marries him. There might've been no real evidence to start with, which could be the reason that I had to agree to so many locations, like casting a net."

"Or it could still be someone trying to make some headlines with that same net."

"Maybe." I looked around outside for his Charger. "Obviously Guy and Pacey know your car. I hope you hid it well."

"I did," he said, then took a long drink of the coffee. "You sweetened the maintenance man?"

"I did." I winked then nodded to the glove box. "Help yourself." Movement across the street caught my eye. Guy jogged down the steps and ran a hand through his blond swoop of hair before jumping into his jeep.

"Nice," Mark said with a laugh after popping the glove box open. "What happened to the rest of the goodies for that fake bachelorette party?"

I started the engine, waiting for Guy to move. "Well, believe it or not, that place doesn't take returns or give refunds."

"No kidding?" His voice pitched with excitement and amusement while he twisted the stick of the dickpop pinched between his fingers. "I'm guessing the rest of those items are stashed back at your place, and I have to admit that I'm not particularly mad about that lie right now." He turned toward me and reached a hand over to my lap, splaying his fingers on my thigh.

"Oh yeah? I think I have an idea why you sound so excited." Keeping sight of Guy's jeep in my peripheral vision, I looked at Mark and lifted my fingers to his mouth, running two pads across the swell of his lower lip. "If you play your cards right on this job, maybe I'll let you take Air Boy for a ride."

The waiting was impossible. I just wanted to confront Guy and choke the shit out of him until he admitted if he was cheating on Pacey. But there was too much at stake to handle it that way. It was Gia's job, and despite my connections to it and the frustrations that brought, I'd agreed to help, not demolish. So I had to sit and wait in Gia's car, ignoring the sexual charge between us to focus on Guy—who was currently pulling into the parking lot of a downtown business complex.

Aside from her running through the things I should or shouldn't do during our spy date, the short drive from the apartment had been relatively quiet. If I really wanted to help her with the job, I needed more info. "Are you going to tell me your guesses?" I slid my hand higher up Gia's bare thigh with the question, hitting the edge or her short cotton shorts as she backed into a spot fifty yards from Guy's jeep and surrounded by other cars for cover.

"Guesses?" Keeping her eyes aimed at the jeep, she grabbed my hand and slid it back to her knee.

I laughed and squeezed her skin playfully. "Guesses for who hired you."

"I have no idea at this point. I was leaning toward Maria again, but with the price tag on the job and the fishing tactic, I'm not so sure." She grabbed her phone from the console. "He's on the move. Let's go."

I hopped out of the car and moved with her, staying close to the other vehicles as we watched Guy disappear into the thick glass door of the closest brick building.

"Slow down a bit and stay behind me. I'm not sure how crowded it is in there and I don't need him spotting you."

I did as she instructed, entering behind her through the glass door etched with the words Gulf Craze. The main lobby of the local magazine wasn't very busy during midmorning. There was no information desk, but there were directional signs to offices located on different floors. Tracking Guy, Gia hurried past a few people waiting at the elevators, moving slow enough not to draw attention. She peeked around then continued on just as Guy disappeared down another hall.

"Well, we can at least rule out Guy, right? What about the other visible players?" I whispered as we moved, glancing into a few open doors along the way. "Pacey would have reason, but if she's worried about Guy cheating on her, she hasn't mentioned anything. And that says a lot since she has an issue keeping her concerns quiet, especially about the wedding." We stopped at the next hallway and glanced around the corner again. Guy stood outside a doorway, shaking hands with a busty brunette wearing a floral dress and a flirty smile. Gia held her phone up to the wall's edge to snap a picture and as soon as they moved into the room, she hurried down the hall.

We slowed when we realized they'd entered a glass-walled conference room. Opaque waves covered nearly the entire panels, allowing us to pass by without a chance of being recognized. There was an identical room a few feet farther, but Gia stopped at the wooden door between the two rooms. We stepped inside a narrow space and closed the door behind us. Cabinetry lined half the room's length with a sink and a counter between. A pitcher and glasses sat upside down in a drying rack beside an empty coffee pot. It was a refreshment prep area, pinned in the middle of two conference rooms, a door to access each inside.

Gia didn't speak. She leaned closer to the door to eavesdrop on the muffled voices in Guy's conference room.

I stepped close behind her and continued whispering my thoughts into her ear. "Rick and Evin really wouldn't have reason to be involved unless they were into Pacey—which I doubt—and I don't think Edena would have Guy followed being family and all. So I agree that it's probably Maria or Leah. They are Pacey's best friends. Or maybe there's an ex of Guy's we don't know about. Have you seen any other crazy stalkers besides yourself?"

She turned her head a little, keeping her ear to the door, and whispered, "No. But they could be just as good at being invisible."

"If that's the case, you should've spotted them right away." I breathed a soft laugh. "You have to work on your stalking."

Her lips turned down as she side-eyed me. "I was pretty good at being invisible until you showed up."

"Is that right?" I grabbed hold of her hips from behind, admiring the extended curve of her ass as she leaned forward against the door. "Good thing I'm not one of your targets then because I see you. I've seen you all along."

Pink spread up her neck and into her cheeks then her lips pulled into a wide grin. "Apparently."

She had no idea what she was doing to me. That look. Her seductive eyes cracking me wide open and lighting me on fire. The sight of her coupled with the risk of being caught spying had me harder than a rock. I sighed.

"She's asking some basic questions," Gia stated absently. "This sounds pretty standard."

My heart raced and my dick throbbed. I couldn't take it anymore. I wanted her. Here. Leaning closer, I slid a hand over her ass then around and down to the inside of her thigh. She tensed and looked over her shoulder at me questioningly but didn't push me away. With my other hand, I pulled her back against my chest and hunched over to capture her lips, kissing her from behind. She hesitated for a moment but joined in quickly, abandoning any thoughts of refusal or cares of consequence. Not wasting any more time, I slid one hand up under her bra and the other into the waistline of her shorts and panties, massaging her, instantly feeling her mutual excitement.

I moaned. *Shit, this spy stuff is hot*. Her hands reached up behind my head, pulling me deeper into the kiss, pressing her breast into my hand, and arching her butt back against me.

The words behind the door grew louder, clearer. "Thanks for coming down today, Guy. It was a real pleasure to meet you."

Gia dropped her arms and broke our kiss, her widened eyes turning toward the door. I stilled my hands for a moment then continued massaging her despite Guy's possible departure. Having a complete hookup was off the table, but I still planned to please her.

"There you are," another voice said. "I thought I was joining you for this?"

I stopped for another moment, worried the small interview could turn into a full-on conference where they'd all want coffee.

"Hey," Guy said. "Courtney, this is my publicist, Edena."

"Oh yes. We spoke on the phone. Nice to meet you, Edena."

I continued on, biting down on the side of Gia's neck. She leaned into me, whimpering a tiny bit as I slipped a finger inside her.

The other room's awkward silence stretched on painfully until finally a voice sliced through. "I better get back to my office. Guy, it was a pleasure. I'll be in touch for the follow-up and photo shoot info. Take all the time you need." A click of a door suggested Courtney's departure.

"What the hell? You were supposed to wait for me." Edena sounded pissed off. Her anger, the harshness of her voice, was like a bucket of ice water tossed on my dick. I tried my best to ignore her, focusing on Gia and her soft sexy breaths as I licked up her neck and massaged her more.

"You were late," Guy replied, "and I wasn't gonna postpone the initial interview because you failed to show up."

"I had to cover for someone at the restaurant. Next time just wait."

"There better not be a next time." Now he sounded pissed off. "I'm not paying you to work for your dad."

"You're right. You're paying me to set shit like this up and to hit the tabloid tip lines so your name doesn't disappear like that stupid show. I know my job, and you know you can't afford to lose me … or have the wrong info slip."

"That sounded an awful lot like a threat." Guy's usual laid back voice had vanished.

The clicking of high-heeled footsteps traveled in from the hall followed by a new voice. "You need to grab the food we ordered from up the street. We have a half hour before—"

Knowing the voices in the hall were about to enter the room, Gia launched herself away from me.

"Shit." I grunted.

Gia lost her balance and smacked her hand on Guy and Edena's door. There was no time to mourn the loss of her heat, only time to scramble. Just as the outside door and the door to Guy's conference room both began to open, Gia jerked the door to the empty conference room open and hurried inside. I was on her heels. "This room looks great for the interview!" she yelled into the new room, laying down some lame cover for our escape.

Clambering toward the room's glass door, we ignored the confused voices behind us—everyone obviously puzzled as they met each other in the small refreshment room. When we finished our sprint outside to the car and slammed the doors shut, safely hiding us inside, I looked at her and laughed through heavy breaths. The situation was so hilariously chaotic that my balls didn't even ache a need for release.

She started the car and tore out of the parking lot, her own heavy breaths the only noise she made. All I could do was stare, thinking how gorgeous she was, how hot the situation had been, and how sexy it was for her to get down with me like that in a public place.

"That was—"

"Fucking stupid," she cut me off, turning the wheel and barreling down the street.

"What?" Apparently, she wasn't feeling the same.

"We almost got caught."

"We got out. No harm was done."

"I'm such an idiot! I can't believe I let you come with me. I can't think around you. This is my job and I can't concentrate on what I need to do."

"Hey," I said, slipping my hand under her arm while she shifted gears and laying it on her thigh for reassurance. "It won't happen again, okay?"

"You're right. It absolutely won't happen again." Her tone was clipped, indicating way more than she was saying.

"Don't, Gia. We made a mistake but everything's fine. We even got to overhear something useful. Edena threatened Guy."

"I could have heard more if I'd been alone." She lifted her hand from the stick to remove mine from her leg.

"You're blaming me for this?" I couldn't help snapping back. "I wasn't the only one in that room."

Her jaw tightened. "That's my point. I can't be trusted to get the job done when you're around."

I wasn't sure if I should take that as a compliment or not. It was nice to hear that I affected her in that way, but the connotation punched me in the gut just the same. Was she questioning more than this? "Look, I won't apologize for being there. Maybe you could have heard something different without me, but there's also a huge chance you wouldn't have. So the only thing I'm willing to apologize for is not being able to make you finish ... because I honestly don't ever want to leave you unsatisfied."

Her cheeks reddened. And while that response would usually make me feel good and maybe indicate everything would be fine, it was the only response I received. There were no more words for the rest of the ride. That had me more worried than I wanted to admit.

"Are we still on for the rehearsal dinner?" I asked as she pulled her car up beside mine back at Pacey's. When she'd initially told me the dates and locations for the remaining jobs, she'd agreed to go as my date. Now, I wasn't so sure she would. "It might look a little odd if not." It was a sad excuse to use, but I'd do anything for more time to discuss what was wrong, to open her up.

"I'll meet you there," she said, glancing at me. Her eyes were the saddest I'd ever seen and it tugged at me. I wanted to fix everything.

But how could I when I didn't even know what the real problem was? She regretted me being there. Was she regretting more?

"Gia, I need to know that we're—"

"I just need some time, okay? If something had happened ... if I ruined this job ... if Guy is guilty, but I had ruined any chance to catch him in the act ..."

"You didn't. There's no reason to feel guilty, to think about what if. It's fine."

"I just need some time. I'll see you at the dinner Friday, but I need some time to think."

"Okay ... I'll see you there," I acknowledged and shut the door. Standing in the street, watching her car disappear, I had no idea why I gave in so easily, why I didn't demand to talk. This was all new to me, different from anything I'd been through in my adult life. Having chosen a path where relationships had no real shelf life, I hadn't had to deal with many emotional issues. There was no time for things to blossom or deaden. There were no cares or expectations. No disappointment. Should I have done something more, said something more? Probably not. Giving her the time and space she needed was likely the best choice. I wouldn't chance making things worse. I could only hope that the time would bring her whatever clarity she needed. About us, about the job. Then, after the job was over, maybe we could move on to focus on us.

27
Gia

One more night. One more night. One more night.

"You haven't left yet?" Kass questioned, walking up to the front of the boutique with material and measuring tape draped across her shoulders. She'd been putting in extra hours all week, preparing promotional designs with the new material we'd purchased.

"You're mistaken. I'm not actually here right now," I deadpanned, sweeping my eyes back to the computer screen and staring as blankly as I had been for the past half hour. The orders hadn't changed. The schedule hadn't changed. My position hadn't changed.

"Weren't you supposed to be at East Bay like an hour ago?"

"That was the time I was given for the rehearsal. The dinner probably just started."

"So that means you're two hours late."

She knew me. I nodded at her joke but couldn't bring myself to humor her with a chuckle. I was too crazed. Too nervous. Tonight was the final night. I'd take one more picture of Guy and the job was over, regardless of whether that picture was of him holding Pacey tightly or some other girl. I had hope that it would only be

Pacey, but after Wednesday's spy session at Gulf Craze magazine, I had my doubts. Edena threatened Guy with leaking some info. That threat had stuck to me for the past couple days like my clothes in August with a hundred percent humidity. What did she have on him? Was he messing around on Pacey or was it something about his career?

"Gia, get your heels on and get outta here. It's not about you, the job, or Mark. This is about Pacey. It's her night and her big day tomorrow. You need to set aside whatever shit is going on in that marriage-hating head of yours, take one stupid picture for the job, kiss Mark on the mouth, and be there for him to support his sister." Kass leaned an elbow on the high edge of the desk and stared at me.

"I know you're right. I just ..."

"You're just getting in your own way. You always have, especially after Landon."

"I know that. I just can't fall like this. Be stupid about it. I mean, I nearly pulled a 'you' and let him bend me over in some kind of office kitchenette while we were spying on his almost brother-in-law, for Chrissake."

Her eyes bulged at my confession, but she recovered quickly, nodding and saying, "Ooh, yeah."

"It was stupid and reckless and—"

"And what? Spontaneous? Sexy? True? Real? It's okay to fall again, Gia. Stop being so afraid."

"I'm not—"

"Oh my God, shut the hell up right now. You are so afraid of what happens next, after the job is no longer an obstacle between you. And that's fine. It's completely fine. We all know you're strong. You're stronger and more independent than anyone I know. You don't need a guy's help or a guy's love. Aunt Aim, Viv, and I know that. Everybody knows that. There's no reason to try and prove it to yourself or to anyone else … over and over and over again." Her head bobbed in exaggeration as her words punched hard through my emotional wall.

"I'm not afraid of love, Kass, that's you," I snapped, not wanting to acknowledge the truthful words that hurt so much. But I knew. I'd known for a long time. I was terrified. It's not easy to offer your stapled heart to someone new, not knowing what they held in their other hand. It could be their own heart, beautifully bruised and ready for an intimate exchange. Or it could be a slew of weapons, malicious and ready to silence whatever loving beats you had left.

"Oh, no!" she said, shaking her head and pursing her perfect lips. "We already know who I am. I may have my faults, but I am definitely not afraid of love. Fear of commitment is far from the same. I love. Many people. A lot. And I'm happy with that. But you, you're guarding your heart as if it's already shriveled inside a coffin."

"I …" Even though I knew the truth, I still tried to think of an argument.

"It's okay for you to accept that you're falling in love again. And it's perfectly fine to let a man do things for you, care for you, make you feel good about yourself, and—gasp—rock your fucking world inside the sheets, inside the surf, with your hands tied, with *his* hands tied, when you're sad, when he's pissed, before you—"

"I get the picture," I interrupted.

"Do you?" she asked, dropping her hands to her hips and silently tapping her bare toes.

I nodded and closed my eyes, picturing Mark's crushing gaze the last time I'd seen him. The conflict raging inside his eyes had been enough to bring tears to mine. "I need to talk to him."

"Yes, you do. So get to it. I'll shut down and close up. Have a good time, okay?"

"I'll try—" She glared at me. "I will."

After dropping my car at the valet and walking the steps into the entrance of the main clubhouse, I smoothed a nervous hand down the sides of my black and white embroidered maxi dress as my mind worried about everything. Was the dress more beachy than rehearsal dinner? Would Guy be stupid enough to hook up with someone the night before his wedding? How would I apologize to Mark? Would there be dessert? I needed sugar. Thoughts blended while I glided across the polished marble of the wide lobby, passing the front desk and lounge areas, heading toward the glass doors at the back. I knew the rehearsal would already be over, but I made myself check anyway—killing more time, prolonging the inevitable.

East Bay's lawn sprawled out behind the clubhouse, with a gorgeous, open view of the bay beyond the perfectly designed displays of assorted flowers, fountains, and shrubbery of the gardens. Without towering trees obstructing the bay's ridge, The District was even visible—only a short drive or a few thousand dinghy rows away. Good to know if I needed an escape during dinner. As long as I wasn't drunk. Drunk dinghy rowing wouldn't get me far.

The wedding party was nowhere in sight. A few employees were folding and removing two rows of chairs used as the temporary aisle for rehearsal. Come tomorrow, the chairs would be back in place to seat all the guests attending the wedding. I turned around and headed toward the elevators. Tomorrow's wedding reception would be held downstairs in the ballroom, but tonight's dinner was upstairs in the clubhouse's lookout.

I fidgeted on the way up, tugging the ends of my loose curls while staring at my mirrored reflection and double-checking the phones within my small clutch. The burner had one more picture to take, and the earlier it was taken the better. I would still continue to watch Guy through the night to be sure nothing else happened, but I wouldn't chance exposure either.

The rooftop restaurant was a perfect mix between club fancy and beach dressy, with a tiki style bar along one side, tables with cloth napkins, and decor of everything in between. With the glass doors retracted much like those at the lobby eight floors below, the indoor fully opened to the rooftop. That was where I spotted the sectioned off wedding party tables. Most were already empty, plates being cleared while some of the people stood admiring the views with drinks in hand. I scanned for Mark with no luck. Pacey stood near Guy, chatting with an older couple. Parents possibly. Guy's or Pacey's. Both were undoubtedly attending. And if they were Pacey's, they were Mark's. My heart punched a few extra nervous beats at the thought. The woman wore a belted short-sleeved dress colored in sandy hues. Her short dark hair had natural looking waves. She was close to Pacey's height. The night's new panic attack kicked in as soon as the older man's head of dark brown hair turned a bit, streaks of silver within catching the rays of the setting sun. Strong, square face and jaw, heavy eyebrows, sexy as hell smile—he could've easily passed for Mark's much older brother. I watched him take a drink from his glass and my stomach growled with even more nerves than before.

I was about to meet Mark's family.

It was too late for dinner but never too late for cocktails.

Tipsy Gia, PI, prepared to find the truth before the world spins. It had a ring to it, comparable to *PI Pleasure, getting bent for the truth.* Ugh.

I made a beeline for the bar, ordering a Blow Job shot—needed to bring the double dose of calm with liquor and an early taste of dessert—and a beer. I threw back the shot then scanned the area again. No Mark. Pacey had stepped away from Guy and her parents, moving toward the end of the bar. I knew I'd be spotted soon enough, so I sucked it up and headed in her direction.

Nameless faces gawked at me with each step, raising my heart rate and flushing my cheeks. Was my dress too beachy after all? I was so used to blending in, but that wasn't happening.

I was nearly to the end of the bar, my eyes focused on Pacey and her exquisite white crocheted lace and baby pink chiffon skirted dress as she ordered from the bartender. Not far from the end, a hand caught my forearm, stopping me in front of the high stools. My tense glare met two pairs of dilated eyes and grins. Evin and Rick. Their cheerful faces looked me over with breathy chuckles.

"Gia!" Rick said, releasing my arm and rubbing the top of his bald head. "Good to see you. You look—"

"Stunning," Mark's voice interrupted from behind me.

I spun to face him, like a magnet unable to control my own movements with him near. His stormy eyes roamed my body while I did the same to him. A crisp, white button-down tucked neatly into a pair of black suit pants, sleeves cuffed at his forearms. No tie. No jacket. If he'd had them on for the rehearsal, they were long gone. There'd be no complaints from me. The top couple of buttons were open, revealing a teasing amount of skin. The shirt's fit was perfect. Tight enough to show the strength in his shoulders and arms, loose enough for them to breathe in all the sighs of the women he walked by. Because I knew I wasn't the only one losing the battle for air around him. I fought the inner bitch inside who wanted nothing more than to glance around at the women, to catch them still staring as they wondered who he was talking to.

I fought the urge, hard, for one gracious second, then lost harder. The inner bitch gloated while I peeked over his shoulder, seeing a couple women doing exactly what I'd thought. But only one pair of those eyes remained steadfast when I caught them. The same woman who had been speaking with Pacey when I'd arrived looked at me from across the room, keeping contact as she tipped her fluted glass to her lips. *Their mom.*

"Way to steal our thunder, Mark," Evin's voice rang with a laugh behind me, breaking my connection with Mark's mom. "We were just about to tell her how ... sweet she looks."

Mark ignored Evin and licked his lips then flashed a tense grin. "Can we talk a minute?" His head nodded back toward the entrance.

"Sure," I replied, biting my lip and adjusting my grip on my beer and clutch while he took hold of my empty arm to lead me out.

My stomach twisted. All the things I needed to say spun, spun, spun inside my head as his hand slid down to mine, pulling me behind him, past some people, out into the nearly empty hall, not stopping until he reached the door to the stairs and moved us inside the empty stairwell. He grabbed my beer and my clutch and set them at my feet.

"I ... I'm sorry ..." I whispered, feeling a change in his movements when we'd stepped inside. *Is he angry that I was late?* "... that I didn't answer your calls or texts. I'm sorry about the other day. That I'm late. I ..." As he stood upright again, close, so close—eyes focused, jaw clenched—I lost my reasons for apology. "You know what? No. I'm not sorry," I said, my voice echoing down the stairs as I stood straight, squared my shoulders, and tipped my chin up to meet his gaze. "Taking you with me was a mistake, so I'm not apologizing for that. I was mad at you, but I was more pissed at myself because I should have known better. And as for not talking to you—I needed that time to myself. So I'm not apologizing for that either." I watched one of his brows quirk, the silent look not giving me any sign of backing down. "If you have a problem with any of that, that's too bad." Still no reaction. My thoughts got more defensive, considering why I'd even taken a chance with him, why I'd bothered to let him in. But then Kass' words weaseled into my mind and the need to push him away slipped. *He did nothing wrong.* "The job's over tonight. So if I'm a problem for you, if you don't—"

"Stop," he whispered, his hands lifting up to my neck, my jaw. "I brought you out here for a couple of reasons. First, you have whipped cream under your nose."

I gaped.

"And as selfish as it is, I didn't want to lick if off in front of everyone." His brow lifted again, this time accentuating the amused twinkle in his eyes. He didn't wait for my reaction as he moved closer. His tongue licked tenderly just above my upper lip before he pressed his lips fully to mine. I opened to his caresses, letting him taste me, take my stupid words away with his forgiving mouth.

He pulled away, touching his tongue to his top teeth with a smile that made me clench my thighs together. His hands moved down to my bare shoulders and his eyes followed. "God, Gia, you look gorgeous ... so fucking sexy. It's going to take every ounce of restraint to go back in there. But there's a couple people who would be extremely pissed at me if we were to leave right now. They were already upset that I may have screwed something up with you."

"Oh. Well, I am really sorry about being late," I admitted.

"It's okay," he said, skimming his fingers down my arms. "I'll forgive your fashionably late entrance if you forgive me."

I shook my head. "There's nothing to forgive. You only did what I wanted. And thank you for giving me time."

He smiled and leaned down to kiss my cheek then nuzzled my neck, inhaling deeply against my skin. "I want to give you my time … and so much more."

I closed my eyes at the admission, letting it all sink in. There would be no barriers soon, and I was completely ready for that. I wanted to be with him, learn more about him, spend an obnoxious amount of time with him. In bed, in showers, in bakeries.

He sighed and straightened up. "First, we have to get through the next hour or so. As far as I could tell earlier, Guy was behaving the same. I didn't spot him doing anything unusual. I'll help you watch him for however long you need to in order to get that last picture. That won't be a problem. The real question is, are you ready to meet my parents?"

"Not really," I admitted as the nervousness crept slowly back through my body.

"I'll make it up to you later. Promise. But I can't be trusted in here alone with you any longer, especially after tasting whatever that sweetness was in your mouth."

I laughed. "A Blow Job."

His eyes widened and I laughed again before pushing through the door.

28
Mark

I steered Gia toward what was left of the rehearsal dinner. Several people had already bailed. I hoped the low numbers would ease Gia's mind some even though I knew she was only worried about meeting two in particular. My dad and mom stood outside, chatting pleasantly with Pacey. I fully believed my mom would have stayed well past midnight to meet Gia given that it had been a few years since I'd introduced them to a girlfriend.

I placed a reassuring hand on Gia's back, rubbing circles over the soft material with the pads of my fingers as we stepped up behind Pacey, who turned around as soon as she saw Mom's eyes divert to us.

"Gia! Thanks so much for coming!" Pacey said, throwing her arms around her and squeezing.

"Easy, Pay." I chuckled. "You don't want to risk injury before tomorrow."

"Way to just throw that bad luck out there," she said, letting Gia go and poking a finger to my chest. "You don't give me enough credit if you think I'd break that easily. And I know I wouldn't break Gia with a hug either."

"Hey, Pacey! Sorry I'm late. I love your dress," Gia said, the words tumbling out. She was still nervous. *Shit.* Maybe I should have given her two more shots.

I added more pressure at her back, rubbing lower just above her ass. I'd like to say it was only for her comfort, but it was also a warning to all the eyes tracking her since she'd walked in here wearing the sleeveless black dress that looked and felt as soft as her skin. The way it wrapped around her—starting behind her neck, dipping low into her cleavage, hugging her waist and hips then flowing freely down to her ankles—conjured thoughts of her wrapped up in only my bed sheet. So the hand was for anyone else thinking anything remotely similar.

"Gia, these are our parents, Kirk and Julie Foster."

"Pleasure to meet you." Gia shook my mother's hand first then her hand was swallowed up by my father's.

"It's very lovely to meet you too, Gia. You are every bit as beautiful as Mark and Pacey described."

Gia smiled and clasped her untouched beer nervously with both hands. "That's very kind. Thank you." Her eyes cut to me.

"We hear you work at the boutique where Pacey's gown was made," my dad commented before taking a sip of his single malt.

"It's my family's boutique. My older sister, Kass, made Pacey's gown."

"Yes, she did a magnificent job," my mom added. "Do you work designs and alterations too?"

"I don't actually. That part never caught my interest as much as it did for Kass or my aunt. I help manage the business side. Scheduling, ordering, bookkeeping. I enjoy handling all the information, solving problems and arranging things behind the scenes."

"I think that's wonderful. And I'm looking forward to meeting Kass tomorrow. I'm sure you'll be handling a lot more business after the next Destination Bride hits the shelves." Mom turned toward Pacey. "The interviewer said it would be in the next issue, right?"

Gia's head turned toward me, eyes scrunched with confusion. *She doesn't know.* I felt her stiffen and rubbed my fingers along her back. She turned back toward Pacey. "I'm sorry, did you say Kass was coming to the wedding?"

"Yes, she'll be here pretty early. Maybe an hour or so before the ceremony," Pacey replied. "I know she normally turns down the invites for weddings featuring her dresses, but she couldn't say no this time because I got a response from Destination Bride magazine. They're taking a couple shots before, during, and after the wedding. They also plan to interview her about her designs."

"Wow, that's fantastic. She didn't mention ..."

"Oh? She probably wanted to surprise you," Pacey offered, smiling. "You should come earlier too! I'm sure the magazine would love to hear from you also."

Guy walked up, sliding between Pacey and my mom. "Hey, Gia. Good to see you."

"You too," she replied.

"Pacey, my parents are getting ready to leave, so I'm gonna see them out."

"Okay, I'll walk with you. You two don't leave yet." She eyed me, clearly knowing I didn't want to stay here longer than I needed to now that Gia had arrived.

I scowled playfully, and she returned the gesture.

"I'm really sorry. Will you excuse me for a second?" Gia suddenly asked.

I tilted my head. "Everything okay?"

She grinned at me then at my parents. "Oh yes. I just need to use the facilities."

"Okay." I grabbed her beer to hold and watched her walk back toward the bar and the bathrooms.

"She seems very nice," Mom said, not waiting for me to turn before diving into her analysis. "Just wish we got to meet her before tonight."

I sighed and spun back around, taking a drink from Gia's full beer since I hadn't thought to grab another for myself. "Things were ... a little complicated before. And she's been pretty busy with work, so it's been difficult for us to get together."

"Well, we expect to have her for dinner soon."

"Yes, ma'am," I said with a laugh then took another drink. "I think I'll grab her another beer since I've almost killed this already. Do you guys need anything?"

Dad tipped his glass, rattling the cubes. "No, I think I'm fine. We should be leaving pretty soon anyway or I'll never hear the end of the beauty sleep issue for the wedding tomorrow."

Mom flicked the back of her hand against his arm. "Don't start, old man. You're the one who demands at least eight hours and will be in bed as soon as we walk through the door. You aren't fooling anyone."

Dad only smiled and rolled his eyes.

I laughed and walked toward the bar, more curious as to where Gia had gone. She was nowhere near the bathroom when I looked, so I changed direction and made my way down to the lobby instead. Pacey and Guy were stepping back through the main entrance when I'd arrived. Not wanting to get caught up by them, I turned down the closest hallway and saw Gia ducking into the first doorway to hide. I followed, startling her.

"What are you doing down here?" she whispered.

"Looking for you. What are you doing down here?"

"I took advantage of them coming down here for a less conspicuous picture. Anyone can take a pic from the lobby."

"Good thinking. Did you already get it?"

"I nabbed one of them near the valet outside while they said goodbye to his parents."

"Did you already send it?" I noticed some movement at the end of the hall, so I stepped forward, pushing farther into the small entry, pressing my body to hers, pinning her to the door.

She tipped her head back to see me, elongating her neck. "I sent it to Viv's info stripper first. I still need to send it to the client's number."

I dipped my face down, trailing the edge of my nose to her neck, inhaling her, relishing the way her sweet scent—a heady blend of her skin and the Baileys and Kahlúa mix still on her breath—triggered a rush, making me harden instantly. "We need to leave soon."

"Yes," she agreed.

"Let's hunt down my parents. They're leaving too, so we should be in the clear to get out of here once we say goodbye."

She simply nodded, and I brushed my lips to hers, lightly sampling what would come later.

Before I lost all rational thought, I took her hand and led us back into the lobby. She trailed behind, tapping through the phone keys despite my rushed steps. She wanted to end the job. The job that could have ripped Pacey's life apart. The job that had tangled us together while keeping us apart. I was ready for it to end too, ready to see where we'd lead without interference.

The elevator chimed and the stainless steel doors retracted just as we turned the corner.

"Oh, there you are," my mom said, running her fingers through her hair as she exited. My dad wiped a hand across his mouth smoothly, following her out.

I glanced at Gia with a wan grin, trying my hardest to ignore the obvious tells of my parents' elevator interlude. She bit her lips together with a tight smile and lifted her brows. "Yup," I confirmed, slowly turning back to face my parents, "here we are."

Gia reluctantly let her hand and the phone fall to her side, pressing a few more buttons before lifting her eyes to give my parents her complete attention.

"We're heading home," Mom said. "Tomorrow's going to be—" A phone chimed and she reached into her purse, pulling out the black phone she'd dropped at brunch on Sunday. She checked the screen, distracted for a second, then finished, "A long day for all of us." After a few blinks of her widened eyes and a soft blow of air through her lips, she dropped the phone back into her purse and looked at both of us with a tiny, composed grin.

The phone was an emergency backup. That was what she had told me on Sunday. Why would it get notifications? Could it have been a wrong number? Was there any other reason ... unless ... *Oh!* I straightened up, suppressing the thoughts for a moment. "We were just about to leave, too, but we need to say bye to Pay first," I replied, leaning in to give my mom a hug. My dad took the cue and shook Gia's hand and said goodbye.

"It was nice to finally meet you, Gia," Mom said when I pulled away. She leaned in to hug Gia, surprising me.

"You too, Mr. and Mrs. Foster."

"Oh, no. None of that." Mom released her and stepped back with a dismissive wave. "Please, call me Julie. And you're still coming tomorrow, correct? Possibly earlier for the magazine pictures?"

"I'm sure I'll get the details when I chat with Kass later."

"Okay then. Goodnight, you two. See you tomorrow."

I moved my hand to Gia's back as we watched my parents cross the lobby to leave. "You just sent it, right?"

"Yeah, why?"

There was a chance it was a coincidence. But there was a bigger chance it wasn't. "I'm pretty sure I know who hired you."

She eyed me curiously until she realized I was still looking toward the entrance then her eyes widened. "Your mom? I thought that as soon as her phone beeped too because I'd just sent the pic, but that could be a total coinci—"

"Possibly," I interrupted. "But that's not really her phone. She'd dropped that one on Sunday when we were at bunch and said she had bought it as an emergency backup after forgetting her phone somewhere. And you said that the referral client was Maria, right?"

"Yes. Are they close enough to discuss this kind of thing?"

"If they had thought something was happening, yes. To protect Pacey. But it could also be like you thought. She got the info and decided to throw a safety net out there for protection, just in case."

"Wow," she replied.

"Yeah."

"It fits. There was never an alternate phone number, so she was screening. And as much as Viv and I were tempted, we weren't going to try and hack the bill pay portal linked to our site. We knew the sender account was fake since the client wanted anonymity from the start, but after the first payment cleared, I wasn't as concerned."

I moved my hand up her back and turned her body against mine. "I'll have to find out why."

"What do you mean? You want to ask her?" She straightened up.

"Of course. I need to know if there was a reason or not. I'm surprised she didn't tell me about it."

"How do you plan on finding out without giving me away as Duplicity?"

"I won't mention you or Duplicity."

She shook her head and closed her eyes. "Just by asking you're telling her everything. How could you possibly know that she had hired someone otherwise? The only conclusion she can draw is that you know the person on the other end. And that would naturally lead her to me."

"I can swipe the phone again or say I saw the picture tonight."

"And she could just as easily lie and say she'd taken the pictures herself, even if most of them are saved on it—which I doubt. And even then, she'd have every reason to act offended by your questions." The last words whipped from her mouth like they wanted to hit me, and her narrowed eyes were practically tossing daggers.

"You really care that she knows after the job is already done?"

"And you don't care?"

"No, but I know my mom. She wouldn't say anything about your job."

"That's beside the point. The fact that you're willing to give me up because you're a tad pissed that your mom didn't tell you about her suspicions is the real problem."

"That's not it," I said, a little sad that she would think me that petty.

"Then why not just leave it alone? Guy didn't cheat. He's clean. Your mom got the reassurance she needed before the wedding."

"And you got paid," I added bitterly.

She scowled and backed away from my touch.

Shit. What the hell am I doing? "I'm sorry. That's not at all how I feel. Look, I'm not sure why this is frustrating me." I touched her arm, trying to ease her anger. "I'm not pissed that she didn't tell me. I'm just really curious to know why, if there was a more specific reason she hired someone."

Gia bit her lip. The tension in her brow faded and her eyes softened, but she looked away from me. "I understand that this job involved your family, and I know that it hasn't been easy for you. But it hasn't been easy for me either." A tiny, sad smile drew on her lips as her eyes swept back to me. "I'm asking you to leave it alone, to keep my professional identity a secret. If that's too much to ask, tell me, please. I battled the idea of dating when we first met, worried that you'd eventually know, if I could trust you, how you'd react to this job—the possibility of me being the one who ruins your sister's wedding—and to the next job, and any others after … if there was an after."

I reached up to her face, my fingers spreading under the side of her jaw, and she didn't pull away. "You're absolutely right," I admitted with a nod. "It was a gut reaction, please believe that. I want to be with you. I want to support you—your choices, your work. My mom had her reasons. Whatever those reasons were, they aren't my business. So, as long as everyone's happy, everyone's okay, I'm okay with that. I won't ask."

Her eyes gazed up at me and she exhaled a sigh. "Thank you."

"Thank *you*," I repeated, watching her eyebrows scrunch with a silent question. "For not acting on the look I saw in your eyes a minute ago. I thought I was eighty-sixed for sure, buried with the bodies back at my place."

She poked her fingers into my sides as the edges of her lips tipped up the tiniest bit. "That look might have changed, but I wouldn't thank me yet. I still have plans for you."

"Really? It doesn't involve something inflatable, does it?"

She laughed at that one, full and adorable, revealing the kind of smile that made me second-guess anything I'd ever considered beautiful before. My heart stuttered at the sight, stunning me, rendering me speechless and motionless.

"Maybe," she admitted through the last breathy chuckles. Her eyes tracked a few people heading for the front desk, and she dropped the volume and tone of her voice. "You'll have to wait to find out, though. Like your mom said, tomorrow's a big day for everyone. And apparently, I have an annoying sister to talk to."

I slipped my fingers farther back into her hair with a smile. As much as I would have liked to take her home and show her how much she meant to me, prove how much of an idiot I had been for questioning her concerns, there was no way I'd suggest it. We needed to get through the wedding then handle us. "Pretty sure I'm supposed to be here at noon to get ready with the guys, but I'll probably be here early to help Pacey with anything she needs."

"And if Kass wants me here, I guess I'll be here early too. Tell Pacey I said bye, okay?"

"You want me to piss her off tonight too? Part of the plans?" I joked, running my thumb along her cheek. She arched a single brow and I added, "Of course I will. Drive safe, okay? I'll see you tomorrow." I pulled her closer and leaned down, pressing my lips to hers softly before letting her go.

The sway of her hips had my full attention as she crossed the lobby toward the entrance. She attracted other eyes as well, but I couldn't bring myself to care much about that. I was more concerned with replaying our conversation, making sure we were still good. I had been honest about not asking my mom for the truth. That didn't mean I wasn't curious as hell, though.

Maybe there was a way to find out without spilling Gia's identity.

29

Gia

East Bay's clubhouse looked impeccable Saturday morning. I arrived close to eleven—the time Kass had told me to show after I'd bitched her out on the phone the previous night. Her excuse for not telling me about the feature for Destination Bride was that I'd had enough happening and she didn't want to burden me. Pfft. She should have known that kind of news for the boutique was welcome no matter what else was happening. In fact, good news like that might have even helped calm my nerves about taking the final picture of Guy and meeting Mark's parents. I forgave her, of course. The bear claws she promised to bring helped a little.

Besides, more concerning issues involving Mark had taken front row in my mind.

If his mom had hired Duplicity, there was a chance Mark would get hung up on her reasons. I understood his curiosity. They were his family and if she was suspicious, he wanted to know why. But in this case, his curiosity could burn me and my business. He said he understood. He claimed he wouldn't pursue it further. Did I believe him? I hoped I could.

White lilies adorned the entrance, in short and tall vases placed on tabletops, ledges, and the front desk. Small accents of ribbon and lace were also positioned through the main area to lead guests to the gardens and to the ballroom, which was where the reception would take place and also where I was to meet Kass for the Destination Bride interview and pictures. Round tables filled both ends of the room, with the grand dance floor in the center and a wedding party table set along the side wall. Cuts of dusty-rose-colored crepe and lace were placed through the room, splashing color over the high-backed chairs and on the white table cloths. Kass sat at a table closest to the rear exit, eyeing the other set of lobby doors. The ceiling-high windows showcased the shady grounds behind her where the wedding aisle and seats were being assembled again.

I passed a camera guy setting up a light stand in the middle of the dance floor as I moved toward Kass. "Where's the apology you promised?"

Her head of thick brown hair turned, the ends of the flat-ironed strands whipping lightly over her shoulder. She raised a perfectly sculpted brow and a corner of her lips. "I was going to share, but you're late so ..."

"Bullshit, I'm late. And I was going to tell you how stunning you look, but you're a bitch and I'm hangry so ..."

She laughed and adjusted the skirt of her sage chiffon dress to cross her legs. "Good thing I'm joking. I left the claws in my bag on the table there, next to my portfolio. You are now free to tell me how beautiful I am."

It was my turn to laugh at her vanity, even though she did look amazing and deserved any and all the eye-fucking praise she'd get in person and between the pages in the next edition of Destination Bride. Hopefully, they'd all pay attention to the dress that was on Pacey too.

I set my clutch down then snatched a bear claw from her bag while looking at her portfolio spread wide and ready for its close-up. "Ooh. They want to see all the goods, huh?"

"Justin, the photographer ..." she said and Justin's eyes snapped up to her from his light assembly, sporting a megawatt smile on his boy-next-door face. Was he straight out of high school? She winked at him then turned back to me. "He said Mira—the journalist doing the article—went to check on Pacey a little while ago, but we were able to get the portfolio shots already. There are a few other sketches in addition to Pacey's."

"And you didn't go find out if she wanted help into the dress?" I took a bite of the bear claw and moved to sit in the chair across from her but changed my mind, knowing Justin had already eye-fucked her a million times everywhere in the room and I wasn't willing to chance getting stains on my dress—even imaginary ones.

"C'mon, Gia. You really think that low of me?"

"No," I said around another bite of almond deliciousness. "And it wouldn't be so horrible if you offered. You made the damn thing."

"Helping her into it is her mom's job. I shouldn't even be here today. I should have made Aunt Aim come with Viv. They are much better with this stuff."

"Well, she wants you to get the credit you deserve. And Viv had to help with the shop anyway since I'm here. Are you staying for the wedding or are you heading back to work today?"

"Aunt Aim gave me the rest of the day off. I'm hoping the interview is quick and that Justin"—she smiled at him when he looked up again—"can get all the pictures they need now so I can split before the wedding."

"I'm sure he'll do whatever you want for a chance to see your split," I mumbled with an eye roll.

"And I'm sure I'm not the only one who'll be anxious to get outta—" She stood quickly, nearly knocking over her chair, and I immediately knew why.

Pacey stepped into the ballroom, muting all the beauty around her, including Kass. The dress. Her perfect hair and makeup ... She was stunning. The lace filigree trimming that began at the sweetheart bodice split and fanned out down to the floor. It caught the light from the windows, making the fit and flare silhouette glow like something otherworldly.

"Kass, Gia! I'm so happy you're here!"

"Wow, Pacey, you look gorgeous," I said, walking to her to give her a gentle hug, careful not to snag anything.

"It's the dress." She smiled with a laugh. "You two look beautiful too. This is Mira," she added and nodded her perfect head of wavy hair toward the woman at her side dressed in a business button-up tank and sky blue pencil skirt.

"Hi," Mira said, extending her hand for Kass and me to shake. Her wide, alert eyes and soft face and smile were framed by a blunt cut bob that swept right below her chin. She had the look of a fashion magazine journalist nailed. "Thanks for agreeing to come. I've been admiring the dress since Pacey sent us the pictures. Your design is phenomenal, the ruching at the waist ..." She pointed at the gathered material. "Truly exquisite."

"Thanks," Kass replied, and I was surprised to see a tad of color form in her cheeks. "I try my best to give the bride exactly what she wants."

"And you did, one hundred percent. This day wouldn't be the same without this dress," Pacey praised.

Mira moved over beside Kass. "We'll get the pictures and then I just have a few questions for you, if that's okay?"

"Sure," Kass said, following Mira as she moved to the center of the room to check Justin's setup.

"He was a little torn up last night, Gia," Pacey said, pursing her lips a tad, though she couldn't hide the small smile in them.

Realizing she wasn't talking about Guy, I bit my lip and looked toward the photo setup. There was something pulling me to spill my guts to her, the secrets I could never tell fighting for their own freedom, probably because I wanted to be closer to her now that I was a part of Mark's life. Or maybe it was the fact that she looked like an angel in that dress, and who really wanted to lie to an angel? Stupid wedding dress.

"I know. I was too. We're just new, ya know? Gotta work some things out." It wasn't exactly a lie. All relationships have issues. Ours just started wildly different than most.

"That's a good thing." She turned toward the back window, watching the club staff continue to place chairs. "Love's never as easy as most people would like, and it's rarely defined by the times that matter the most. The hard times. The times we fight about where to go on holidays or what house to buy. We like to base everything on the good. The positive. The perfect times, like proposals and weddings and shiny presents. When everything goes right." She sighed and tapped the back of the chair. "We shy away from the uncomfortable hardships, the times we cry. But I think the bad days are the most important. They show the strength and truth of the relationship, build the foundation, patch the pieces that don't fit quite right, make people grow together." She shifted her body to face me, the lace and tulle swaying with her. "Nothing's ever perfect. Nothing should ever be perfect."

"Wow." I nodded. "Deep stuff. Tell me those are your vows," I said, only half joking. Her excitable personality had taken a backseat on her wedding day. But I guessed seeing the final product after months of planning could have a calm, contemplative effect on a person.

"I wish," she teased back, though there wasn't a trace of humor on her perfectly made up face.

"Oh, I'm so glad you didn't start without me!" Pacey's mom scooted into the room, drawing everyone's attention. Her beige, knee-length taffeta dress had a scooped neckline and soft ruffles at the gathered waist that gradually smoothed out, giving her a classic Jackie O look. "I had to take a quick call from distant family about directions."

"We were just about to get started, Mrs. Foster," Mira said before turning her eyes to Pacey.

"Right, let's do this," Pacey said, grinning softly at me before shuffling onto the dance floor.

I barely moved as I watched Mira and Kass stage Pacey and the dress in several spots around the room for Justin to take multiple shots. For some reason, I couldn't shake the unease Pacey's words and calmness left behind. There was something there, more than friendly relationship advice, but I couldn't put my finger on it.

"Hey," Mark's strong voice said from somewhere behind me.

I spun around as he entered, the ballroom door closing behind him. One hand gripped the hook of a hanger at his shoulder, draping a garment bag over his back. "Hey."

"You look beautiful. Purple suits you." He eyed all of me with a smile, then placed his other hand at my waist and leaned in for a kiss.

His lips were soft and inviting regardless of how quickly they pulled away. We weren't the focus of the eyes in the room, but I wasn't about to push for something more, especially when those lips could easily make me toss all etiquette into a raging fire of incivility. "Thank you. It's one of my favorites. I have a thing for the ombré look." I smoothed a hand down the gradual change in color.

His eyes shifted, peering around me to take in the activity in the room. His mom glanced back at us and waved him over.

"I'm going to say hi real quick. You wanna—"

I shook my head. Even with others around, he needed some time with his mom and sister without me in tow. "No, I'll hang back here unless they need me for something."

"Okay." He scrubbed his hand through his hair and walked toward the photo session. The pictures stopped long enough for Mark to give Pacey a quick kiss on the cheek, say hi to everyone, then speak to his mom briefly.

I watched him, studying the way he stood—tall and confident—the way he smiled—soft and genuine. My stomach fluttered with excitement, ready to skip past our awkward start and move on with him, with whatever he wanted with me. Just from looking at him, I knew life was about to get a whole lot better.

Shifting my focus, I caught Kass staring past Pacey at me. Her head tilted and her mouth popped open, silently forming the word "Aw." I narrowed my eyes.

Mark moved into view, blocking Kass' stare. "I'm gonna change. The rest of the wedding party should get here pretty soon. The guys were bumped back so they wouldn't walk in on this."

"Smart," I said absently, thinking again of Pacey's words and glancing her way. "Hey, I wanted to ask you something."

"No," he responded flatly.

"You don't even know what I was—"

"It can't be good with that look in your eye. I already know that look is trouble."

I screwed up my face. "I—you—"

"And now you're thinking we haven't been together long enough for me to know. Tell me this, what is my look telling you right now?" One of his eyebrows rose as his gaze ran down my body. His lower lip pulled slightly between his teeth.

Oh. I definitely knew that look. Suddenly, the ballroom's temperature soared.

A mischievous smile spread across his lips. "See."

"Well, yes. That look is hard to mistake," I admitted with my own cocky grin. "I see it a lot."

He laughed. "We'll be talking more about my look later. But I'm guessing yours involved something that should already be finished."

"Well, yeah, kinda. But I can't ignore it." When he only responded with a silent nod, I continued, "Pacey's oddly calm today, and when we were talking a bit ago, she seemed ... I don't know. Distant. She was talking about love and all, but it was as if she were detached."

"It's probably cold feet. I'm willing to bet it happens to most people, wondering if they are making the right decision since it's one of life's biggest."

I pressed my lips together with a nod. "That makes sense, but I'm not sure. Our conversation just took an odd turn."

"Gia, I'm sure it's nothing. She seems happy enough right now," he added and both of us watched her smile for Justin's camera, teeth and dress sparkling brightly.

"You're probably right." *Her words, though.*

"Okay, I'll see you in a bit." His lips kissed my cheek as Pacey's words continued to tumble around in my head.

The difficult times. The times we fight. "Mark?"

"Yeah?" He stopped just before he walked away.

"After we met, when we talked about you approving of Guy, didn't you mention them not really fighting? Or her never really telling you about any fights with him, where she probably normally would?"

"Yeah. She's never mentioned them fighting that I know of. Why?"

"Just ... thinking. Maybe they're perfect after all."

Too perfect.

30

Mark

I left Gia standing in the ballroom, the odd, far-off expression still plain on her face. What she was thinking had me slightly worried, but I wasn't about to get into the conversation with Pacey in the room, especially if it was what I thought it was about. The job was over. Done. The last picture was taken the previous night. And even though I was itching to confirm my mom was the one who had hired Duplicity and find out the reason why, I'd promised Gia that I wouldn't pursue it further.

So the question was, what exactly was going through her head? She could be right about Pacey. If she thought she was acting oddly, cold feet was the most obvious problem. Marriage is huge, and maybe Pacey finally realized she jumped in too fast. Our quick hello inside the ballroom wasn't nearly long enough to see how she was acting. I'd have to talk to her when she went back to the dressing room before everything started.

I finished rolling the sleeves of the white dress shirt then pulled on my gray linen pants and matching vest, grateful Pacey and Guy had been sensible enough to forgo the full jacket suits and went with a more relaxed look for the groomsmen. As I slipped the pink-colored tie around my neck, my mind started wandering back to Gia and how much I'd wanted to haul her into the changing room with me. That purple dress she had on was so hot, formal enough for the wedding and sexy enough to make me wish the day was over and I was slipping her out of it and into my bed.

A door slammed somewhere out in the hallway, more hostile than accidental. I moved around the standing mirror and yanked the door open, unsure what would warrant the noise in the wedding hallway. A pink-colored bridesmaid dress swayed hurriedly down the hall. A tamed mess of brown hair was tacked on the back of the girl's head, its wild thickness struggling against the pins securing each section. Judging by the hair, her tall frame, and the stomp in her step, I knew it was Edena. Definitely not Leah or Maria. My brain quickly dismissed the scene, but my gut wouldn't let me retreat back into the room. After all, she had threatened Guy at his interview. That information might not have been enough to make me follow her, because technically it was none of my business, but if there was a chance at something or somebody ruining this day for Pacey, it became my business.

I moved my bare feet down the cool polished floor, staying close to the wall and listening to the sounds from the lobby fade as noises from the nearby kitchen rose. I slowed before reaching the end of the hall, questioning my motives, my plans. What would following her accomplish? Maybe she just needed a drink of water. Or maybe she was fetching something for Pacey. But then I heard her talking.

"No, I'm not waiting for you to get here. Tell me now."

I palmed the wall and peered around the corner, spotting Edena pacing halfway down the deserted hall. Her head jerked back and forth while holding the phone to her ear, looking nervous or anxious. When her body turned in my direction, I lurched back out of view.

"And you didn't think it was important to tell me that some bridal magazine was doing a feature on your wedding day? I'm supposed to know about any authorized publications. That's my job." Her heels clicked sharply back and forth along the floor. "I don't care. You should have called me even if you found out two minutes ago so I could try to check all their info. I don't like surprises. They might be all about dresses, but I'm betting your name was really appealing."

I clenched my jaw, biting back the temptation to squash her anger before she brought the whole wedding down.

"I know that ... Yes, but ..." Her words lightened. "No, I'm still pissed you ditched dinner last night. When you get here, you're making up for it ... I don't care ... Hurry then."

Those last words made less sense. Something grabbed my shoulder from behind and I nearly jumped to the ceiling.

The sound of a sweet, familiar chuckle followed. "If you're spying on your next victim, Serial Killer, you really suck at it." Gia's voice was low, conspiratorial.

I turned my body slightly and pressed a finger to my lips to quiet her. Her small grin disappeared and her eyebrows drew together, instantly recognizing my seriousness.

"Just text me when you get here." Edena's heels clicked closer and I looked around quickly, knowing there was no time to run down the hallway or duck into a closer room.

The only escape option was our connection. I grabbed Gia and spun her against the wall, pinning her body and crashing my lips to hers. Her hands slid up my chest, my neck, holding tightly as I pushed my tongue inside her mouth. My focus was split, half on Gia and how my body surged from the contact with her, and half on the sound of Edena's shoes clicking around the corner. Maybe it was closer to an eighty-twenty split because Gia sucked on the end of my tongue and—

Footsteps stopped right behind me as Gia and I continued what had the potential of being one of the hottest hallway make-out sessions. Edena cleared her throat, but wisely chose not to speak. Her steps began again, a bit more hurried, then disappeared for good when a door snapped closed.

I bit Gia's lip and tugged it lightly with a little growl before pulling away. "Goddamn."

Her face was flushed, her dark lipstick smeared around the edges of her plump parted lips. "Good ... cover," she whispered, letting her hands slide down my chest, fingers trailing affectionately over the vest. "You look sexy as hell in this, but not sexy enough to stop me from asking why you were spying on Edena."

I ran my hands down to her hips, squeezed, then backed up fully to get my bearings. After that kiss, I couldn't think straight. The hall was clear. Distant noises came from the kitchen and bodies moved way down by the lobby, but there was no other movement. "Thanks. And I wasn't planning to spy on her, believe me." I glanced down at my bare feet, and she did also.

She giggled and pulled her hand up to cover her mouth. "Guess not."

I smiled at her, in awe of her. Everything about her.

"You gonna tell me what's up? Or you just gonna stare at me with googly eyes, Happy."

"I'm definitely Happy now. Looking at you, being with you, touching you," I admitted, gently pinching her chin lightly between my thumb and my bent index finger, fighting every urge to kiss her again. Somehow I knew I'd never have enough of her.

Her eyes widened at my words then glossed over with a dreamy stare. "Still not gonna let you off the hook."

I laughed. She was right. Not exactly the time or place to really talk the way I wanted to. The day wasn't about us anyway. It was

Pacey's day, and I had to make sure it wasn't going to get fucked by Edena and some weird publicist issues. "I heard a door bang, saw her out here, so I followed. After what we'd heard at the interview, I was curious."

"Curious?"

"More so when I heard her ripping into Guy on the phone. At least, I'm pretty sure it was Guy." Voices sounded in the hall toward the kitchen. "Let's move." I grabbed her hand and led her to the room set up for the groomsmen then into the bathroom sitting area inside, closing us in the space.

I leaned against the slim vanity ledge and offered her the studded armchair. She stood in front of me instead then slipped the clutch off her wrist and dropped it on the counter before grabbing a tissue from a box at my side and peering into the mirror behind me to clean the smudges from her mouth. "So she was mad at Guy again? Did you hear why?"

"The bridal magazine. She was pissed she didn't know about it ahead of time so she could do her job."

"I saw her peek into the ballroom a few minutes ago as they were finishing up Kass' interview, but she didn't come in. Do you think she'll calm down before the ceremony starts?"

"She mentioned them meeting when he got here, so, I don't know, maybe he'll calm her down. But she also said she was mad that he'd ditched dinner last night. That had me wondering whether it was him or not because everyone was here for the rehearsal dinner."

Gia hooked her hands on her hips and tilted her head back, squinting at the ceiling. "Ditched dinner?" Her focus returned to me. "But you were positive it was him before that?"

"Well, she said his name was the obvious draw for the magazine. So, yeah, I thought it had to be him. What are you thinking about?"

After a few moments of her biting her bottom lip and tapping her fingers on her hips, she whispered, "Holy shit." Her eyes fluttered as her head shook back and forth. "Holy shit."

"Holy shit what?"

She was suddenly really interested in the floor, staring downward with a hardened gaze as if she were cramming for a final on carpet patterns.

"Do you think she's pissed enough to wreck the wedding?" I replied to her silence.

Gia stepped closer, looking up. Her brown eyes were wide, their lashes fanning up under her brows. "You're not going to like what I'm thinking." Her body pressed against the slight bend of my knees until I spread my legs apart, making room for her to stand between my thighs. There was a cleverness to her expression that made pieces click into place.

"You're thinking about the job still," I said, having a hard time keeping my irritation in check. "It's over, Gia. Guy's clean. We were all here last night. There's no way he was out with anyone else, so I have no idea what the hell Edena meant. It can't be related to the job."

"I have to tell you something, and the idea of it is kind of out there. I mean, it's somewhat taboo, but I know it happens a lot," she said with a tiny, manic chuckle that fizzled into a stone cold serious murmur. "I think it might be the truth."

I sighed. "Gia, I don't think I want to hear anything right now, except that Edena won't fuck this day up for Pacey."

"She might have already. Well, she and Guy." Her words were soft as she gauged my reaction. When I didn't respond, she continued, "So, the night of the adult store." A tinge of pink crept across her cheeks and my mind went exactly where hers did, thinking of her in my car, legs hooked over my shoulders, moaning … She coughed a bit then continued, "My lies that night may have been a tad more than just picking up a fake bachelorette party order. I mean, you obviously know I was there to spy on Guy. But when … after … you and I …"

I grabbed her sides and pulled her closer, amused by her sudden shyness. "After I had the most incredible takeout in my car."

She nodded and bit her lips together to stifle a broad smile. "Yes, after that … You had Guy's phone that night."

"Ah. And you switched it with yours on purpose." More pieces falling together.

"It was too tempting. It looked like my burner. There were no other leads. So I chanced a peek. I only had time to scroll through some of his text threads. None of them showed anything suspicious, but I wasn't surprised since Pacey probably has regular access to it and he'd have to be pretty stupid to leave any evidence there. Anyway, Edena's thread was normal, too. Normal business texts about interviews. Normal family texts about *dinners*." She stared at me like I was supposed to know something.

"And?"

"He's always having dinner at their family's house, often without Pacey. And Edena lives there …"

"Wait." It sounded like she was implying … "Are you seriously suggesting that 'dinner' is a code for …?"

"That is definitely what I'm suggesting."

31

Gia

"They're family. Families have dinner all the time." Mark shrugged with a head shake, totally ignoring my theory. My theory about something completely possible, a little twisted but completely possible.

"They're a step family. Her dad. His mom. If I remember correctly, they married around five years ago. Edena's only like a year older than Guy, right? So they would have been like sixteen and seventeen when they moved in together, or even younger depending on how long their parents dated. It all could have started well before Guy met Pacey." I was thinking out loud now, working through some details as Mark squirmed in front of me.

"You were right. This is out there," he said, his denial slipping as the idea started to settle.

"Not too far. Could have happened when they first met, or maybe later. One lonely or drunk night. Parents asleep. Their compulsion maybe not even disguised with trivial excuses."

"Uh. Just ... no more details."

"I can't help it. Look at it this way, if our parents had married and you and I were in the same house ... not technically related ..." I looked into his eyes, wondering if I could have denied myself then. Probably not.

He chose to ignore my analogy, but it obviously got him thinking. "Okay, say it is true, why continue it all? Or why propose to another woman? That makes no sense."

It was my turn to shrug. "Love's a bitch. Sometimes you just don't know who you'll fall for."

"You're suggesting it's more than stepsiblings with benefits? That he probably loves her and Pacey both?"

"I'm sure it's not the first time in history that one person has loved two people. And with the business I'm in, I'm by no means making excuses because there are *none* for cheating as far as I'm concerned. But he obviously has enough feelings for Pacey to want to marry her. She could also be the safe bet, knowing that he can't have who he might truly want. I mean, technically he could have Edena, but if he's worried about his newfound fame and how that might look to a larger amount of people, he would have to disappear from public eye, right? Not sure how that would work. Being in the spotlight only added to the complications, I'm sure. And really, Edena looks miserable all the time. It makes you wonder if she's always that way or only around them."

"I think we're getting too far ahead. Let's back up a bit. We don't even know—"

A door opened and closed in the main room and voices flooded into the area.

"Sounds like Evin and Rick," Mark whispered. His gaze swept from the sitting room door back to me. "If any of this is true, how can we prove it in less than an hour?"

"I'm not sure," I admitted. "We'd have to have something solid for the wedding to be called off. Most brides won't buckle to catastrophes easily, even if the venue catches fire. And I already ditched the job's burner phone last night."

"So we won't be able to report this to the client or to Pacey under your business anonymity," he acknowledged.

"Right. No anonymity. What—"

A couple of hard knocks hit the door.

Mark stared at me, eyes wide.

I whimpered sexily then whispered, "Ooh," loud enough to be heard outside.

"Shh," a voice said.

Mark's brows scrunched at me and I smiled, pressing my hands onto the vanity ledge on either side of his butt and pounding repetitively, just hard enough to make the sounds heard. "Ah, yes." I moaned.

His head dropped to the side of my neck then, and a soft chuckle pushed his breath along my skin. "Shh, quiet," he said in a loud whisper, catching on and playing along. His lips skimmed my neck and moved closer to my ear. "They better leave soon or we'll really start making noises."

I smiled as his teeth pinched down on the outer edge of my ear.

A couple of hard laughs bounced around the other room then a door closed at last.

"Oops. That probably wasn't the smartest idea for a cover since we need to go stalk Edena to see when Guy arrives," I said, backing away from him a little.

"Wait." He tightened his grip on my waist. "I'm not exactly thrilled about pulling some covert op at my sister's wedding. I hope this day turns out like any other, but it's probably best to assume the worst, where my sister ends up crushed. I love her and want to make sure that she's aware, but I'm also worried about hurting her, even if it's indirectly."

"That's exactly why people hire Duplicity. I'm not sure how I'll handle it if everything's true, but I'll get it done."

"No. You already did your job, and keeping it a secret is an important part of how you run your business. If what we find out is bad, I'll break the news. It won't be easy, but if it means you aren't hurt today too, that's what's going to happen."

I smiled solemnly. His intentions were honest and the very definition of chivalrous. All concerns of him searching for answers about his mom's involvement and possibly outing me in the process washed away, like writing in the sand. He had me swooning … at a wedding. I never thought there'd be a day that would happen. Granted, it was a wedding we were likely about to wreck, but still. "Thank you."

"I never want to hurt you." His hands lifted to my neck, fingers sliding under my jaw and into my hair. "Now we need to kiss, for luck or something."

I leaned closer and placed my hands on his firm chest, feeling the soft linen of his vest under my fingertips as he held my face, guiding me. Our lips met, tender and calm. He pressed in, opening his mouth, his tongue coaxing me to do the same. The rhythm was a living dream, never waxing or waning. My chest ached at the sweetness, at his touch, so gentle and loving. Loving me. Caring. He was willing to do so much, willing to protect my identity and my job. All of it made my head spin and my heart hammer for him.

After pulling away, I couldn't help but to stare into his eyes for several moments, lost by what he'd become to me and seeing the promise of more between us.

"So what's the plan for this? Edena's probably in the room with Pacey right now if Guy's not here yet. Do you want to go in or wait outside for Guy to show?" he asked, slipping his hands back down to my sides and smoothing out my dress.

"You should go in to talk to Pacey since you haven't spent any time with her. That might also flush Edena out of the room. I'll hang near the lobby and wait for Guy to show, then tail 'em to see where they meet up."

"Sounds good. Let's just hope that nothing happens today except drunk people and bad dancing."

I laughed lightly, attempting to ignore what I truly thought. He could hope all day long, but I was pretty positive something was going down between the stepsiblings. The pieces fit.

"Let me throw on my shoes then we can go," he said, guiding my body so he could stand fully.

I grabbed my clutch, and after he checked his reflection in the mirror, wiping a small amount of lipstick transfer from his mouth, we moved into the main room where he quickly slid his feet into socks and a pair of black oxfords. Within a second of stepping out into the hallway, a couple of throats cleared, purposely doing a poor job of camouflaging chuckles.

Men. Always such boys. As Mark glanced back at the waiting duo with a chin tilt and a cocky bro-code smirk of recognition, I rolled my eyes and kept moving toward the lobby. But there was no shame in my walk. Even if Mark and I had had a quick hookup, pride would still put the sexy sway in my hips. He was all mine, and my God, that thought was thrilling.

"Good luck with Pacey," I whispered, sliding my hand down his bicep and over the roll in his sleeve to his bare forearm, knowing our audience was still watching from down the hall. "Text me updates. I'll do the same."

"Okay," he replied then planted a chaste kiss to my forehead.

I didn't wait for him to enter Pacey's dressing room to start my march to the lobby. Finding and tracking Guy was essential to uncovering the truth and revealing it before Pacey made the biggest mistake of her life.

The lobby had filled up with more activity. Employees in white shirts and beige pants bustled about, tending to last minute touches on displays, while penguin-suited kitchen staff moved in and out of the ballroom to finalize placings and centerpieces. Out front, valets gathered, preparing for guest arrivals. And at the other side of the building, through the back retracting doors, the altar had been set up, an arch of branches woven with strands of white crepe and calla lilies throughout. All the wooden folding chairs had also been placed, with pillars of the same height along the aisle row, capped with matching crepe and lilies. Aside from the poised Mira and photog Justin setting up a position just outside the retracted doors, no other guests had arrived. There was still time. Still hope.

I moved around a bit as I waited, not wanting to attract attention, even to play into being some creepy stalker guest that arrived an hour early. Wait ... technically ... Oh, semantics.

My phone chimed a text, so I pulled it from my clutch and got cozy beside a ficus by the ballroom. *Maybe I should have worn green instead of purple.*

Edena just left. Gonna follow her.

No sign of Guy—I started to text the reply until a blond swoosh of hair passing the window caught my eye. When Guy's lithe body appeared through the retractable doors, I jumped closer to the ficus and deleted and retyped hastily. **Guy here. Watching him now. Heading toward kitchen.** I pushed away from the plant, batting wayward branches from my face, then shuffled down the hall, maintaining a safe distance behind his long strides.

My phone chimed again and I scrambled to silence the short sound while ducking into the closest door alcove.

Wow! That could be fun. I was only planning to break his legs. Heading to lobby.

Huh? I scrolled up to my message. **Guy here. Wasting him now. Heading toward Kraken.** I snorted, unable to control my laughter. The humor extinguished pretty quickly, though, as the threat Mark made registered. *Shit.* I hadn't fully thought of what might happen if we actually discovered the truth because he hadn't fully acknowledged the possibility.

Guy took a turn under at the stairwell exit sign to the right of the kitchen doors. **Back stairs**, I texted Mark then turned my phone to vibrate and jogged down the hall, slowing only when a few employees passed by.

She's on the elevator. No floor numbers. Just got waved down by my mom.

We lost her. I pushed the heavy door to the stairs open and eased inside. Rushed footsteps echoed above me and I moved to follow. Only, the clacking of my heels carried just as heavily through the hollow space. I flicked them off and continued up the cool tiles, careful to stick close to the wall. As soon as a door clicked shut, I hauled ass up to the next flight and quietly cracked the door open.

Seeing no movement, I rushed through and peeked around the corner of the closest hallway of guest rooms. Aside from a fully stocked cleaning cart, the hall was empty. Nothing.

4thFloor. I texted the update with my slingback platforms and clutch dangling in hand. Acting on the worry that he'd already entered a room, I crept past a few doors. Well, I did until my stomach twisted at the sudden thought of him being another floor up. If I'd lost him, any chance of finding the truth was gone.

Maybe, I added to the text hastily then continued to look around. The only thing I heard was a rich voice humming from somewhere inside the room with a propped door and the housekeeping cart parked outside.

Before I had the chance to turn around, a messy stack of brown hair and a floor-length chiffon bridesmaid dress moved through the sand-colored hallway like a dusty rose desert tornado.

Edena's eyes were pointed toward the phone in her hands, giving me enough time to take two steps and launch my body through the open door. I stumbled, nearly falling onto the carpet. The humming continued, louder now. The owner of the voice had to be in the same room, but the fear of Edena disappearing again outweighed getting caught by the maid. So I pressed my face to the doorjamb and peeked out just enough to see her stalking straight toward me.

Sheer panic rocked my body, spiking my temperature and forcing terror sweat from every pore.

Don't let this be her room. Don't let this be her room.

I scrambled farther inside but instantly regretted that decision as soon as I caught sight of Guy standing outside on the balcony, looking down on the wedding area. I backtracked and rushed into the small bathroom, almost smacking into the well-cushioned backside of a lady, who was bent over the toilet with a scrub brush clutched in a rubber-gloved hand, a gray bun of hair fastened atop her head, and earbuds plugged in her ears. She hummed a few new notes, and I scooted behind her to the only place I could hide: the shower. A shallow pool of suds and water at the bottom of the tub covered my feet and the smell of bleach cleanser stung my nose, but I was thankful for the thick curtain to hide behind.

"I thought you'd beat me up here." Guy's voice cut through the maid's humming.

"I did," Edena's voice snapped. "But I had to go grab a Coke for my rum since I drank everything in the mini bar last night waiting for you."

She had a room here the night before? I tucked my phone into my clutch, pressed my hands flat to the tile wall, and leaned my ear close to the sliver of open curtain, attempting to tune out the humming and sloshing toilet water.

"Last night was impossible. You knew I couldn't disappear from my rehearsal dinner. What the hell do you want me to do?"

"I want you to tell me why the fuck some goddamn magazine was just downstairs taking pictures without me knowing about it first."

"I didn't know about that until this morning. She forgot to tell me. She's had a million other things to think about—"

"She's had a million things to think about? Oh, how horrible," Edena cut him off then laughed harshly.

The toilet flushed and the maid hummed on, standing upright and removing her gloves on the other side of what suddenly felt like a very thin layer of material. I inhaled a fearful breath, hit with the pungent bleach aroma. The urge to cough and gag was fierce, but I held it off, slapping a hand over my mouth, letting the tears well inside my eyes. The sink turned on and I released my breath, watching through the crack as the maid wiped it down.

"I would have told you if I'd known. I'm sorry."

"Show me how sorry," Edena replied, her voice almost too low for me to hear.

"There isn't time, and the maid ..."

"You owe me. And I don't care if she sees."

"Tell her to leave, then maybe ..."

An age-spotted bare hand slipped through the curtain, and I scrambled my slippery feet to the back of the tub. While I was worried about being seen, I'd neglected to think about a fate nearly as bad. Her hand wrapped around the faucet and twisted, and the shower head spurted to life. I held in a gasp and pulled my clutch and shoes behind my back, instantly protecting my phone as hot water pelted the front of my dress. *Mother fuck!*

Her hand lifted to the shower head and rotated, spraying me from the neck down. Even though I was drenched, with no extra clothes to change into, a pang of hope still weaseled its way through my gut at the thought of not being caught. She must have been too distracted, must have done the routine a million times and was too complacent to even care. But that hope was squelched with a big bucket full of "nope" when the maid's face peered around the curtain.

Her green eyes widened and she grabbed her chest with a loud, raspy gasp. I held my free hand up in surrender and took a step forward out of desperation, forgetting the water that immediately pelted my face. I sputtered and backed off, pulling my fingers to my lips, pleading for her silence. Her thick brows furrowed. But before she could make a choice, Edena's voice cut into the room.

"Are you done in here?"

I almost pissed myself. If she caught me, if she saw that I was spying on her, all hell would break loose before I even got the chance to tell Mark or Pacey. I stepped back as far as I could, pressing my body against the shower wall, my feet almost slipping on the bottom curve of the tub.

The maid's sizable figure blocked the opening of the curtain, but she couldn't block Edena's loud voice. I cringed for her when I saw her remove her earbuds.

"I said, are you finished in here?" The tone of Edena's voice was so stern, I cringed again. Decapitation would have been less painful.

The maid's hand grabbed the curtain and I inhaled another breath, horrified at the chance of being thoroughly exposed. But the hand only yanked the curtain fully closed.

Phew.

"I'm finished in here, but I haven't finished the room," her raspy voice answered.

"You're finished," Edena snapped.

"Yes, ma'am. Let me just grab the new towels for you." She never looked back into the shower, only scooped up the dirty towels and moved out into the entryway.

"If you'd like to step out here a second," the maid said, followed with an exaggerated throat clearing, "you can also choose whatever I have for the mini bar."

Oh! A signal.

I eased around the curtain then slid my wet feet toward the door, the water dripping from my dress landing on the tiles in deafening tiny splashes. Guy stood in the entry, one hand pressed to the top of the doorframe, facing the hall where Edena and the maid stood by the cart.

The maid bent and grabbed one towel slowly, stalling. "I'm sorry I don't have all the mini bar items. I could go and bring some back."

Using her diversion, I backed toward the balcony. My clutch buzzed, alerting me to a text message. *Mark. If he could see me now.*

"No, we can do without," Edena replied curtly.

"Edena," Guy uttered in an irritated tone, standing straighter. "Time's ticking here."

I hastened my backward steps, clipping the arm of a desk chair with my thigh and instantly biting down on my lip to stifle a pained grunt. Luckily, he'd left the sliding glass cracked enough for my wet body to slip through without much noise.

Gia, the super soaked sleuth. I had to admit that the alliteration sounded pretty catchy.

I stepped close to the balcony's side railing and looked over, letting the humid breeze whipping up from the ground smack the reality of the fourth floor in my face. It may as well have been the hundredth floor. If it had only been the second, I could have pulled off the patented cheater jump maneuver. At least I had wet clothes on, and that was better than naked balcony traversing. But otherwise my luck still sucked. Naturally, I blamed the wedding ... which was actually due to start really soon even though the setup below remained empty, oddly enough. Early birds always happened, no matter the occasion, so it was surprising that there wasn't a single ass in a seat with a set of gaping eyes locked on the wet chick four floors above.

Edena's and Guy's voices grew louder from somewhere behind the sliding door and the curtain that was drawn halfway—my only cover.

"There's no time," Guy said. "I have to get dressed and—Why is the floor wet?"

"Shut up with your excuses. There's always time for dinner." Edena's voice was husky and stomach churning. *Ew.* They really should have used another code word.

Guy groaned. "Ahh, baby. I can never deny you my meat. It's so good for you."

After choking back an actual gag, I was torn between escaping and attempting to snap some pics. But with the bed so close to the door and the curtain only drawn halfway, I'd surely be seen. Mark would have to believe me. And Pacey. Oh, Pacey. My heart ached for her, for what was about to happen.

I stared mournfully down at the rows of empty chairs and delicate decorations, swung one wet leg after another over the railing, and stretched a hand and a foot toward the neighboring room's railing. But that was nothing but a cruel joke. The gap was entirely too large. I'd have to make an actual leap ... in a sopping wet dress that apparently had the ability to hold water like a damn raincloud.

Water continued to drip down my legs, soaking the narrow balcony ledge, and before I could even plan the most basic of jumps, my feet slipped.

32

Mark

As mother of the bride, my mom looked perfect. Great dress. Beautiful makeup. But while everyone else's view of her would be just that, I could see turmoil the moment I saw her eyes. They were tired and weary. I'd seen it when I'd first arrived and was quick to shrug it off as wedding emotions. But as I halted my steps in front of her, I knew something was up and I forgot all about Edena disappearing into the elevator.

"I have to talk to you," she started, her voice coming out in an exasperated sigh. "There are a lot of calls I still need to make, but since Pacey's going to be a bit busy here in a minute, I should be the one to tell you."

"Okay," I replied, confused as to where the conversation was going.

"No, you must not have heard me. I'm here for the Pernell & Foster wedding," a woman's voice called from the lobby's front desk.

"Ma'am, please," an attendant's voice followed, a whisper by comparison, then dropped off completely.

"You look so handsome in this suit. Gia's a lucky girl," Mom said, stepping in front of me as I tried to decipher what the issue was at the front desk. She smoothed a hand down my vest and pressed her lips together with a nod. "I need to go handle some things, but I have to tell you …"

My phone buzzed in my hand and I glanced at it, seeing Gia's text about being on the fourth floor.

"The wedding is canceled," Mom said, letting her hand fall from my vest and taking a step back.

"What?"

"I can't really explain right now. I have to keep making calls and turning away the people who couldn't be reached. Your father's busy doing the same."

"Oh wow. That's …" I shook my head, unable to focus on a single thought or question. Was everything true? Did Pacey find out? Or was there some other reason? How could I ask my mom without giving Gia away, without admitting that I knew?

Mom's phone rang just as mine buzzed in my hand again. "Everything's going to be fine. The girls are in with Pacey to keep her company. Give us a few minutes to take care of this stuff then we'll explain."

She walked away without waiting for a response, answering her phone on the way to the front desk.

What is happening?

After reading Gia's last text, there was a possibility that she had lost Guy too. Maybe we wouldn't get any evidence, but there was a chance we didn't need it anyway.

The wedding was off.

I stood by the elevator and stared down the hallway toward the dressing rooms, debating whether I should find Gia or go see Pacey. Since Gia likely didn't know about the cancellation, finding her seemed the logical choice. I took the elevator up to the fourth floor, pacing inside the small box as my worried thoughts continued on a repetitive loop.

The elevator landing area was quiet and empty but voices traveled out from the back hallway. I glanced around the corner and watched a clubhouse maid exit a room and move behind her cart. Her thick body scooted around the end and she grabbed a single towel from the bottom while Edena stepped out beside her.

"I'm sorry I don't have all the mini bar items. I could go and bring some back." She slowly pulled another single towel.

And where was Gia? There was no sign of her at the opposite end of the hall. Was she somewhere else?

I slipped my phone from my pocket and sent a text. ***Where are you?***

Edena towered beside the gray-haired lady. "No, we can do without."

"Edena, time's ticking here," Guy said. There was no denying it was his voice. He should've already met with her and been getting dressed. Unless he already knew the wedding was off.

I inhaled, fighting the urge to run down the hall, bust inside, and demand answers with my fist. There was so much adrenaline pumping my blood that my eyes strained to focus on anything except the color red. But jumping the gun and kicking his ass, no matter how satisfying it would feel, was ridiculous. If they were actually doing something wrong, they wouldn't admit to it. And then I'd look like the asshole who'd just broken a room door and Guy's face.

Their door clicked shut, but the maid remained, staring at the decorative number plate with a look that I assumed held more than a simple annoyance toward guests. With her brows drawing together and her teeth chewing her lips, there was no mistaking worry.

I needed information. And I needed to find Gia. The maid was my best option. I jogged down the hall to her. Her eyes widened and she took a few steps back with my sudden approach.

"No," I said, careful with the volume of my voice. "I need some help. Have you seen a short brunette wearing a dress with different shades of purple?"

Her green eyes narrowed just a tad. "Yes, why?"

"She's my girlfriend and I need to find her. Was she on this floor? Anywhere near the two people in this room?" I nodded to room 426. "I know them too, but I don't want them knowing I'm out here looking for her."

"She's in there. She came into the bathroom while I was cleaning and—"

"She's in there? Do they know?"

"No, they don't. She went to the balcony when they were out here with me."

"Shit. Shit." I paced a few steps and wiped a hand over my mouth. "Do you have the key to this room next door? Is there anyone in there?"

"I'm not supposed to—"

"Please? I really need to help her get out of there."

She nodded, understanding how detrimental the situation was, and pulled a keycard from her pocket. I hovered behind her until the door clicked then I rushed past, the room blurring, my only focus on the glass door. Within a second, I had it open, my eyes scanning the empty balcony and landing on Gia's hands gripping the railing on the opposite side, her body swaying with the struggle to hold on. Everything else fell away.

I hauled my body over the railing, and only then did the grunts and moans from inside the room filter through my tunneled concentration. There was no denying what was happening just behind the layers of curtain. Guy was fucking his stepsister.

He's dead.

With her arms extended above her, Gia glanced over her shoulder and locked eyes with me as I launched myself right beside her. I swung over the railing, not caring if they heard, if they saw. With the better positioning, I grabbed Gia's arms to hoist her up.

"Mark," she whispered. "You shouldn't have—"

"Really?" I asked, hooking my arms around her wet waist and pulling her over the railing. "You can't just let me have this moment? I kinda liked saving you." Even in the face of death, looking like a drowned rat, she was gorgeous. I smiled and watched her pouty lips slowly grin back at me.

"Thank you. But this isn't exactly the best place to let you gloat." Her smeared raccoon eyes shifted toward the back lawn then toward the room. "I'm surprised they didn't hear such a magnificent rescue."

I grinned at her playfulness. "Guess they aren't focused on what's happening out here."

"Right. So how should we ...?" Her body turned as she considered our options of escape.

"I would say the same route, but ..." There was no way I'd risk her falling.

She followed my thoughts while tracking the movement of my eyes toward the sliding glass door. "No. We can't just—"

"Walk through the door."

"There's no way," she whisper yelled. "They'll see us."

"I want to be seen."

"Are you crazy?"

"Feeling a bit, yeah. Now that I was told the wedding is off and that I know this piece of shit is fucking another woman on the day he's supposed to marry my sister."

"It's off?" Her hand wrapped tightly around my arm. "How? Why?"

"My mom told me downstairs. She said they'd explain more later after they finished dealing with the guests. I have no idea if this is the reason. I don't know what Pacey's doing right now. And I'm not sure whether the douche inside even knows yet."

"He doesn't. They were talking about—"

Through the continuous breathy grunts, a familiar message tone beeped from somewhere inside. I knew the sound. Guy's phone.

A groan was fast to follow.

"Don't ... you ... stop," Edena said in loud bursts. "Ah yes!"

"That's it." I couldn't take it anymore. I'd never known a fury like the one building inside. I no longer cared why the wedding was called off, just that it was. That was all that mattered. And as far as I was concerned, if there was another reason—cold feet, another man in Pacey's life—no one would even know. Because for the next week at least, Guy's betrayal would be written in black and blue, on his face for everyone to see. "Let's go."

Gia squeaked and pulled back against my grip, ready to protest, until we locked eyes. Watching her tense look soften, I could tell she saw all the emotion inside me. Her arms went slack and her resolve crumbled.

"I can't duck outta here and pretend this didn't happen, Gia, not even for a minute."

"Please just don't ..." It wasn't a plea to refrain. It was a plea for restraint. Guy was lucky she was here. On one hand, I wanted to wreck him, to make his outsides mirror the mess that Pacey's heart would be. But Gia mattered too. I didn't want to hurt her. If the situation made her uncomfortable ... There was always the next time I ran into him.

I grabbed hold of the door and flung it open the rest of the way, watching Guy clumsily detach himself from Edena and scramble backward.

"What the fuck?" he stuttered out as he slammed back against the wall, almost knocking down the mounted TV.

"Ah!" Edena screamed and spun around in the bed, hastily wrapping her body inside the covers.

Before any more questions could be shouted, any excuses spewed, I pried Gia's hand from my arm and moved her toward the door then stopped in front of Guy with a smile and a clenched fist at my side. I gave him enough time to process what was about to happen, to understand he had no chance to leave the room unscathed, even if he chose to run scared and leave his clothes and bitch behind.

That realization only took a moment, and I reveled in seeing the change snap in his eyes. As soon as it happened, I happily slammed my fist into his face.

His nose cracked and he let out a groan, covering his face and falling backward into the wall again.

"Mark," Gia uttered, calling me back down from the rush, just loud enough to be heard over the noises Edena made as her sheet covered body stumbled over to help Guy.

"Stupid motherfucker," I grunted.

Gia's soft hand wrapped around my forearm and led me outside. "We should go talk to Pay."

Pay. *Fuck.* I was the one who'd have to tell her. Picturing the look in my baby sister's eyes squeezed my insides and made me want to run back to the room so I could drag Guy out by his hair and dump his bashed face at her feet. That feral compulsion was almost too much to ignore.

"Hey." Gia eased her soft hands along the sides of my face when we stepped into the elevator. "I'm with you. He deserves every bit of what you're wanting to do. But I don't want you locked up either. That wouldn't make the day better. Pacey has enough to deal with. Besides, we don't know what is happening with her yet."

I breathed deeply as I listened to her, letting her calmness, her touch, bring me down again. "You're right. Let's go find her."

33

Gia

"**I** can tell her," I offered as Mark and I approached Pacey's dressing room. I was still wet and coming down from one hell of an adrenaline rush, but I was more than willing to tell Pacey what I'd seen upstairs, even if there was a chance at exposing Duplicity. I would do it for Mark. I wanted to help him any way I could, to take away some of the sorrow I'd seen build inside his eyes after the rage had faded.

"No chance," he replied, pulling the pocket square from his vest, pressing it to my dress to dampen it, then gently dabbing the makeup beneath my eyes. "I'd like you to come in with me, though. Or if you'd rather leave to get changed, that's okay. Are you cold?" He tucked the material into his front pocket then placed one hand at my back.

I grinned sadly. "I'm fine. I want to make sure she's okay. You're okay."

He pursed his lips. "Are you worried about me or are you just worried I might kill that fucker if I'm left alone?"

"Both maybe." I chuckled and glanced at the hand that had hit Guy.

He smiled and lifted it for both of us to inspect. "It's fine. And I'll try to control myself. Promise." He took a deep breath and rolled his neck, shifting his focus toward the door. "Okay, I'm ready."

Decorative mirrors lined the inside wall of the dressing room, and a few more were set up at the back, flanking a snack table full of finger foods that looked as though it hadn't been touched.

"Hey," Leah greeted us with Maria at her side. Their dresses had already been discarded for shorts and tanks, and their purses were already slung over their shoulders.

"How is she?" Mark asked as I finally saw Pacey standing close to the window, gazing out over the clubhouse's back lawn with her back to us.

They both spun their updos around to take another brief glimpse. "She's been waiting to talk to him. He hasn't shown yet." Maria was able to hide her anger in her hushed voice but there was no hiding her expression. They knew. Which meant Pacey knew the truth too. How much detail was still uncertain.

"He'll be here in a minute or so. After he gets his clothes on and wipes the blood off his face." Mark scowled.

Both their eyes popped wide-open and their lips instantly curled into approving smiles. "We're hoping to see Edena soon too."

They knew it all.

Maria looked at Pacey one more time. "She's planning to stay with your parents for a while. We'll drop by tomorrow if she wants."

Mark nodded and waited for them to leave before moving across the lengthy room, dodging the plush seats and a table with an unraveled bridal bouquet spread out on top, a few of its loose flowers lying on the floor below.

Pacey pulled some of the tulle from her dress repeatedly through her fingers, her eyes pointed toward the empty seats beyond the windows. Not bothering to turn, she said, "I know how to plan a good one, huh?"

Mark wrapped his arms tightly around her. "I'm sorry, Pay."

"They were upstairs?"

"Yeah," he confirmed, releasing his hold and pulling two chairs close together for them to both sit. "How long have you known?"

"A little while." She sat beside him.

"And you didn't call this all off?"

"No."

"Why?" I piped in, unable to quiet my curiosity. She'd known and yet she'd continued to act like nothing was wrong. Why endure more pain? Why torture herself longer?

She glanced back at me for a moment. "I'm pissed, a little selfish, and maybe a bit foolish. If it was true, I wanted to embarrass him. To really make him feel like the ass he is. I also didn't want to lose the magazine feature. This dress"—she smoothed her hands over the material at her knees—"Kass' dress, deserved to shine whether it made a trip down the aisle or not. Then there was the tiny, stupid part of me that felt like it wasn't true. Maybe I'd find that I was just being paranoid all along, worrying for nothing.

"But I found that wasn't the case by setting my own traps. The only person who really knew was Mom, who helped me hire a specialty PI after Maria leaked some contact info one night." She shot another glance in my direction and grinned ruefully. I immediately locked eyes with Mark. She had hired Duplicity?

"I know it's supposed to be anonymous, but I'm guessing you both know what I'm talking about."

"How did you ...?"

"When Mark told me he ran into you at The District the night he was with Guy and you happened to show for mini-golf the following day, I was curious. Then he told me he ran into you again on Wednesday night when he delivered Guy's phone for me. But I still wasn't one hundred percent until you showed up to the beach and Mom forwarded me that day's picture. The time it was taken, the angle. It put you behind the camera."

"Oh. I'm pretty stellar at this gig apparently," I admitted sheepishly, sneaking a glance at Mark, who lifted the corner of his mouth in a sympathetic grin. *Gia, double O busted.* My gut twisted at the thought of failing, of never being successful.

"No, you absolutely are, Gia. If I wasn't the person who hired you, I wouldn't have known. Besides, one of the pics you took—the mini-golf day—was the one that actually opened my eyes. I was unsure about Guy cheating, having that feeling that something wasn't right but not really knowing who it could be. That picture, though. You caught Guy and me facing each other. I think you were trying to focus on Leah and Maria at Guy's side, but Edena was the person I noticed. The look on her face as she stared at us ... Well, it was far more expressive than her usual pissed off look.

"From there I just pieced more together. We never fought. He went to his parents' and stayed overnight a little too often despite our apartment being a short drive. God, I was so stupid," she said with a strangled sigh, sweeping her fingers under her eyes.

"No, not stupid," Mark said, putting an arm around her. She leaned into him, accepting his comfort as her body shook with sobs. "Not stupid at all. Trusting someone is not stupid. Loving them is not stupid, Pay. He's the stupid one."

I watched as he let her cry in his arms. Maybe the moment should have been just between them, but I was grateful that I had been let in, to see who they were. If I'd had any doubts about him before, they had exploded into bits. He was more than I ever thought possible.

The door opened and Mark's parents came in, quietly observing the room.

Pacey's head popped up from Mark's embrace and she wiped her eyes.

"Everyone's been contacted as far as we know," Julie said, answering Pacey's silent question. She looked at me with a tiny grin, and I backed away a little, giving the family more space.

"Has he come to see you?" Kirk asked, stepping beside Pacey and gently touching her shoulder.

Mark stood from his chair, letting his father take his seat. "No. Gia and I saw them upstairs. He definitely knows it's over now." He took a few steps to stand beside me.

"You stole my finale," Pacey replied to him with a soft laugh that was far from convincing. Even if she'd initially wanted to tell Guy herself, she sounded grateful it hadn't happened that way.

Mark held his hand up to inspect his knuckles. "I'll gladly recreate the high point—"

The door opened again and Guy took a single step inside, not bothering to close the door behind him. His eyes were bloodshot, his nose red and swollen. Both Mark and Kirk straightened up and took their own steps forward—a subtle warning.

"I'm ... I'm really sorry, Pacey. For everything. Can we maybe ... talk."

Pacey stood, her dress spreading out on the floor around her as she pushed her bare shoulders back. "No, Guy. I'd originally planned to talk when you got here, but you didn't even have enough respect to keep your dick in your pants on your wedding day. So, no, I don't want to hear your bullshit."

"I—"

Pacey's hand shot up with her palm to him, halting his words. "I'll be by the apartment to get my stuff sometime this week. If anything's missing or broken, all the local magazines and all the national tabloids will have their fill of information. Destination Bride is honoring my request to keep their article about the dress, but I'm sure they'd be more than willing to shift the tone if I wanted. So all that's left to say is"—she took a steady breath and closed her eyes for one long blink—"take your sister's penis and get the fuck out!"

Whoa.

When Guy hesitated a moment longer, his gaze flitting around the room as if he'd find something that could help him, Mark took another foreboding step. Guy nodded then, and with a sad frown, he backed outside.

Pacey collapsed to the floor like a marionette, a long cry escaping her.

Julie and Kirk rushed over, dropping at her side and wrapping her in a cocoon of hugs and whispered assurances.

Mark stepped back toward me and slid his hands down my arms. Locking his stormy eyes with mine, he lifted my hands and pressed his lips to my knuckles. The sweet gesture made my heart flutter. I looked at his knuckles, still red and angry, wanting nothing more than to reciprocate there ... and all over. "How are you? Cold?"

My dress was still wet, yes, but there was no way I'd be cold around him. "I'm good." He lifted a skeptical eyebrow. "Honest."

"Okay." He grinned with a nod. "I'm gonna help finish up here. I'll probably crash with them tonight too. You want me to drive you home?"

"No, that's okay. You stay," I replied as he released my hands.

"Thank you, Gia. For everything."

"Don't. There's no reason," I whispered with a head shake. I'd done my job, sure, but it was different now when he was concerned. I knew I'd do anything.

"There are plenty of reasons, and lots of ways I want to thank you later." His fingers grazed lightly up my neck.

I shivered, not from the cold but from his words and his touch. "Well, if you insist ... baked goods would be nice."

"That's all, huh?"

"Maybe," I said with a smile even though I wanted so much more. I savored the feeling of his skin on mine, needing far more than a small touch of his fingers. I craved more. I craved him.

"Anything for you." He leaned in for a quick kiss then walked me to the door where I waved and said a quiet goodbye to Pacey and their parents as they began to stand up.

There was no reason for me to even offer to stay. Pacey needed her family. Having pretended to not know about Guy's affair for at least a week, she'd obviously been balancing a lot of emotional cards, and all of them had just crashed. She would need some time to recover, and being with family was the start.

As for me, it was all finally official.

The job was officially over. Pacey's wedding was officially off.

And I was officially in love.

34

Mark

The night with Pacey and our parents had been an exhausting one. Prior to the wedding day, Pacey had done a good job holding herself together, considering her fiancé was nailing his stepsister. At least, she had until we'd gotten back to our parents' house, where the rest of Saturday and well into Sunday could only be described as manic depressive. The highs reached well into the clouds of empowerment, full of laughs and cries of strength. And the lows hit the bottom of despair, with uncontrollable fits of sadness and anger. There had also been a ritual burning of any disposable materials connected to Guy and lots of alcohol consumption, which probably fueled all of the above.

Dad had busied himself negotiating potential refunds. The previously prepared food at the clubhouse had been sent to a few local homeless and women's shelters. The cruise ship was contacted to reschedule the Caribbean honeymoon. Concerned family members continued to call, wanting more information. Our mom was successful in fighting her own urge to blast the once beloved Guy's indiscretions to anyone with ears. The news would leak eventually, but it would be on Pacey's terms. Having that piece of control when her whole world was spinning was the catharsis she needed to get life back on track. She would be okay, though.

She was tough, resilient, and she'd always been able to recover and move on quickly.

I was certain she would.

And because it was all over, I could move on too. With Gia.

Smart. Strong. Shit, I was falling for her. How she had handled herself at the wedding was amazing. Even after getting trapped in a room with Guy and Edena, then hanging from their balcony ... She didn't want to give up, didn't particularly want me to save her. She was independent, confident, and determined. I had no idea how much of a turn on that was until her.

All that tenacity and strength wrapped around a soul that cared fiercely, for her family, for her goals. I had hope I could be wrapped in there too because being with her was already erasing the linear life I'd led before. I felt stronger and more focused. Everything was clearer with her, like the world had finally opened every door I'd ever pounded on.

I was willing to be anything for her, do anything for her.

With my everyday normal returning on Monday morning, I left my parents' house Sunday evening, agreeing to check in with Pacey during the week and help retrieve her stuff. But work was hardly the main reason to get home. I was also hungry for time with Gia.

I'd missed her.

A few minutes after arriving home, unexpected knocking had me a little worried. Dealing with anyone else was not part of my plan. I just wanted to shower and head to Gia's apartment as soon as possible.

"Open up! It's the cops!" Gia's deep-toned shouts were loud and strong. "We have it on good authority that you're stashing dead bodies in there!"

I jerked the door open and glanced around the open hall. "You really trying to get me arrested? A guy like me won't do well in jail. I'm too pretty."

Her hand swept her hair back over her shoulder before pressing against my chest. "Pretty boring maybe. Those boys won't want anything to do with you, so don't fret." She laughed then pushed past me.

"Didn't your text agree that I'd be at your place in a half hour?" My eyes zeroed in on her ass as she moved toward the kitchen, and my hands twitched, jealous of the white denim wrapped snugly where I wanted to place them.

She dropped her purse on the breakfast bar and spun around. "I did. But I couldn't wait."

"Thank God," I admitted, moving to her in a few long strides and crashing my lips to hers, diving in with no thoughts of curbing my enthusiasm. I needed her.

After a minute of making out, she pulled back a tad and licked her lips. "How's she doing?"

I brushed my fingers along her cheek and stared shamelessly at all her lovely attributes—the curve in her silky lashes, the shades of brown in her bright irises, the pink tinge in her soft cheeks. Her asking about Pacey only added to my attraction, to my feelings. "She'll be okay, eventually. She was really hurting, no matter how much she tried to hide it."

"I know that feeling," she admitted, running her palms over my chest.

"They all told me to tell you thanks, by the way. My dad knew about hiring you too because he helped set up the account transactions."

"Ah. Well, I wanted to talk to them about that."

"Nope. Don't even think about it. And that's coming from them. You did a job. You got paid for it."

"But I just don't feel right—"

"Gia," I said, brushing my fingers along her jaw before slipping them into her hair. "Stop. There's no way to fight this. They won't accept the money. You needed it for the shop, to help start your business, right?"

"Yeah. We ordered more material for Kass, and Viv grabbed more supplies for Duplicity too. But the money I was saving for my PI classes—"

"You're keeping for your classes," I interrupted then pressed my lips to hers softly. "Stop thinking about it."

"Fine." She sniffed the air, her nose still close to mine. "What's that smell?"

"What smell?"

She twisted her head to look toward the kitchen. "That smell. Sugar. Cream. Something smells delicious."

"I don't smell anything."

"I'm so lucky you're a horrible liar." She shoved me away and rushed around the breakfast bar and into the kitchen to investigate.

I laughed and waited until she opened the refrigerator. Her face popped out from around the door, an eyebrow lifted, a stunning smile stretched wide.

"I know we both have work tomorrow. But tonight, since you couldn't wait for me to get to your place, *my place* is now a deserted island and I'm supplying the cannolis."

"You're insane!" She rushed around the breakfast bar and slung her arms around my neck. "But what are you supposed to survive on?"

"Ha! There's not enough to share? I could've sworn I made enough during downtime at my parents' place. I guess I'll just have to live off you then."

"Don't tell me you've added cannibal to your killer résumé."

"Maybe. By the time I'm done with you tonight, there might be nothing left." Her lips pursed. "Too much?"

"A tad."

"Okay, let me try again." I looked up at the ceiling, feigning serious contemplation. "By the time I'm done with you tonight, it's going to feel like you died and went to heaven."

"Too corny."

"Shit, I thought that one was pretty good. Hmm." I moved closer, tilting my face back down to hers, and ran my lips over her cheek, down below her ear. "By the time I'm done with you tonight"—I kissed her neck, using my tongue to tease her skin—"you'll be begging for the real kind of boring."

She laughed, and I pulled back to stare at her, a full feeling swelling inside my chest. Happiness? Love? Everything.

"What time do you work tomorrow?"

"Late morning," she whispered, a smile still gracing her face as her giggles died.

"Stay with me." I would beg if I had to. I wanted so much with her, an endless list of things, experiences, but what I wanted most right now was to be inside her and for her to be here with me in the morning.

"Maybe, but only if my friend can stay too."

"What?"

"Well," she said with a smirk, backing out of my arms. "I happen to remember someone being pretty excited about my accidental sex shop purchases, so I brought Air Boy with me just in case. He rode shotgun."

"You're serious?"

"Yes."

"So why didn't you bring him up with you?"

She squirmed. "Well, I didn't want to hurt his feelings if you weren't really interested."

"And it had absolutely nothing to do with having to walk him all the way through The District, past the shops and restaurants, by yourself?"

"Of course not." She giggled again, her guilty smile crinkling her gorgeous eyes.

"Well, I can assure you"—I grabbed her waist and pulled her body back to mine—"my only interest is you, so I'm glad you left him in the car." My hands wrapped around to finally hold her lovely ass.

"My only interest is you, too."

"No Air Boy? No possible beignet suppliers?"

"No. Only you," she said, her smile saying the same. "I was so worried you would hate me from the start. I wanted to drop the job so bad, wanted to forget all about it and just be with you. But I couldn't just give it all up."

"But you were willing to yesterday, even before finding out that Pacey knew. Why?"

"Because I realized I trusted you. I feel like I know you so much more." Her hands moved away from my back and slid up my chest, her fingers drawing circles over my heart. "I know the kind of man you are. Loving. Generous. You'd never hurt me the way I've been hurt before. You're genuine and someone I never thought I'd meet, especially the way we did. But the longer we were together, the more I trusted your word. Your family would never expose Duplicity, and I wanted to help Pacey any way I could."

"God, you're amazing. I will forever be grateful for that broken air conditioner."

Her hand slapped my chest. "You are not grateful for the air conditioner!"

"Oh, yeah, I am."

"Stop," she said with a laugh.

"And I'm grateful for Pacey. Her taste in wedding dresses ... and her bad taste in men. Because I'm thinking you wouldn't have given the boring maintenance man a chance otherwise."

"I may have." Her eyes were transfixed on mine as her fingers started moving affectionately on my chest again.

"I'm mostly thankful that you did despite everything else. I hope you have an idea how much I care about you, how much I trust you, how much I want you."

"I think I do."

"I want to show you." I pressed my lips to hers, and she opened for me, our tongues meeting eagerly, anxiously. I broke away and kissed a trail down her neck. "I want you in my bed all night. I want you in my arms." My tongue laved her skin, tasting her, cherishing her. "I wanna wake up next to you."

Her pulse quickened beneath my lips and she breathed, "What else do you want?"

"All of you, Gia."

"Show me."

"Happily."

two years later

Gia

Another day, another douchebag. The next target was rumored to be a repeat offender, and not very organized with his affairs. The contact: someone who found Duplicity on its spiffy new public site.

A few months had passed since I'd completed all my courses, taken my exam, and finally applied for my PI license. Despite not having a brick and mortar hub, Duplicity was completely legit and thriving, practically drowning in douchebags ... and douchebagettes?

Is douchebagette a word? Well, I'm making it one. Great, now I'm suddenly hungry for French bread. And tacos too ... but that hasn't changed in the last few months.

"Pacey, I think you might have sent me the wrong address. Didn't you originally say it was an apartment near The Villas? I'm getting closer to Destin Commons and I'm a hundred percent not in the mood to be around clothing stores. I've done enough shopping lately." I rubbed a hand over my swollen belly. "But they do have a Mexican restaurant ..."

"Oh, oops. I think I mixed that up earlier. Don't worry, though. You're heading the right way. And no, you can't stop for food yet,"

Pacey's chipper voice said through my car speakers. It wasn't like her to mix things up.

Not long after her wedding debacle, she and I got really close. While finishing school, she helped at the boutique and with Duplicity, which was more than welcome since the boutique had blown up following the Destination Bride feature. Kass was well on her way to becoming a go-to bridal name. She and Aunt Aim had to hire more people for retail and seamstresses for Kass' label, especially when Viv graduated and was accepted to FSU. She'd been gone the better part of a year and a half. And though she was close enough for weekend visits, they had become less frequent with school and a new Geek Squad job at Best Buy keeping her busy.

Pacey had pretty much been my right hand since Duplicity's legal kickoff. I relied heavily on her organization because my brain had entered pregnancy and threatened to never return.

"What do you mean 'oops'? And don't mess with me about the food, Pay. I'm getting hungry and I may need to stop if this turns into a serious stakeout."

"No, no, it won't. I promise. The contact stated that this should be straightforward regular scenario, just like the rest of the low profiles we're taking right now. No worries. Just follow the GPS and let me know if you need anything. Good luck." Her tone was higher than usual, even more excitable.

Hmm. Maybe she'd gotten closer to her latest boyfriend? I could only wish her the same as what I had with Mark. The last two years had been a dream. I couldn't have imagined a better person to love, to want to live the rest of my life with, to want to raise children with ... and possibly walk down an aisle for one day soon.

My baker maintenance man.

I rubbed my stomach again then took a few more turns before slowing the Velostar past the entrance to a residential neighborhood. Apparently, Pacey had been wrong about the apartment aspect too. Houses stretched out before me, spaced on spacious lots landscaped to tropical perfection, with rows of palms and leafy Elephant Ear, decorative flower beds and rock beds.

Beds. I yawned, tired already.

"Get a grip, Gia," I scolded myself as I counted down the house numbers. Napping was not an on-the-job option, no matter how hormonal and tired the final four months became.

When I realized the house number was the next up, I parked along the sidewalk and rolled down my windows. All was quiet. The nice cushion distance between houses was good and bad—no direct pedestrian activity to blend in or stick out. But if I were to be spotted, people would likely assume I belonged in the area with my hard to miss stomach.

A woman's laugh caught my attention. The sound came from inside the house on the corner with a single black sedan in the drive and a staked 'For Sale' sign in front. I couldn't move and park somewhere else without raising any flags to possible onlookers, so it was best to go in on foot. I turned off my engine and slid the seat back to kick the door open. Exiting my low car had already become a chore, even when I had all the time in the world off duty. I rocked my body a few times and used the wheel for leverage, my stomach rubbing against it a bit as I pushed up to a standing wobble, looking like a damn duck getting out.

Gia, double O belly roll.

I walked as normally as I could down the sidewalk until I reached the drive, then I crouching-duck-hidden-belly hustled my way around the black sedan toward the front door and bay windows. The house looked empty inside. No blinds or curtains blocking the view of the bare walls. I didn't like the full exposure. If I could see in, they'd have an easy time spotting me around the short plants out front.

But none of that mattered when I heard his voice.

"I'm glad this place was first."

Mark? Mark! What the ...?!

With a pounding heart and tunnel vision, I rushed around the corner and slung the front door open. All other thoughts ceased as one sent my mind into a frenzy strong enough to force tears from my eyes before I even had a chance to focus.

"Gia, I—Oh Christ, are you okay? Baby?"

He was in front of me within a second, one hand on my cheek, wiping at my tears, the other at my belly.

"I ... I ... What the hell are you doing here?" I asked in a whisper when I really wanted to scream. *Scream, Gia! Dammit!*

"Oh, shit. You thought ... Shit. Maybe this wasn't the best way to surprise you ... but we've both been so busy. Can you give us a minute?" he asked the well-dressed blonde. With a round, plump ass and really thick thighs, she was gorgeous. He would make pretty babies with her. What the hell was wrong with me?

"Babe." He grasped my face in his hands and locked eyes with me. "This is for us. I wanted to surprise you with this but wasn't sure how. I want to buy us a house. The condo is only one bedroom and—"

"What?" All this was a surprise? "You aren't ..."

"No, no, babe. Have I ever given you a reason to doubt me? Us?"

"No." He'd never given me any real reason to be jealous, even when we'd first met. God, my hormones were all over the place. "I'm sorry."

"No, baby. Don't be sorry. Be happy. This is for us. We're shopping today. For a baby room. Maybe two."

And then the flood started again, fat tears streaming down my cheeks. "You ... We ... This is ...?"

"Could be. I wanted to start looking, to add to our promise."

I pressed my face to his chest and inhaled—the baby dulling the heavenly sugar smell embedded in his shirt that I wanted so badly to love in that moment—and then I cried some more. He'd been taking culinary classes as he continued to work at East Bay Resort, working hard for his own dream. "But the bakery?"

"We're fine. With the condo being in the middle of rental heaven at The District, the sale will go well. We'll still be on schedule for that plan. And the other plan that involves a couple of rings."

"I'm a mess," I mumbled with a sigh and melted into him as much as my stomach would allow.

"You are." His arms cinched around me for a moment then his hands moved to my face, tipping my chin up to look into my eyes. "But you're my mess. My smart and sexy mess."

"Remind me of that in another couple months."

"I'll remind you every day and every night, forever." The pad of his thumb touched my bottom lip before he kissed me, proving his truth again with every touch. "I love you."

He had every piece of me, of my heart. "I love you, too."

"Good. Now, let's find a home for our family." He dropped to his knees and planted his lips on my stomach.

I ran my fingers through his hair, thinking of all the things we'd done and all that was yet to come. "Only if it's boring."

"It'll be the perfect kind of boring."

Acknowledgments

I have to start by thanking my family. Will and Zoe, I'd be lost without you both. Thank you for accepting and supporting my dreams. I'm sorry that sometimes I get lost inside my office and often forget to make dinner. To Mom, Aunt M, and Uncle J, thanks for always being there even though you're really way too far away.

Tonya and Cari, thank you for offering all your thoughts in group chats and frozen vid calls. I—I—I love ya, you crazy bit—Call me back. I hope you liked your cameos.

Kim Chance, my amazing Disney princess CP, you can brighten even the darkest of writerly moods. Thanks for being there when the comedy wasn't. Your help is invaluable. I'm so excited for you and *Keeper*.

Amanda Clark, I'm thrilled that I can call you my friend. I'm not sure what you call me, but it can be whatever you want. I'm just glad you didn't run away when I sent you life-threatening bookmarks and (s)talked you into reading more of my stuff. Thanks so much for all your feedback.

Jenni Moen, stop kicking so much ass. Just kidding. Keep kicking asses and twisting hearts. I can't say thank you enough. You are an amazing writer, and I value all of your input. When we put our heads together, we can conquer websites and newsletters like pros. *throws confetti*

Emerson Shaw, you are fabulous! Thanks again for your blurb help and for taking the time to beta read.

Amy Concepcion, thank you for everything! Your beta notes are always on point and so helpful. Also, I am forever grateful that you agreed to be an admin in the reader group.

Emily Lawrence, I love your wonderful editing skills. Thanks for setting things straight.

To Ena and Amanda, thank you both so much for your help with the release blitz. You ladies work so hard and are always on it!

Huge thanks to all the bloggers reading and reviewing, and those who are part of release blitz! I really appreciate all of your help and support. Your words help get ours out there. Thank you for your generosity and love!

To the BFFs, you ladies are inspirational. Never give up!

To the Dreamers, thanks for joining the reader group. I appreciate you hanging out with me and chatting all things books and animal memes.

And of course BIG hugs and MANY thanks to everyone reading this! I really hope you enjoyed *Spied*. My goal with this one was to make a few people smile, maybe even laugh. We can always use extra love and laughter in our lives. So if *Spied* added a little more to yours, I'm feeling pretty blessed. <3

About The Author

J.M. Miller J.M. Miller lives on Florida's Emerald Coast with her husband and daughter.

When she isn't spending time with her family or being distracted by social media sites, she writes contemporary and fantasy romance novels.

Website:

jmmillerbooks.com

Books:

Dead & Lovely

Senior Year Bucket List

Fallen Flame

Scattered Plume

Hidden Ember

Sever

Deep Breath

The Line That Binds

The Line That Breaks

www.ingramcontent.com/pod-product-compliance
Lightning Source LLC
Chambersburg PA
CBHW060902210726
48293CB00006B/1918